I0543442

HARBINGER

Book Three of the "Celestial Creatures" series.

Olga Gibbs

RAGING BEAR
PUBLISHING

Harbinger

Published in 2020 by Raging Bear Publishing.

Copyright © Olga Gibbs 2020.
The rights of Olga Gibbs to be identified as the Author of the Work have been asserted in accordance with the Copyright, Designs and Patents Act 1988.
All rights reserved.
No part of this publication may be edited, reproduced, stored on a retrieval system, or transmitted, in any form or by any means without prior written permission from the publisher, nor be otherwise circulated in any form of binding or cover other than that in which it is published and without a similar condition being imposed on the subsequent purchaser.

This book is a pure work of fiction. All characters, names, places and events in this publication are fictitious. Any resemblance to real persons, living or dead, or to businesses, companies and institutions, or localities is purely coincidental.

A CIP catalogue record for this title is available from the British Library.

Paperback ISBN 978-1-9164710-2-3

Cover design by Perie Wolford.

For upcoming publications visit www.OlgaGibbs.com

Praise for "Celestial Creatures":

"Celestial Creatures" series is filled with dynamic characters, intimate portrayal of visceral emotion, realistic characters and compelling twist endings in every book.

Reader.

A story unlike any I have read before.

Reader.

Hallow weaves in several important themes into its already complex mythos. These themes are not at all fictional, and speak to important problems in society. From abuse, mental health, and economic deprivation, Hallow pulls no punches in including some heartbreakingly real depictions of inequalities and injustices that blight society. It is the inclusion of these themes that I most admire the ambition of Hallow's narrative, and it is for this reason that I hope Hallow finds itself of the bookshelf of many young readers.

"Fraternal Philosophising" blog.

"Heavenward" reaches back into the actual lore and religious accounts to bring us more accurate representations of angels, powerful entities who, though light in nature, are violent to the success of their cause. I also very much enjoyed the depiction of Ariel's mental struggle and accurate representation of schizophrenia.

Sahreth Bowden, author.

I would definitely recommend this book. It is perfect for lovers of fantasy, magic, all things angels and celestial beings without the religious part, a realistic MC and an amazing world-building.

Esmée van der Weide, book blogger.

I really enjoyed the rich, descriptive language because it really made me feel like I was alongside the characters in the story experiencing what they were.

"The reading chemist", blog.

CHAPTER 1

I'm pelted through the air for a few painful seconds. My body is pulled and twisted as if I'm fighting my way up from the bottom of a bog whilst being electrocuted in the process.

Suddenly my body slams into a wall and my skull hits the solidity of it, bouncing back. If I wasn't an angel, the impact would've been the last thing I would've experienced in my short life.

Tentatively, I open my eyes.

I'm lying on the familiar polished grey stone floor and the bright sunshine from above washes over me, bringing with it a sharp sense of déjà vu.

I know we are in Uras. The open, bright, spotlessly-blue sky above is unmistakable and the air is saturated with oceanic scents of sea salt and ozone brought over by a gentle breeze.

But the obnoxious and overpowering smell of tropical fruits barges into the soothing symphony of the ocean, I find this annoying and irritating. The roofless hall stinks of sugared fruits as if someone had washed the floor with a fruit smoothie. It tickles at my nose, bursting with popsicles of sugar rush in my brain.

Welcome to your new home, Ariel.

As I'm about to lift my head and shake it to dislodge the pain, something drops on top of me, crushing me under its weight and my head hits the polished stones. The air is expelled from my lungs with a violent "puff".

"Shit", I mumble, breathing a few times, before lifting my head.

I wrestle my twisted arm from under the warm body atop and gingerly touch my head, rubbing at my forehead and temples. My head feels in one piece and doesn't hurt, apart from a dull ringing in my ears.

Blindly, I reach behind me, ready to push the body off, when my hand travels over the familiar clothing and the small shape.

Jess!

Pushing with my right hand at the floor, I rise. I shuffle and adjust the position of my arm, bringing it closer to me, pushing myself higher, while keeping a hold of the body on my back with my left hand.

I wriggle and move underneath the body, trying to gently slide Jess' body off me, but my grip loosens, then slips and Jess' body rolls off and her head hits the stone floor with a dull thwack.

"Shit."

No longer caring for gentleness or speed, I rise up on my knees, spinning towards Jess.

"Jess! Jessie-boo", I call to her as I shuffle on my knees closer to her.

I stroke her face, pushing hair away and stroking her soft skin.

"Jessie, Jessie-boo?"

She doesn't respond and in the silence of the immense hall without a roof, my voice begins rise with the first wave of upcoming hysteria.

"Jessie?!"

"She's fine."

I snap my head up, turning towards the voice.

Rafe stands behind me, watching Jess over my shoulder. His jaw is set tight and a fine sheen of sweat coats his pale face. I had almost forgotten about him.

"She is fine", he repeats, "it might take a few days for her to wake up. The shard of essence that I gave her is battling with her soul at the moment, but they both should settle soon, once they realise that they are both staying."

He comes closer and standing over my and Jess' bodies, he adds: "The essence shouldn't be inside a human, but mind you, neither should a human be in Uras."

I turn my attention back to Jess. I lean towards her and I can hear her deep measured breathing, as if she is asleep.

Rafe takes a few heavy steps closer, and listening to the shuffling of his feet, I wonder if he is still unwell.

Without another word, he bends down and scoops Jess' small body in his arms.

Nestled in his large arms and pressed against his chest sealed in a black armour of a rigid tactical vest, Jess looks smaller and younger. She looks paler against him. She looks lost and alone, breakable and defenceless. The contrast between their bodies is so stark, that watching her twig legs swing in Rafe's arms, I wonder if I've made a mistake bringing her here.

But Rafe's gentle arms close protectively around her, hugging her close.

"Let's go", he nods to me.

"Yeah. Let's go."

Rafe leads us away from the small, round hall where we have crash-landed, down the open roofed, white-walled corridor with the same grey stony floor, through a wide and tall arch of a white stone, hidden under a dense greenery of a trailing rose bush, with white rose buds winking through the green draping of leaves, that move gently with a breeze.

The heady scent of a breezy spring evening spins my head as I walk through the arch.

The white miniature rose buds dot a green living fabric of green leaves: living, breathing, producing that heady scent of spring.

The strangled echo of my shuffles and Rafe's heavy footsteps floats and dissipates into the sky the moment it's born.

I'm following Rafe, not yet knowing where we're going. I'm walking behind him, mindlessly watching the swing of my sister's feet in time with his steps.

Another decision has been made, another path was chosen, and only time will tell how well I have chosen both for myself and others.

Rafe's bottom wing drags along the stone floor with a soft "swish", snaking side to side with his steps radiating a soothing rhythm within the silent corridor.

My gaze travels towards his right, wingless side and I brace myself for a fresh stab of the familiar guilt. But instead I stumble, trip and almost fall at an unexpected sight. I stop, holding on to the corridor wall, keeping myself up.

"Rafe..." A strangled whisper is all I can muster.

Through the black rigid plastic of his tactical vest, through the thick fabric of his jacket underneath, the purple stumps of his new wings have begun to sprout.

It's just the two thick feathery stumps, matching the *base* of his left wings to a "T". The purple stumps end abruptly, as if drawn with a pencil on paper and then erased by a sure hand, leaving behind only the base.

The bases of his wings sport two thick, fully developed humerus bones – the central limb bone of a wing – one growing up and one growing down, covered in a purple fluffy afterfeather.

The edges of the feathery stumps are raggedy and raw.

Rafe has stopped following my call and is now looking at me over his shoulder, holding Jess in his arms. His eyebrows are raised, conveying his silent question.

"Your wings... The *right* wings are..."

I don't know how to finish this sentence. Growing, materialising, coming back from the dead?

He turns his head and his gaze briefly drops behind his back, but he doesn't need to see what I'm talking about.

He just nods.

"Yes, I know."

But as I take two cautious steps closer, Rafe suddenly throws his head upwards, clamping his mouth shut, but not before a pained cry escapes past his clenched teeth.

He stands immobile for a few seconds, with his head up to the bottomless sky and his breathing is as raggedy as the sharp edges of his growing wings.

I shuffle closer.

Under my stunned gaze, the red blood rises from the depth of his stumps, bubbling, spurting like boiling water, surging to the top and then pooling at the raw, charred ends of his stumps.

The thick blood rises, gathers at the top but doesn't spill.

Rafe moans.

His breathing is shallow and his eyes are closed.

The blood sits at the top of his stumps like tree sap, coagulating & burgeoning in uneven volcanic layers, turning under my gaze from the deep red colour of the blood to the purple, shimmery colour of his wings, before it begins to shape, morphing into another inch of wings' purple bones, covered with a soft fluff of a purple down.

I release a choppy breath.

I don't know what I expected to see in terms of angels' wings growth and development, but this certainly wasn't it.

I never gave much thought about how his wings would grow back or if they'd grow back at all, but if anyone would've asked me, I would've imagined a soft spell bringing them back as if by magic, all while a happy smile plays on the recipient's lips. I would've imagined the right wings growing over time from small, miniature wings into the larger ones, just as animals and plants do.

Not in a million of years would I have imagined the process of wings re-growth to be so brutal, violent and bloody.

"Are you okay?" I whisper, struggling to pull my gaze away from his wings.

He still holds Jess in his arms and I take another step closer, ready to take her from him.

"Yes", he barks at me in a rough whisper without opening his eyes.

"Do you want me to hold her?"

"No. I am fine."

We stand like this for a few moments, before his breathing evens out and his gaze snaps back to me. Rafe glares at me and without a further word, he turns away, returning to marching down the stony narrow corridor, and I follow.

Since I gave Rafe half of my essence – *is it mine if it belonged to Uriel before me? Shouldn't I still call it "Uriel's"?* – and he woke up, he hasn't said much to me.

He didn't acknowledge the transference. He didn't make a comment about it, didn't say a word. He hasn't spoken or shown a gratitude for my decision nor did he object to it. After he drew in his first breath and opened his eyes, lying on the ground and he looked at me, I knew straight away, that he was aware of what was inside him.

His gaze was searching, maybe wanting to say something, I don't know, then suddenly, startling me, tears had bloomed and spilled from his eyes, sliding to his temples.

I've never seen Rafe's tears, and seeing him like this, powerless, lost and exposed for the first time I truly understood what he had lost.

His grief and loss were so bare and raw, that I didn't want to watch it any longer, so I got up and walked away, unable to help to think that maybe I've screwed up again, that maybe everything is my fault after all.

"Are you sure about it?" were Sam's last words to me, and the soft pressure of his fleeting kiss on my lips with a taste of sweet blackberries on my tongue was his goodbye.

I've updated Rafe on my decision, on what I've decided to do, but I didn't add that his dead girlfriend was okay with this plan, that the plan is the only way forward for me and my survival. Watching him lying on the ground crying, the words of my needs and my survival stuck in my throat. It my selfish decision, but I wasn't so cruel as to rub it in.

Rafe didn't argue with my decision and my plan. He didn't try to talk me out of it. Suspended deep in his grief, I wasn't sure if Rafe even heard my words, as he sure didn't acknowledge any of them.

And now, following Rafe down this corridor, I began to wonder if maybe Sam was right and that maybe, sharing Uriel's essence was beginning of the end for me, that maybe Rafe's resentment will be the end of me.

The stone corridor bends right and then sharply down, and Rafe, leading the way, follows its path.

Rafe takes a right turn and abruptly stops. Not expecting it and keeping my gaze on the floor, I ram into his solid body.

"Sorry", I mumble to his wings and stumps in front of my eyes.

Rafe doesn't acknowledge me nor does he say a word to explain the stop, and after a few seconds of silence and unable to see anything past his wide back, I take a step around him.

CHAPTER 2

I huff and roll my eyes at the sight in front of me.

Here we are. Shit and the fan are right on time.

A large crowd of warrior angels, sealed in shiny white armour are jammed into a tight space of the corridor, with at least forty or fifty standing ahead of us.

The wings of the angels are pastel, pale in colour. I spot a few pastel blue wings, a few powdery grey, lightest peach or lilac. Not a single angel could flaunt the pure white wings of Sam or the crow-black wings of Baza, or the shimmery purple of me and Rafe.

It's hard to tell, looking at this tightly crammed crowd, if any of them has four wings, but it's clear that their wings are much smaller than mine or Rafe's.

They stand shoulder to shoulder in a solid, breathing mass, taking up the entire space of the corridor, from wall to wall and from the ground upwards, rising into the open air like a frozen mid fall tsunami wave.

The angels at the back are floating high in the air with a further row of them in front of them floating slightly lower, and the row in front of those floating lower still, until the ones at the forefront stand on the ground.

Their formation is of a church choir settled on bleachers, and I briefly wonder if they are here to welcome me, *Uriel*, home with open arms and a heartfelt performance of "Ode to Joy", or some other glorifying performance. But if they were here to greet me back with open arms, they wouldn't have their swords of white, rippling fire out of the scabbards and raised.

They are not here to greet their new ruler.

What the crowd have in common is the colour of the tunics underneath their white sparkling armours. The different shades of blue, from dark navy to pale, turquoise blue and covered in silver intricate heavy embroidery, poke from under the breastplates. The trousers of the shades of blue are encasing their legs.

Although all angels wear silvery-white armour, some have only breastplates shielding their chests, while others are sealed tighter, sporting pauldrons, vambraces and even gauntlets.

The angels long hair stream down their backs, floating softly in the breeze. Only a few angels have their hair plaited, and one of them is Chamuel.

Chamuel stands at the forefront of this "blue clad" regiment. His silvery-grey hair is cut short at the top, while at the back it is long, plaited into a thick and intricate plait, resting over his left shoulder, with a string of white glistening pearls weaved into it.

"You have returned", he calls, raising his bushy grey eyebrow at me, bowing slightly, but the smirk that is dusted over his lips is anything but respectful.

He speaks in a weird gurgling language, but my mind processes it with ease, and when my attitude barks the response in English, the angel understands it too, unflustered.

"Weren't you expecting me?" I open my eyes at him with feigned surprise, as I pull my lips to form a small "o".

"Oh no. I hope I didn't ruin your seating arrangements for the dinner."

I take a step forward, standing shoulder to shoulder with Rafe. I want to ask him about the language translation but I know that now is not the time.

Chamuel's sharp blue eyes dance between me and Rafe, lingering for a few long seconds on Jess' body in Rafe's arms.

"Wardums are not allowed in our sacred place", Chamuel remarks, nonchalant.

"Don't call her that", Rafe growls low in response. Although his growl is quiet, it's menacing enough for a couple of angels behind Chamuel to flinch, fighting with their feet, wanting to take a step back.

I don't know the word Chamuel just said, but it's clear that it was an insult.

He takes a few steps towards us, away from his soldiers, unfazed and confident. He is not afraid of us.

"Traitors that made a deal with The Endless Harvester may never enter the great halls of Uras", Chamuel calls, raising his left arm above his head. His deep voice booms and amplifies, rising like cathedral music in a church. Although he addresses me and Rafe, I can hear the call of righteous indignation to his followers.

I settle, preparing for his long rousing speech to the masses, when he snaps his gaze to me, while his right hand travels to the armour belt around his waist, housing a selection of weapons, settling on the hilt of his sword. His glare is silent, but his message is clear.

"The deal that *you*, without a doubt, have made with Baza", he continues.

Then dropping his voice lower so only I and Rafe can hear him, he adds, "as there's no way, you'd still be alive."

"That's right", I snap, "I shouldn't be alive... Thanks to *you*."

But he ignores my remark.

"No traitor ever should be allowed in Uras", he bawls in his strong commanding voice, turning away from me to address his troops. "We should not soil the Grand halls of the Daughter of An's residence with presence of Baalzebu's followers. We should protect the purity of Uriel's teachings. We should stand strong in the face of this temptation", he yells, throwing his accusing finger at us, "and coercion that Baalzebu's horde may bestow upon us. We should be advertent to his dark games and preaching. We should be watchful of his disguises and we should be wary of these *willing* traitors."

He looks at me and Rafe over his shoulder and a fleeting smile tugs at the corner of his lips, before he turns away.

"The traitors of Uriel's teachings should be banished from this sacred place and must never enter these divine halls", he roars, throwing his head up to the blue sky above. His voice bounces off the walls, met by the humming, approving roar of the angels around him. The noise seems to vibrate deep inside their chests, rising upwards.

But I've had enough of this show.

"Traitors?" I ask, shaking my head and taking a step forward.

Chamuel spins to face me and angels around him fall silent.

"Traitors?!" I call louder.

The hysteria and anger set in. I meet the calculating gaze of Chamuel's icy eyes. There's no fear or doubt in them.

"You're calling *me* a traitor?" I roar and my wings fly open.

I take another step forward.

This performance clearly was orchestrated with clear purpose and precision. This public rousing accusation is a brief court hearing, which will leave no doubt in anyone's mind how guilty we are, and when the time comes and followers will be called upon, we will be executed without a second thought.

"*You?* Of all people? You're calling *me* a traitor?"

The hysteric shrill of my voice is accompanied by a low grumbling vibration to the floor.

A few angels on the ground exchange glances, dropping their gazes to the moving floor underneath their feet.

"That's rich coming from you", I bark at Chamuel.

At this point, I am only an arm's length away from him.

My wings stand rigid behind my back. Maybe in response to the opening of my wings or maybe answering my words, but Chamuel's four blue wings, open wide around him too.

His hand strokes the hilt of his weapon in a warning.

"What?" I laugh bitterly. "Are you going to kill me? Kill *Uriel?* Right here? In front of everyone? No more hiding, huh?"

Chamuel says nothing.

"Someone feels bold today, bold enough to progress his conspiracies from backstabbing and scheming to open confrontation", I hiss and then bitterly laugh.

"I don't need approval to execute the traitor and Baza's votary in order to save Uriel's legacy and Uras, from marking it by the dirty apostate", he grumbles low.

His hateful eyes are on me.

"You are full of shit", I bite out. "Making things up as you go along. What's in it for you? Take Uras for yourself? Find a better "beyelai"?" I mimic Chamuel's bowing from last time, by placing my four fingers to my forehead and bowing at him.

"Nobody's going to believe you. Nobody's going to believe any of this bullshit", I say.

"I don't need proof", he hisses at me. "They will believe me because they trust me. They'll follow me and that's more than I can say about you. You always will be a lowly human to them. You'll never be Uriel to them, no matter how many times you proclaim that you are her."

"And I'm not planning to be her", I interrupt him. "I don't claim to be her. I am me."

Irritated, I push the hair from out of my eyes.

Only now I've noticed my hair whipping around my face, as a strong wind gushes through the halls of Uras.

I lift my head up and see that the bright summer-blue sky above has turned thundery grey, ominous and pregnant with promise.

Chamuel and a few angels lift their heads upwards, following my gaze.

"Waiting for something?" he asks.

I drop my gaze down and ignoring him, I step sideways around him.

Standing in front of the "blue" army of beautiful angels, I address them: "I am Ariel. Yes, I was born human, but I was also born an angel. I was born as Uriel. She didn't choose me and I didn't choose her, yet it was decided. Ophanims have made the decision.

"Uriel is inside me now. Her essence is inside me, with all its powers. Now she is me and I'm her. All her battles are now mine to fight, her oaths are mine to keep", I repeat what she said to me. "But all of her powers are mine too."

I have the attention of all angels. They're listening to me, to what I have to say.

I scan the crowd. My silence is brooding and promising just like the sky above.

"I spoke to her", I yell to them. "She's not coming back. She couldn't, even if she tried. She is in Udhad but she approves of me. She said so herself."

I try to remember how the angelic oaths go.

"I swear to An to uphold Uriel's teaching of a free will. I swear that fight of Uriel's will not die in vain."

I try to sound as pompous as Chamuel was. I'm trying to speak their language, but right now, apart from the free will, I don't know what else to promise them.

The stillness of angels is offset by their hair and clothing lashed around by the gale wind. The angels in the few top rows, the ones which were floating in the air, are struggling to keep their earlier solid formation, as now and again, the wind would push a few of them to the side or take them higher into the sky, separating them from their comrades, and they would open and beat their wings, fighting to regain their earlier position and composure.

"The time has come for you to decide if you still support Uriel's teachings, if you still believe in free will. It's time for you to decide if you can overlook and move past the fact that I was born human, that my loyalty might lie there as well."

I look at the army of still beautiful faces in front of me and I clearly see that I am out of my depth in the angelic scheming warfare or angelic lifestyle.

I want to cry. It's the first of many battles and I feel like I have already lost this one.

My wings are wide open and the wind pushes me off my feet.

I look up at the open sky. The wind roars above our heads like a wounded animal, and the sunlight has disappeared under a heavy veil of storm clouds, but the rocking and rumble of the ground has settled.

I know that I need to do more to show them that I'm not human, not anymore. I need to flex my muscles and show my strength. I need to perform my miracle.

I push with my foot off the ground and my wings take me up, first to the level of the lower "bleachers", then bringing me face to face with angels floating in the top row, and finally, above them all.

I float above the pale-winged army, above Rafe with Jess in his arms, above Chamuel. The face of every angel is directed at me. I read attention and curiosity on a few open faces, hostility on others, and surprise on Chamuel's.

I'm battling with the wind to keep myself anchored in one place.

I look down at the angelic faces.

Fake it 'til you make it.

I know that I need to be the leader they can believe in. I need to be strong enough for them to stay, and I need them to stay if I'm planning to fight for my freedom, freedom to choose what will happen to me and my life.

I draw in a breath, willing for the words which will come out next, to ring strongly and decisively.

"Everyone will need to decide where their loyalty lies", I call to the angels below. "If it's not me, that's fine. I'm not going to hold anyone against their will. I don't need the service of the scared. I want the service of the strong.

"Uriel and I, we were both thrust onto this path by one treacherous act. Uriel was savagely killed, slaughtered, by the ones she trusted the most and I'm not going to make the same mistake. Everyone will get one pass from me and it will be granted today. Everyone will be excused for their earlier wrongdoings but it's only today. From today the treachery will end", I call to them above the wind.

"Every one of you will get one mercy from me. But only *one*", I reiterate, looking pointedly at Chamuel.

"Only one", I repeat, yelling to the crowd, "and the time for mercy is now. My gift to you is the same gift Uriel bestowed upon my kind – free will. Uriel fought and lost her life to protect the freedom of choice for mankind. I will follow her teachings and return the favour to *her*, now my, kind. I'm giving you the freedom to choose for yourself, to choose if you'd stand with me."

I scan the crowd, pausing, desperate to read their minds.

"But that's only now! It's only today!" I yell to them.

I can hear a distant rumble in the dark sky, but I'm too preoccupied with my battle for their loyalty that I'm trying to win here, to pay attention to that obscure noise.

"From this day forward, I expect loyalty from everyone who decides to stay. I will not be betrayed. Not anymore. Every betrayal will be met with swift retribution", I roar above the wind which has picked up.

"I am not human anymore. I am Ariel: The Harbinger of Doom, The Keeper of Gates", I glare at Chamuel. I don't remember all of Ariel's titles that he rattled off earlier, so I add, "The follower of Uriel's teachings, The protector of her ways."

I'm completely making things up, assigning myself random titles, directing my own rousing speeches, but I hope to relay the main message: I am here to stay, to be the leader they need, and that I am the "new", improved, Uriel.

I pause.

A sudden gust of wind shoves me and then, following close on its tail, a tidal wave of bone-shaking buzzing and humming cascades from the sky, vibrating the air and my body with it, reaching deep inside me, raising the hairs on my body.

The air shudders.

It's like a shock wave.

It seeps through the air, colliding with me, before it passes through me, descending through my skull, down my body, escaping through my toes. The shock wave escapes me, plummeting towards the ground, leaving behind burned and exposed nerves.

By the disturbed looks on the angelic faces, I know that the wave just hit them and then the floor.

The angels, standing on the ground, wearily shuffle on the spot, scanning the stones under their feet, raising their heads upwards, checking the screaming wind in the sky.

Chamuel's gaze shuttles between me, the brooding sky, the rocking ground, and the wrinkles deepen between his brows, his lips pressed into a hard line. He is on the ground, on his own, a few steps away from his warriors.

Although the vibration wave has passed, the wind hasn't stopped marauding the sky, bringing with it a new noise.

It's a deep and low grumbling of thunder. It rumbles in the sky, shaking the air every two seconds. In the stunned silence, the thunder is deeper, yet clearer, defined.

The "thunder" is a buzz. It has a rhythm. The buzz's deep throb finds an answer in my bones. It is low and throbbing, with the deep rhythm of a double bass. It's a sound of an airplane engine in foggy air, with a… pulse of a heartbeat.

As I float mid-air, trying to decipher the new sound, while looking to recover my royal commanding equilibrium and remember where I was in my speech, when a white bolt of lightning zooms past me.

It hits the ground between Chamuel and his "pastel-winged" army, spraying the shards of chipped stone and dust in the air. The chipped stone and dust, picked up by the wind, dances in the air among angelic bodies, rising upwards on the air streams.

The angels are quiet. Their confused and scared gazes are raised toward me, as if I'm an author of this mayhem, as if *I* have produced it all.

Have I?

Every sound suddenly dies, leaving only the billowing of the wind behind.

Everything is quiet for a second, before the stone floor groans, splitting a second later with a strident screech, and a zigzagging, narrow ravine appears between Chamuel and his army of angels.

The ravine sits for a moment, as if thinking what it should do next, and once it has made up its mind, it runs up a wall, disappearing through and behind it.

The wall crumbles into a pile of white stone, some of which fall into the ravine.

Shit! Here we go again… It must be me. Although I don't remember asking for this…

Holding their formation, angels on the ground shuffle away from the narrow crack. Although clearly concerned, they're calm and organised, not scared enough to disperse. The narrow yet deep crack between them and their leader doesn't concern them.

Chamuel snaps his head up, glaring at me.

"Can't control it yet?" he growls, livid yet smug. His voice rises above the billowing of the wind, and the returned pulsating sound of the engine.

Maybe I don't, because suddenly, another bolt of lightning sizzles past me from the open dark sky, narrowly avoiding me. I fly out of its way, watching it leaving a crisp, burnt out hole next to Chamuel's foot.

CHAPTER 3

His eyes open wider in surprise and his nostrils flare with anger, and I could swear I can hear the grinding of his teeth.

The angels are agitated too. Their guttural language rumbles among their rank. They try to keep their formation, but some of them, at the back, drop into the lower level or straight to the ground, and the gaping holes begin to appear in previously unified battalion.

From this high up, the erratic movements of their pastel wings gives the crowd a resemblance of a flock of colourful butterflies. The angels turn their heads, beating their wings in the air, floating, straightening their ranks, unexpectedly dispersing again. They keep their position, but they are on the brink of a panic.

They keep their distance from Chamuel. Maybe they're waiting for his command or maybe afraid of the wind and lightening, keeping their distance from Rafe as well, not braving to charge at the "traitor".

Chamuel is an island between the two warring parties.

Chamuel lifts his head and his livid gaze meets mine, even the sly smile of his is forsaken. He flashes his glorious icy-blue wings open and takes to the sky, towards me, while tugging his double-faced axe free from his belt.

That answers that question...

Keeping my gaze on the Chamuel rising body, I pull out my two small swords.

But suddenly, as if a hidden sun on a rainy day covered by eclipse, the sky above our heads grows black. The darkness sucks in the last of the light, and with it, everything around us turns grey, even the bright, polished silver of Chamuel's armour is now charcoal and dull. The inky air is of the colour of black and white movie.

I want to look down to the ground, to understand what's going on, but I'm too afraid to draw my gaze away from Chamuel and his axe.

The pulsating roar of the engine is louder. It's here. It's above me.

The shiver comes over my spine, as my essence whispers incoherent warnings, knowing what's coming and how bad it is.

But Chamuel is too preoccupied with me and his hate for me, to pay attention to this noise. Or maybe this warning is only for me to hear.

His deep-set, piercing blue eyes under his bushy grey eyebrows are fixed on me and alight with hate.

"A dirty wardum leading this army?" he yells towards me, as he's rising, jerking his head to the ground.

He is next to me now.

"Not on my watch", he growls low, his gorgeous face is level with mine.

His wings wrap around him for a second. His body draws back to give him the space, and suddenly, he launches himself forward, towards me, swinging his axe, his face contorted with rage.

I throw my arms up, in front of my head, protecting myself.

Dzuu-u-um.

Metal collides with metal. The vibration from the connection of our weapons shakes me and I'm pushed back by the force of Chamuel's attack. I tumble backwards through the air.

I right myself, but I feel dizzy.

Chamuel looks at me and a corner of his lips lifts, as he pulls his axe back, readying for another attack.

He is pleased. His eyes tell me what I already know: he is a seasoned warrior and I wouldn't have a chance against him in a fight, that I should have crawled into a hole when he graciously gave me the chance, but now I will die.

The next moment, his four wings fold behind his back and he drops for a quick second, before his wings open and he glides, turning and twisting mid-air, as his wings take him beneath me, around me.

He moves fast.

He is to my right and I can feel the air movement from the beating of his wings. I can hear his breathing, and then he swings his axe.

The axe cuts the air, screeching on its way.

I duck, barely saving my head and my neck.

But I don't manage to save all of me. The blade of his axe finds the top of my top wing, slicing the tip off.

The round, fat drops of my blood float in the air in front of my eyes, caught by the roaring wind.

"Argh!" I scream into the already busy air, but nobody hears me as the buzzing, pulsating noise is finally upon us.

The noise is above me. It blankets the air around as it's vibrating with a living heartbeat. It screeches and cries. It's a buzz of millions of high-pitched shrills, millions of children' cries, millions of agonising hungry wails, and it's coming my way.

Something inside tells me that this noise is more dangerous than Chamuel, and I raise my head and look upwards.

The new cloud has completely covered the sky. The living cloud is screaming and talking. It's breathing and moving.

I don't know what it is, what it's doing here, how it ended up here or who called it, but one thing I know for sure is I can feel it, the danger and *hunger* that is radiating off it.

The blacked out sky, the dark air, the roaring wind, the pulsating, screaming cloud above, I can't get my bearings in this cacophony of noises. I don't know what to do.

I spin on the spot, looking for Chamuel, who has changed his position in the air. I glance at the dark living cloud above, towards the ground at the barely visible once blue and now grey army, Rafe and the small ravine between them.

And that's when I sense rather than hear a new movement.

I turn just in time to see the blade of Chamuel's axe, covered in my dripping blood, slicing the air next to me. I've missed his move.

I throw my arm with my sword in the air, but I am too slow to deflect this strike, and as if in slow motion, under my surprised gaze, the axe flies past my sword, toward my blocking arm, and I wail.

I thrash, spinning away.

Chamuel's hold on his axe is released and I'm free.

I look down at my arm. Chamuel's axe is deeply lodged in my radius bone.

Suddenly, all four of my purple wings close around my body, and losing their support, I drop towards the floor like a stone.

The drop.

Scared and in pain, I try to scream but my screams are shoved back into my throat as I fall backwards, tumbling, flapping my useless arms, while my wings remain closed. Chamuel disappears into the distance, under the approaching cloud.

I watch Chamuel as he watches my fall. The cloud and the dark air are above him.

The pain and the fall are unending. It's short as a second, yet long as the excruciating pain.

The impact.

The air is expelled from my lungs. I ride my roaring wails, until my body hits the ground, hard. It feels as if all my bones are shattered upon impact. My skull vibrates and I can't draw any air into my lungs, and it feels as if my chest has caved in with the impact too.

Lying on my back, I look above but I can't see a thing past the darkness.

My wings sense the "pastel" army to my right and Rafe to my left but I can't see anything.

I need to get up. Chamuel is coming. I try to move but my every movement is answered with agonising pain that is drawn from the wobbling axe, lodged in my arm and from my bruised body. Blood pools under my arm. The bloody puddle grows, spilling, seeping into my clothes.

I need to move. He'll be here.

I grab hold of the axe handle.

"You can do it. You can do it. You can do it", I whisper, praying to myself and in between my whimpering cries.

One, two, three...

I yank the axe out, howling with the wind. Tears come to my eyes, spilling, as I clamp my mouth.

But my scream is not the only one in the air.

Chamuel's agonising deep roar has filled the air, bouncing off the white stone walls, disappearing into the grey sky.

I lift my head. With the tune of his scream, the eclipse of the pulsating cloud begins to dissipate and fade, disappear as fog under a sun, leaving only the wind to abuse the halls of Uras.

The air is brighter and so is the sky, and in this brightened air I clearly see Chamuel floating mid-air.

Laying on the ground, bleeding and in pain, all I can do is to grab the axe's handle tighter in my grip, readying myself for Chamuel's descent.

But Chamuel is still in the sky.

His arms, legs and four wings are spread wide like an eight-pointed star, and as I rub the tears out of my eyes, I see that the colours are drained from him, not only from his wings, which are no longer zingy blue, but from his clothing, from his skin, his hair. It's as if he became a dull, grainy photographic, sepia image on the background of crisp, blue sky.

But this sepia image is alive.

It's roaring in absolute agony with his head thrown back.

His pained roar and whistle of the wind is the only noise left to echo in Uras. The pulsating shrill of millions of screaming children had vanished too.

Holding Chamuel's axe tight in my hand, I turn my head toward the "pastel" army, ready to ward off their attack.

But nobody's interested in me. The "blue" army is silent. Their heads are drawn upwards, watching Chamuel.

I turn my gaze back above me.

Chamuel's plait has unravelled and his waist-long hair floats, dancing around him. His hair is the reason why it takes me a bit longer to understand what's going on.

I narrow my gaze on him and I can see that his body is covered in something. It's all over him: his face, his arms and legs, his clothing.

The layer is brown and it's moving. The living layer ripples over him and I lift my head off the ground, rubbing at my teared up and blood-smeared eyes, straining to see what it is...

I gulp for air.

I try to breath. I swallow back the rising bile, when I discern the nature of that layer, when my eyes zoom in on it, even so far from the ground, and I can make out every single one of *them*.

My mind refuses to acknowledge it, protecting the last shreds of my sanity, but my eyes drinking the sight in.

Chamuel's body is covered by a swarm of odd-looking brownish-grey flies or insects. Busy and agitated, they crawl over his body.

They are fat stick insects, with spikes covering the entirety of their bodies. They are slim and long, with the bottom end curling upwards like the tail of a scorpion.

Four slim dragonfly wings flutter behind each insect's back, producing that buzzing, throbbing noise of children's screams. But while wings of some insects are clear and see-through, others' wings are burgundy, blackish-red.

The insects with clear wings are more frantic. They push the ones with red wings out of their way, and when they succeed, I watch the ones with the red wings fly off Chamuel's body with a burdensome, slow speed. When the ones with the clear wings take their places, Chamuel's agonising screams begin to ride of a fresh wave of torment.

The number of the 'red-winged' around Chamuel is growing. The swarm grows darker and with it, quieter grows Chamuel.

I push my body up, clutching at my arm, trying to get distance between myself and Chamuel's strung high-up, screaming body with the hideous swarm of the insects on him.

I push my feet at the ground, finding the balance to get up, while keeping my gaze on the swarm.

Suddenly, as if following a command, the swarm, as one, lifts off Chamuel's body, and unsupported, Chamuel's body crashes from the sky, and I scream.

With the resonating thud of rattling bones and clanks of metal, the body lands in a white pile of bones and metal armour just a yard from me, and I scream again.

Eventually, with my lungs empty of air, I close my mouth shut, forcing myself to breathe through my nose. I was holding the bile down for so long that I don't know how much longer I will manage.

The white bones next to me are polished like a shiny marble. The bones are covered in sparse rags of Chamuel's blue tunic and trousers, lie in a messy heap. The four wings' bones are bare of any feathers. No skin, blood or meat is left in sight. Discarded bones, the armour and a few clamps of long silver hair are all that is left of Chamuel.

They ate everything of him; even the pearls in his plait are gone.

The swarm of red-winged insects propels down, whizzing above me, and I cover my head, but they fly above my head, just an inch away from my eyes, and I can see the insects' veiny wings, filled with Chamuel's sloshing blood, and countless rows of small yet razor-sharp teeth at the front of every insect's face.

The swarm makes a beeline for Rafe.

I roll to my side, pushing through pain, drawing a breath ready to yell, to warn Rafe, when the blood-filled cloud stops above Rafe, who still holds Jess, then fans out behind Rafe's back, settling there.

The wind has died down.

The dark rain clouds are gone too, and through the glistening blue sky, the sun shines down on shocked Uras.

Swinging on my knees and one arm, I look at Rafe, who is calm and collected.

He looks at the silent pastel-winged army.

Not a single one of them is in the air anymore. They all stand on the ground and their weapons are lowered down.

CHAPTER 4

"He said traitors will be dealt with", Rafe's calm voice rings in the still air. He nudges his head towards the pile of Chamuel's bones, addressing the pastel-winged army.

"I agree with him. Traitors will be dealt with, and swiftly. Every high treason and its attempt will be punished by death, sentenced and carried out immediately", he yells above the silence of the hall.

He scans the "pastel" crowd with a heavy, brooding gaze.

I wouldn't call what stands in front of us an "army" anymore. They have lost their bravery together with their leader. Hesitant, they shuffle their feet on the stone floor, unsure of what to do next. Confident in his win, Chamuel didn't prepare them for defeat, haven't issued instructions should he die.

"Uriel had lost her life because of traitorous kyriote, *ibnatum*", Rafe practically spits the last word, "whose qal should've been extinguished a GA ago, and he was executed for what he's done."

"I'm not going to allow the treachery again", Rafe says into a weary silence. "The high treason to Uras and Uriel *will* be punished by death."

"AnshaanKataaru will stand!" Rafe roars. "It will stand today and until the end of Anunnaki. But it will stand with the righteous ones! Only the righteous will be allowed to dwell high with the daughter of An. Only the righteous will be walking the great halls of Uras.

"Declare yourself to Kataaru now, because as the Great Enki, Firstborn of An of Nibiru had prophesised: "The Judgement Day will rise upon us when we fight, and anyone who's not with us..." he pauses, scanning the angels with his heavy gaze, "is against us, and our foes will no longer receive the mercy from Uriel."

He stops, scans the group, and then adds: "Just as Chamuel received."

One sharp intake of air by dozens of angels in unison rustles through the hall.

I'm upright now, sitting on my heels.

I turn my head towards the pastel-winged. I watch them, their confused, scared faces, easily reading into their afraid minds. Without a leader, I see them clearly for what they are.

I can't believe that this weak crowd is Uriel's army.

It's no wonder she's dead.

Between these weak and pathetic peacocks with swords and backstabbing Chamuel, Uriel didn't have chance to survive. Even unorganised, malnourished, raggedy Baza's lizards are more fierce than this inadequate "army".

For the sake of my future, I desperately hope that there are Uriel's soldiers elsewhere, that those soldiers are braver than this over-dressed, privileged, pampered bunch. But something tells me that what's in front of me is all that Uriel has.

I'm screwed.

A single sword clanks to the ground. I turn my head from Rafe towards the "pastel" crowd, watching, trying to figure out who it was.

There's a silence. No movement.

Then another sword drops to the stone floor, then something heavier: judging by the sound, it's either an axe or a mallet.

Three men, one in navy blue clothing, decorated with heavy silver embroidery, with silver armour over his torso, and two younger men in lighter, almost turquoise, shades come forward, pushing through the front rows.

The three stand at the front. The one in the navy clothing is a sixty-human-years-old man, but I know now, looking at him, that he is probably as ancient as the universe itself.

Two young men stand to each side of him. Their tunics carry less silver embroidery and only a narrow breastplate covers each of their chests. They don't have the full armour of older warriors.

The narrow ravine runs between them and Rafe and me. But the ravine is not the only issue that divides us, as all three stand, silent, glaring at Rafe, and I can read the resentment in their faces and their stances.

I turn and look at Rafe. He doesn't say a word either. The swarm of flesh-feasting insects buzzes above his head, but the insects are quieter now, their pulsating screaming has gone.

Clumsily, I rise to my feet, using Chamuel's large axe to help myself up.

I'm next to the pile of Chamuel's white bones and armour. I am in the middle of this stand-off, just as Chamuel was before me.

"You – ", I start but my voice is tired and weak. My throat is raw from my earlier screams. I clear my throat.

"What are your names?" I address the three men.

I shuffle closer to the ravine, using Chamuel's axe as a walking stick. It accompanies my steps with its heavy thuds. The eyes of all three of them are on the axe, watching it's moving with me.

I stand at the edge.

Rafe and the swarm are behind me and the blue army with pastel wings in front of me.

"Names", I demand, straightening my back and pushing back my fears and self-doubt.

"Fake it 'til you make it", Rage giggles in my ear. Cheeky cow!

My blood runs down my arm, down the axe, coating and painting it red, and begins to pool on the ground where it rests.

The scent of the tropical fruits and the ocean of the halls now holds the metallic tinge of blood.

"Hadriel", the old man barks, narrowing his eyes at me.

"Tzatkiel", one of the younger men answers.

"Gazartiel", the other young man replies.

"You want to leave?" I ask.

"We have no business serving the human", the old man answers. The angry slits of his eyes are ablaze.

"You are no Uriel. Everyone knows this Qal was portaged by mistake", he spits at his feet.

I don't know the "portage" but I know the word "mistake" only too well. It was said to me all of my life.

Next to me, Rage bulges her eyes at me, while nodding her head at the old man, demanding to know if I've heard him.

Yeah, I have.

But I grind my teeth against Rage's incitement to violence. Nobody's going to say that I haven't tried.

"So you're not going to give me a chance? You don't believe that Uriel's essence is in me?"

"Uriel wasn't the only leader we had", he barks, nodding his head at Chamuel's bones. "You've promised the safe passage to everyone who no longer wants to share the quest with you, yet you have broken your oath. How do you expect to keep anyone with you? You don't know anything about us and even you word is worthless."

He points his finger to the pile of Chamuel's bones, while glaring at me.

"You were born human, you'll remain human and we'll never serve a human", he says.

He is the only one who speaks, while the two young angels stand on either side of him, quiet, their gazes dance between the ground, white bones, the old angel and me.

"Is that how you feel?" I look at the younger men, who haven't uttered a word.

They cast their gaze to their feet and give a short nod.

Fine. No persuasion or explaining myself will help here.

I will not tell them how wrong they are about me. I will not tell them that I am an angel now just as they are. I will not be convincing them to give me a chance.

I will not give them the satisfaction of seeing me, as a hot, bubbling mess, trying to persuade them to stay, explaining that I planned to let them go without bloodshed and that the Chamuel thing happened without my knowledge. All that will only make me look weaker in their eyes.

I grind my teeth.

Rafe!

"You know what?" I say, glaring at him, "stay, don't stay – I don't give a shit. I'm sick of trying to convince you that I'm as good as your dead leader! Your Chamuel didn't protect Uriel from Mik'hael's sword! You", I hiss, point finger at the man, "didn't protect Uriel from Mik'hael."

"Chamuel had failed. More than that: he betrayed her and that's why he was punished", I roar.

I need to look godly, fierce, a contender for the essence of Holy Uriel.

"Fake it 'til you make it!"

Rage is running circles around me, giddy with excitement of upcoming bloodbath. She's a blood-thirsty little thing.

"Uriel is in Udhad because of you. All of you! Her Qal is lost *because* of you!" I point my finger at the small army behind his back. I carry my heavy gaze from one face to the next and some of the angels drop their gazes under my stare. "And you have the audacity to throw the humanity in my face? After you being the reason for not having the leader anymore? You have failed to protect your leader. You are culpable. All of you! You've closed your eyes to the betrayal after you swore to lay your life for your Uriel. You've enabled what happened to her! All of you!"

A croak, which has very little resemblance with a laugh, escapes me.

"You're a bunch of weaklings, running around, bitching that your world changes, that it no longer revolves around you."

"I'm sick of convincing people, sick of proving myself all of my life", I mumble.

"You know what?" I snap my gaze back to the old man, "don't like me – there's the door!" I throw my finger, pointing somewhere to the side of me.

"But as he said", I nudge my head in Rafe's direction, "be careful what you wish for. We'll come for everyone who crosses us", I call to them, rising on my shimmery purple wings above the ground. The chopped wing with a missing tip is killing me, but I grind my teeth, pushing through pain.

The wind picks up, following my mood, but I need it right now. I need it to instil the fear of God into these arrogant angels.

"An in the skies and Uriel in Udhad be my witnesses, I will come for everyone who crosses me, and no amount of magical swords", I jerk my chin to their weapon on the floor, "will protect you."

"Leave now!" I bawl to the angels below, spreading my arms wide. "Everyone who wants to leave, drop your weapons and leave, peacefully. That is the mercy I have promised you, and here I'm delivering it."

I turn and glare at Rafe and the brown, flesh-eating, buzzing cloud behind him.

His gaze meets mine for a moment and he gives me a sharp nod, before turning away, his teeth grinding.

Tough-freaking-love, pal! You can slaughter them later if you like, on your own time.

"If you want to leave – leave now!"

An array of weapons clanks to the stone floor, producing a weird and rough melody.

Pause.

Then a few more weapons drop.

"Fly", Rafe's voice rumbles from below. It's clear that it would be the last of his warnings.

There's a quick scuffle on the ground. Angels' wings brush over each other's. The bodies are pushed and someone falls to the floor.

One after another, angels rise to the sky like a flock of birds. The beating of their wings disturbs the brooding silence.

Their colourful wings bring them to the level with me. Some angels don't meet my gaze, while others openly glare at me with hate or despise.

But one by one, they disappear in the boundless blue sky, the beating of their wings fading.

Only a handful of angels are left on the ground below. The earlier unified and tight army now looks patchy and pathetic.

As if it were possible.

But it's better than nothing.

Rage stomps away in a huff. She can't believe that the rousing speech of mine hasn't led to a mention-worthy bloodshed.

But I ignore her, as I descend to the ground.

I close my hand over my wound, trying to stem the blood flow. Maybe because of the stress of the situation, maybe because of the blood loss, but suddenly I feel bone tired.

I think about making another speech, thanking them or rousing them for battles to come, promising the endless perks of bountiful Heaven coming their way, but I have nothing else to add.

Amongst the remaining angels stands one of the earlier young men.

I fly over the ravine, landing next to him.

"Why are you still here?" I demand.

"I swore the oath to serve Uriel and I will obligate myself to my oath, just as my father taught me", he answers.

"Even if he has forgotten his own lessons", he adds quietly.

I look at his young open face with sincere grey eyes, framed by blonde shoulders and long curly hair. His face is smooth and beautifully proportioned with timeless beauty of an ancient Greek statue. My gaze slides over his slim young body.

He is either naïve or very cunning. I guess only time will tell.

"Thank you", I say. I don't have any speeches left in me and I don't have the energy for interrogation. At the moment, there's nothing more to say.

I look at Rafe. His head is drawn up as he surveys the red veil of the overfed, toothy brown stick insects above him.

After a few long seconds of fascinated scrutiny, he gives to the red cloud a small nod, and sluggishly the bloated swarm takes to the sky. Their dark bodies obstruct the light for a few minutes, before disappearing in the depth of heaven.

The sky is clear and still again.

Rafe's wings burst open, and he jumps over the ravine in one long stride, landing next to me and the young angel.

"Hold."

He shoves Jess' small body at the young angel.

The startled angel catches Jess' body against his chest.

Turning away from him, Rafe walks to the pile of Chamuel's remains. He bends over the bones and picks up a navy blue rag – the piece of clothing that's left of Chamuel. He shakes it and the small loose feathers, chipped bone and dust rise from it, spiralling and landing softly to the ground.

Rafe comes over me.

"Give it", he huffs, tugging my hand off my wound. He wraps the blue rag around my bleeding arm, once, twice, tying it with a double knot.

He struts over to the angel, scooping Jess in his large arms.

"Come", he calls to me over his shoulder, marching out of the damaged hall, leading me away, leaving the small crowd of befuddled angels to roam the ruins of the once immaculate hall, questioning themselves and the choice they had just made.

CHAPTER 5

I was seething since we've left the angels and the wrecked hall behind. I was livid then and I am livid still.

I wanted to confront Rafe right there, to demand to know what that "swarmy" stunt was about, but mainly: how dare he undermine me.

I need to know if he thinks this how things will work from now on. I need to know if it was a mistake giving him the essence.

I have already begun to regret it.

But he had Jess in his arms and I didn't want to quiz him while we were walking the halls. I didn't want any extra witnesses to my weakness, witnesses to my slipping control on ruling this place and on my emotions as I began to feel Rage's presence around me. Her hot whispers caress my earlobe even now.

I was set out to prove myself to them but I've lost the battle – within two seconds and in spite of my rousing speech, I've lost soldiers and followers. Instead I've obtained glaring evidence, delivered in a most blatant way, that I'm not the leader they hoped for or wish to follow.

So, I grinded my teeth, following Rafe down the white corridors, watching him strut decisively with Jess in his arms, her feet swinging with his steps. The corridor ended with a small hall, out of which three new corridors sprouted, one sharply to the left, one straight ahead of us with steps down and one slightly to the right, Rafe took the one to the right.

The opening of the right corridor is wider than the others. Two columns of white polished carved stone stood tall at each side of the entrance.

We walked down the passage for a while, but eventually the corridor came to an abrupt end, giving way to another hall and crossroads. Rafe has chosen another corridor, but I've stopped counting them by now.

As much as I wanted to ask Rafe about these corridors, how I could find my way in the maze of them if I needed to, I didn't. I was afraid if I open my mouth, I wouldn't be able to shut it until everything I needed to say was dragged into the open, and that is exactly what I was so desperately trying to avoid.

Finally, standing in the privacy of a large room, I could exhale the strangling rage.

We are in a large bright circular room the size of a theatre hall a hundred, maybe two hundred feet in diameter. Tall and large windows adorn the entire circle of the wall. The windows are twice my height, and encircling the room, they make this room the brightest room I've even been in.

A dozen tall, carved stone pillars are erected within the room and positioned to create a smaller circle inside the circle of the room.

The second floor of this room rests on these pillars and a narrow staircase is carved into the opposite side of the room, leading up to the next floor, and who knows where else. A table with two small angelic statues on top, propped to the side of the staircase.

The tall rotunda dome sits above the second floor, above the pillars.

A large four-poster bed is positioned within the pillars' circle and in the centre of the room. Purple, almost black, heavy drapes are tied to every post of the four-poster bed by the thick silver ropes.

There are three of us in this room: me, Rafe and Jess in his arms.

Rafe walks over to the bed and lays Jess on the purple covers.

My Rage gives me a swift kick, my mouth opens and words begin to roll.

"What the hell, man?" I demand, following him.

Rafe turns to face me.

"What, the actual hell, was that?" I screech, losing the slipping control on my breathing and my Rage. Oh yeah, she's smiling alright, pleased to be in control again.

But we need to have this conversation and he needs to hear everything I have to say.

I take a breath, pushing down the lid on the bubbling Rage and take a step closer, looking up at Rafe. I need to see his face.

He stares down at me, not saying a word.

"What, was, that?" I growl, jamming my thumb somewhere behind my back, brushing my wing. Only now I've realised that my wings stand rigid around me.

"What are you referring to?" he asks, unfazed by my attack.

"What am I referring to?" I repeat in disbelief. Sometimes, when he talks to me like this, all stiff upper lip and royal, I want to drown him in that fiery lake myself.

Playing dumb, huh?

As my self-restraint begins to slip, I shove my hands into the pockets of my jeans so they don't fly out, connecting with his face. I so badly want to grab hold of him and shake him, make him hear me.

"I'm referring to the pile of bones we left behind. I'm referring to you slaughtering one of them, after you watched me promising everyone that they can walk away peacefully. After I've made that speech, telling everyone that I am the Uriel and then *you* swoop in, undermining me! In front of everyone! But above all, I'm referring to us losing Uriel's army as a result of your cowboy attitude. That's what I'm referring to!"

Every new sentence comes out of me shriller and louder than the one before, and the blood begins to pound in my ears.

Rage, the sneaky cow, laces her red Doc Martens, while humming "Highway to Hell".

My gaze drops to Jess' white face, stark against the deep purple of bed covers. I've brought him back from the dead for her.

"*Are you sure about this?*" Sam's gorgeous face rises in front of my eyes.

No, Sam. I'm not sure about anything, let alone this!

I spin away from Rafe, marching two short steps to the nearest slim marble column, and my fist flies at it. The column creaks and a razor sharp crack sprouts on its virgin surface, running the height of it in both directions.

"For your future reference", Rafe utters calmly behind my back, "although Uras is made for angels and their angelic powers, it's no match for Uriel's strength."

I spin towards him.

"Exactly. Uriel! I am Uriel", I jab the finger at my chest. "You had no right to undermine me like that in front of everyone."

"I didn't undermine you", Rafe growls, narrowing his eyes at me. "I've made a decision, just as you did before, and so it happened, my decision was different from yours. The decision, which was mine to make as much as yours, may I add."

"Yep", Rage whispers, inciting my hate, "he can slot in perfectly as a new Uriel. Hell, he is the best candidate for the job if there was an audition: angel born and bred, Uriel's original soul mate. And unlike you, they will follow him, will drop you and follow him, because he is one of them and you'll never be."

"We'll never serve the human." The words of the old angel echo in my head.

I grind my teeth, telling Rage to shut up.

I swallow past the shock and burning hate.

What have I done?

"That wasn't your call about Chamuel", I repeat, growling whilst glaring at Rafe.

Rafe scowls. His nostrils flare up, his eyes spark with the heat of emotion and veins bulge on his neck.

"It was. He needed to die."

He turns away from me.

"Why?" I don't let go, but I try a different track and Rage rolls her eyes at my maturity.

"Because he didn't want a human as a master? He wasn't the only one. Or was it because he betrayed me by, apparently, letting Mia in? He wasn't the first one to betray me and he wouldn't be the last", I say, looking at Rafe's back.

Just as you did.

"If he had committed a crime, there should've been a public hearing, tribunal. I, we", I add for Rafe's benefit, "should've shown everyone that new Uriel is fair and could be trusted."

"For An sake, Ariel, open your eyes!" Rafe roars, spinning to me. His two purple wings flash wide open to the sides of him. I close my mouth.

"Will you ever learn? I did you a favour! I've shown you to be strong and capable. I've demonstrated to everybody that Uriel's powers are brimful. I've weeded your garden of the weak and treacherous, and I've delivered a swift justice. I've acted the only way angels understand: powerful, authoritative and vengeful."

When he looks at me, his eyes are blazing eyes of a crazy man.

"You think they don't know what Chamuel did? You think they needed to be told? Oh, you're mistaken. They did! They all did and yet stood by! You know why? Do you want to know why?"

His deep voice holds hysterical notes that I've heard in my own voice so many times, yet never in his. His voice is a high-pitched shrill of a mad man, and then he laughs.

"Because our kind forswears a weak leader", he says and laughs, looks at me and laughs, his laugh changes into something weird and tad hysterical.

I raise my hand and the sound of a slap rings and hangs in the air.

One crazy at a time, please.

His eyes fly open in surprise, together with his raised hand. He is about to strike me.

"Argh", he grumbles, turning away from me and dropping his hand.

I draw in a breath, steadying myself.

Maybe it is the time to admit that I gave half of the world-changing essence to a mad man.

"I should've killed them all", Rafe grumbles.

"So what did Chamuel do that deserved an execution on the spot?" I ask calmly, but I'm pretty sure I know. I think I can connect the dots between his newly-acquired essence and his violent anger. Only a few crimes can earn such a severe reaction.

He rakes his hands through his brown hair, messing it up even more than it already is after the crazy wind. He closes his eyes and exhales.

"You were not the first one he betrayed. Mia's appearance in Uras had nothing to do with you or with you being human. Even if you and

Chamuel became the best of mates, as you call it, he still would've betrayed you, because it all began long before you."

He stops speaking and walks towards the window.

"He is the one who betrayed *her*", he says, looking out of the window. "He was swayed by Mik'hael's promises."

I can't say that I am surprised by this disclosure.

Rafe turns to face me, but the blistering sun shines behind his back, keeping his face in the shadows.

"He lost belief in Uriel's ways. He had enough. Enough of playing for the losing side, had enough of constant sacrifices, which brought no rewards. Or maybe Mik'hael promised him something – I don't know. But he knew that Uriel would've never swayed from her path. She fought far too long for it. So there was only one way to end the millennia long impasse that divided the Sarukh: Uriel needed to die and her essence needed to be nullified, voided."

He stops.

"He is the one who welcomed Mik'hael and his erimnate into Uras. He opened the seal."

"Why didn't you tell it to others?"

"I told you, they knew. Some of them at least knew, and the ones who didn't know for sure, they suspected. Sarukh doesn't forgive weakness. The impuissant ones are not raised in our world: they either fall to Arllu or die. The strong are revered and will thrive, while weak ones are preyed upon. There's no loyalty when the ruling is concerned, there are only fear and calculated alliances. Authoritative hegemony is the only way to rule and lead. Your earlier call for democracy would be laughed at and just by suggesting it, you would've become a target and would be killed."

Rafe falls quiet, and when he eventually speaks, I can hear a trembling in his voice.

"She had missed the warning signs, and now she's gone."

He stops talking. He slides down the window, down the wall, resting his back against it.

I walk closer to him. I see his beautiful face, awash with tears.

"Since you gave me Uriel's essence, I feel so close to her, closer than ever before. I love it, but it breaks me too. I feel her pain, the memory of her pain, the pain of her death. I feel her pain when she was killed and it hurts me. It hurts me so much more because I am powerless against it. There's nothing I can do and I have failed her when she needed me. I've failed to be there for her, protecting her against all of them."

He looks at me.

"I have failed my Arcanum. Only the defaulter would fail to protect the most precious gift the universe can grant one! Yet I am alive and she is in Udhad, and she's disappearing from there too, and soon she will be no more. She will never come back to me, as no one ever comes back from there."

His words become rushed, urgent and hot.

He sits on the floor, rocking himself from side to side. His hands are in his hair.

He begins to mumble.

"I've failed her. I've failed her. What ureeq-taran would fail his own Arcanum?"

He swings his head backwards and the back of his head collides with the wall behind him. He draws his head forward only to smash it again.

He mumbles some words under his breath, but I can't understand him any longer. He is breathless. He screams out one word, only to whisper the next.

"She's hurt... fire...Mik'hael's sword... when they... burning and ripping... The great darkness... taking the last away... The pain... and her pain... Darkness of Udhad eating... it will be the end... at the last of her..."

He raises his wet face to me. His eyes are of a mad man and he says in a loud whisper: "I can hear it sizzle."

Shit! Shit! He lost it. He completely lost it.

And the earlier anger is gone, replaced by the sadness and pity. My heart is breaking for him and somehow I feel responsible, which is totally crazy as none of it was my doing. It was all done before me. But seeing him like this feels as if I have stolen their lives somehow, as if I am responsible for their broken fates.

For the first time I see how broken, really broken, he is.

Having her essence inside him has tipped him over an invisible edge, and I don't know how to reach him.

I don't know what to do or where to go for help. I don't even know where to find the infirmary with the female angel, or if she'd still be there. Maybe like most of the others, she had left.

I slide down the wall next to him, under the window.

I reach out to his moving body, and it takes a while to catch him, to calm the rocking of his deep misery.

I hug him tight, pressing his body to mine and I begin rocking with him. If that's what soothes him, it's the least I can do.

"Shh, shh. Shh, shh," I repeat it over and over again. I begin to say something, something to soothe him, but only platitudes come to my mind and they feel so superficial, banal and empty to comfort this pain, that I stop speaking, and just rock him in the silence of the room.

CHAPTER 6

I am awoken by the painful end of the usual dream.

My throat is sore from my screams, which are still ringing off the walls. But I can hear another agony-laden voice swimming in the room with me, it's a male voice, and for a second I think it's just my imagination until I hear a pained heaving next to me.

I turn my head.

Rafe swings weakly on all fours next to the wall.

I shuffle towards him on my knees. My wounded arm and the sliced tip of my top wing hurt more now. The living pain pounds at the wounds with my every heartbeat.

"Are you okay?" I ask Rafe.

I reach out to him, gently touching his back just under the growing wings' stumps.

The stumps grew overnight, now flaunting a half yard of two wide bones, densely covered in a soft purple down and boasting a few complete, fully-grown large purple feathers at the base.

"I..." he starts, "I..."

He starts twice but falls silent each time, unable to finish his sentence.

He takes a raggedy shaky breath – once, twice, thrice, trying to steady himself.

"An save me!" he eventually whispers. "I just saw Uriel's last moments. I was *her*!"

Welcome to my nightmare, mate.

He turns his head to me, his shocked eyes scream at me in pain.

"Ophanims guard my Qal! I saw everything! I *felt* it!" he whispers.

His troubled eyes search my face for something. Maybe for reassurance that it was real and he's not losing his mind... But maybe he'd rather be told that none of it is real and he's just going insane. I know it's easier than to witness the pain of a loved one.

The sorrow comes over me.

I can't even imagine what it must feel like, to live the last moments of a loved one, to feel their pain, while knowing that you are powerless to do anything to stop or change it.

"Is that what you see?" he asks in a throaty gasp.

I sit back on my heels.

"Yeah. It's kinda the same dream I've been having for as long as I can remember."

Rafe's gaze dances over me.

"How can you withstand this agony on a daily basis?" he rasps.

His pale face is coated with a fine sheen of sweat, and he looks as if he's going to throw up.

"I don't know", I say, shrugging my shoulders, "I guess, you get used to it. I learnt to live with it. Humans are great like that, eventually we all adapt to our environment no matter how painful or miserable it might be. Humans are strong in that respect, probably even stronger than angels. I have lived through much worse."

I draw my gaze up to the window above.

The light in the room hasn't changed. The room is still flooded with the same bright sunshine, which hasn't faded or moved. Staying in this room, it is impossible to tell the time.

Do angels even measure time? Maybe being immortal, one simply wouldn't care about it?

Clumsily, while nursing my arm and hugging it close to my chest, I rise to my feet and plod to the bed in the centre of the room.

Jess is still there. She looks the same: peaceful and still, like Sleeping Beauty in her glass box.

A heavy shuffle of Rafe's footsteps breaks the silence of the large room.

"Is this how it's going to be from now on? The dream?" he asks my back.

"I guess so." I shrug my shoulders, without looking at him, "it hasn't changed for me, so I try not to sleep unless I have to."

I feel sorry for him, but there's nothing I can do about the dream. If I could, I would've changed it for myself by now.

He walks around me, inspecting my wing, before he comes back facing me and tugs at my arm: "Let me have a look."

He takes my arm and unwinds the layers of Chamuel's tunic. The tattered fabric had lost its blue colour, turning dark with my blood.

"The wound is not very deep", Rafe says after inspecting my arm for a moment. "That braggart's axe wasn't even Hannomian. The dirty ibnatum had not thought to acquire one. We'll fix your wound now."

He walks towards the two white slim double wardrobes, carved out of polished stone and erected on the both sides of the entrance door. The wardrobes' surface shines like murano glass.

He opens the door of one of the wardrobes, rummages there for a while before straightening his back, turning towards me and kicking the door shut.

He plods towards me, carrying a black sphere in his hands.

The sphere's weight pulls at his hands, straining the muscles on his neck and twisting the muscles on his arms, under his rolled up sleeves.

"Here. Hold it."

"What –".

But before I have a chance to protest, he shoves the sphere into my hands.

Unexpected, I almost drop it.

"Shit."

I adjust my hold on it, pressing the sphere closer to my chest like an oversized watermelon. It's not the sphere's size I struggle with, but its weight. It's heavier than Jess ever was in my arms.

"What's that for?" I huff, through my teeth, wheezing. "I'm gonna drop it."

"No", he says, "you hold it. Hold until it's done."

"What's done?"

As I say it, the pitch-black sphere comes alive with a soft speckle of golden glow at the centre. The glow, like a light, disperses the darkness within the pitch-black orb. The next second, another speckle is added to the one in the middle, then another one, then the next. As if drawn by a magnet, the specks stick to each other within the centre. More of them appearing, attaching to the ones at the centre, and the sphere in my hands grows brighter.

I look at the bulky dark orb, noticing that the sphere is lit on one side by the external light, and the light is coming *from* me.

I look at myself. The soft beam of light is coming *from* my chest.

"Aaa", I scream. My hands are about to open with panic.

"Hold!" Rafe commands.

My chest is aglow with the golden light of the same colour as the specks inside the orb.

The golden specks keep gathering within the sphere, and some of them swim within the orb like goldfish in a tank. The specks are mesmerising. They're alive, soft and warm, and maybe I'm starting to lose my mind, but I think they talk to each other, softly whispering and laughing.

The dark orb is even lighter now. Then another wide ray of light, this time from above, hits the sphere with external beam.

Standing next the bed, I lift my head to the dome ceiling above.

"HOLD!" Rafe roars, reading emotions on my face.

The dome ceiling above me is the *universe*. Not the crude symbolic drawings, realistic painting, or even a photograph. It's the *actual* universe, I know it, and it's alive.

At the base, the dome is full of windows and flooding with light, but the dome doesn't end where it should. Instead it rises up into the sky, endless and infinite, disappearing into the depth of the deep space above me.

The dome is a magnifying glass, a telescope, which brings the universe to me.

The galaxies of purples and yellows, blues and reds, the dark spots of swirling black holes, the shine of constellations with twinkles of their suns, the sharp pops of exploding stars are all alive above my head.

"Hold!"

But my hands open together with my mouth.

The sphere doesn't fall far, before it's shoved at me with Rafe's hands.

"For An sake, hold it", he says next to me, holding the globe of "gold fish" bowl for me.

I look at him. I look back at the stars.

The beam of cold, silver light comes from the depth of universe, from one of the constellations. It shines at the orb like a searchlight, and when I look close at the beam in front of my eyes, I can see silver tiny speckles of dust, travelling on the currents of that light *into* the orb.

I no longer hold the sphere. I don't know when I had stopped. My arms hang lifelessly by my sides.

I am shocked and mesmerised by the astonishing magic in front of me.

I drop my gaze. The sphere is filled with gold and silver fidgety specks. The light from my chest and the beam from the universe illuminate the sphere.

And then specks begin to swim, down my beam and... *into me.*

I scream. I push at the orb, at Rafe's hands holding the orb. I want to get away. I take a step back, but the beam connecting me and the orb, doesn't break.

Like fish down the stream, the golden and silver specks swim into me, chasing each other. One by one and in clusters, they disappear inside my chest.

I want to throw up. My legs fold underneath me and I crash to the floor.

A faint echo of Rafe's voice comes to me through the fog.

I raise my eye up to him. I read his lips rather than hear his words.

"Look. Ariel, look at your arm."

I drop gaze to my injured arm.

My skin shines, illuminated from within. The luminescence of specks gathers under my skin. Specks tickle my skin and bone. On the stream of light, they rush towards the cut, which has already stopped bleeding.

The mixture of gold and silver rises to the top of the cut. It covers my wound in a living mercurial layer, and the tiny voices of laughter are louder around me.

I raise the arm towards my face, to my ear.

The swirling mercury is talking and what scares me the most is that I understand what they're saying.

CHAPTER 7

"**A**re you okay?"

Rafe's face is above me.

"I think so."

My body is almost submerged within the soft bedding.

I turn my head to my right. Jess' body is next to me.

"Good", Rafe says, withdrawing his head from my line of vision.

"Oh, god..." I breathe out at the round, telescopic rotunda dome above me.

That wasn't a dream. I haven't imagined the universe with a light.

The dome above me has three storeys of windows, each one above is smaller than the one below, which are then crowned by the hemisphere of the universe.

The universe is alive and real as it was before.

"What's with the stars?" I ask, trying to keep my voice unruffled and failing miserably.

"Universe?" Rafe asks from somewhere by the window, but I keep my gaze glued to the dome above. "An has created it, Uriel and Mik'hael were ordained to its safeguarding. Uriel's", he stumbles in his speech and falls silent for a moment, before continuing, "*your* powers are drawn from it, Qal's nourishing, healing. Your life energy is tied to it and as long as it stands, you'll stand too; for as long as it's here, you will always regenerate."

He falls quiet before he adds: "My *saana-mata* loved looking at it. She was determined to keep it going until An roused again."

I see why she loved looking at it. I am mesmerised by the living universe above. Looking at it, I feel powerful, strong and invincible, yet young and small. There is nothing like a window into the universe to empower and humble someone.

"Does Mik'hael have something like that?"

"Mursu sadhu", Rafe growls and then in a few rushed steps he is by my side.

He leans in, hanging menacingly above me. His hands are to both sides of my face, his arms and his face caging me in.

"He needs to die", Rafe growls low, leaning even closer to my face, "that pig *has to die*. You hear me? Die. I don't know nor do I care how big his army is, how many followers and worshipers he has or how far will I have to go to find him. But mark my words, his days are numbered and he's going to die."

He leans into me. His breath strokes my face.

"He must die."

Rafe's warm scent around me, pulling at me, confusing me.

"Okay, he must die", I answer, repeating his words, "and he will. But what happened yesterday... Rafe, you've made the wrong call. We've lost the army because of your rash decision and your need for blood. You haven't executed Chamuel for me. You did it for yourself."

I don't often find myself in this situation, having to preach the restraint to others.

I push him away and sit up.

"You've killed him for your own satisfaction, for your vengeance. It had nothing to do with what was best for Uras, Uriel's legacy or *me*. You did it for yourself."

I swing my legs and stand up.

"You have made my survival harder. You took my army away from me, leaving me open to Mik'hael's attack."

I drop my voice.

"So, next time, when you undermine me, threatening my life directly or with your stupid actions, I will kill you. I will not die because of you."

"We set off today", Rafe barks at me, ignoring my comments and my threat. "I know in which part of Sarukh he resides. We will go there and we are going to kill him, slaughtering anyone who'll stand in our way, who's dumb enough to stake their lives to protect his. We'll slaughter his every follower, every malakhims that pledged to him, every kyriote that serves him. We'll demolish his castle, leaving no memory of him. It will be like he never existed. We are going to kill him, or we die trying, but the *marsu* is going to pay for his deeds."

He didn't hear me. Or he chose not to.

"Rafe, did you hear me? Did you hear what I've said?"

He walks away from me.

I wasn't heard. My reasoning and promise have fallen on deaf ears.

Okay. Let's go with your topic.

"Rafe, how do you exactly envisage the execution of your plan?" I call behind him. "How are we going to fight Mik'hael? Just the two of us? To sneak in and assassinate him? Like he did to Uriel? But I think we won't have that element of surprise, and quite frankly, I don't think we'd manage to sneak in. Or maybe you're planning on an open confrontation. Correct me if I'm wrong, but I think, if you're planning to take on another god, with an army and followers, we would need an army ourselves, like Uriel's army, which we – oops! – don't bloody have anymore", I say, raising my eyebrow at him. "There's no army. All that's left is a bunch of angels of questionable ability and loyalty. How do you exactly imagine to pull this one off?"

I stand, glaring at him.

"You want to go against Mik'hael with a handful of angels or just the two of us? Just tell me which suicide would you prefer, a slow or a fast one? Do you want to have a very short scuffle or caught and slaughtered straight away?" I bristle.

I want to repeat my threat again, remind him that his earlier actions are the reason why we don't have the army, but looking into his crazed eyes, listening to his shallow breathing I change my mind and shut my mouth. Right now is not the time. I don't think it's the time for "I told you so". I am not being heard.

"Do you honestly think that this pitiful bunch of angels is going to follow you or me?" I start again, calmer. "Let's think. Let's think together. There's a difference between keeping loyalty..." I stop. "Ish", I add.

Forever, I'll be questioning these angels' loyalty, "and agree to marching in a neat formation to commit a group suicide. Because going into Mik'hael's place and openly confronting him is committing a suicide. If you stop for a moment to think, you'd see that too, and you'd agree with me..."

I hush my words as softly as I can. I lay my hand on his arm, stroking it in time with my quiet words.

"I don't care. I don't care, anymore", he roars into my face while anger, anguish are splashed over his, and he pushes my hand away. "He must die. He killed her, do you understand that? He just came and killed her, An and her rules be damned. None of what you say matters anymore."

Since he has received Uriel's essence, something had snapped and shifted inside him. I see a change in him: he began losing it. Whatever has happened at the arrival of the essence of his beloved, and is maybe still happening, it is twisting him inside. He is unravelling. He's no longer the rational Rafe I remember. He snaps; he screams, demanding illogical actions and unneeded sacrifices from everyone around him.

I don't know how much deeper he is going to fall or how I can stop him. All that I can do at the moment, is watch him, pushing him away from the edge and soothing his crazy, which is lately a good contestant of mine, and I have to keep him away from doing anything stupid. I don't want to fulfil my promise.

I change track, trying to reason with him.

"Okay, Rafe, let's think for a moment please, together. Where do you think the angels who left went? Where did they go?"

I take his hand into mine, stroking it softly.

"Judging by this old dude's rant, I'd guess at least a few went to join Mik'hael's ranks", I say, "and if we're going to fight him, we need to get ourselves an army. We need to build our ranks again. You told me that Mik'hael's army is vast. Now, it's even bigger. And we have none, zilch, nada, squat. I won't risk you, myself or anyone else for that matter, to take on the fight which is mine. We need to figure this one first."

I can't believe the responsibility for our survival fell on me and I became the military strategist for Uriel's army.

The Scouser has clearly illustrated that running away from who I am was not an option, that Earth never was the "safe heaven", and never will be. Baza's speech and his grey army demonstrated that I'm out of graces with him.

"If you're not with me – you're against me": his ultimatum was clear.

Of course, I didn't hope just to slide in to Uriel's world-changing shoes but I didn't expect that much of a push back and being scorned as if *I had* killed her. When, I've fought Baza, naively I thought I had an army. I hoped that I would arrive into a safe refuge of a safe place that is mine, where I'd be able to catch a break. I hoped to have some induction, "immersion time", where I would be able to ease into the lifestyle chosen for me. And I hoped that Rafe's backing and support would help me navigate and manage the murky waters of angelic politics, his presence would win me the followers – hence me giving him half of my essence.

I didn't expect to fight a vote of "no confidence" the moment I stepped into the halls of Uras and to lose my army the next second.

Standing across from Rafe and watching his crazed eyes, I fear that my survival is again up to me, and only me.

"You want Mik'hael dead?" I ask Rafe, keeping my voice soft and a smile firmly on my lips, while stroking his hands. "Consider it done. We just need to do a bit of preparation, a tiny bit of planning, some research. Not much and not for long", I add quickly, before he interrupts me, "and once everything's all in place, we'll go and kill that scheming bastard, and take everything that's Uriel's, just as you want it, okay?"

I put my hands on his chest and add: "I promise."

But Rafe doesn't answer. Rafe's eyes are glazed and directed somewhere over my shoulder. The caged and torturous thoughts swim behind his eyes, internally directed, and I wonder if he'd heard me. Looking into his crazed eyes, I half expect him to begin talking to himself.

I'm afraid Rafe might have lost it and lost himself to his grief.

Living with my constant nightmare has taught me the feeling it leaves behind, every morning: the feeling of raw anguish, pain and torture, and watching him, I wonder if his feelings are worse than mine, because he is witnessing the pain and suffering of a loved one, of his beloved wife.

And with that thought, the chilling wave comes over, leaving behind the realisation that I'm on my own again.

It's all mine to handle. It's up to me to survive, and I won't be rescued or helped. My life hasn't changed. The location of my suffering has changed, bringing me into divine halls of angels, but not the pain of fighting ugly for my survival, with my every breath.

A rushed drum of knuckles dances on the door and, immediately, the door rattles on its hinges.

Startled, I fall silent. I scoop one of my small swords off the bed, where Rafe placed them after collecting them off the floor in the damaged hall.

Rafe marches to the door, throwing it wide open, without asking who's on the other side.

"Rafael, my beyelai. We're here to follow your instructions", a deep male's voice says past the open door. "We came back as soon as we heard."

Without a word, Rafe walks away from the door, leaving it wide open.

Taking it as an invitation, two males stride into the room, freezing mid-stride by one of the columns, in the outer-circle of the room.

Both males are tall and large, larger and taller than Rafe, looking very alike like only two brothers could. Their jet-black hair is cut short and their skin is dark. Two identical, pastel yellow folded wings protrude from behind the shoulders of the each one of them. Their upper bodies are sealed in silver armour which covers their torso, necks and arms. Their sparkling armours are crossed by large weapon belts, housing various weapons, and another belt full of weapon encircles their waists. The trousers and edges of their tunics underneath their armour is dark blue.

Old white scars mark their hands, which rest ominously on their weapon's belts. One of the angels carries a thick jittery scar across his forehead, while the other's skin is pulled and twisted around his ear, as if covering a healed burn or a torn wound.

These two are Uras' answers to Baza's Butcher.

Both of them study me while I study them.

"Is it her?" The one with a scar across the forehead asks.

"*Her* has a name and she can hear you", I bristle at the one who spoke. "I'm Ariel."

After opening the door, Rafe returned to stand by the window, ignoring expectations of the introduction.

"Our apologies, my beyelai", the one who spoke earlier, answers, "I'm Domiel and this is my brother, Dumah."

"Nice to meet you", I answer.

The regal room, their armour and their formal reply, all of it stinks of some medieval curtsy requirement from me, and I battle with my head and knees for a second, which are itching to drop into curtsy. Instead I keep my gaze up and back straight.

We both fall silent, unsure what else to say. Domiel's gaze travels to Rafe's back.

"Beyelai", he addresses Rafe's back, but Rafe ignores him.

Jingling his white armour, Domiel walks over, and standing behind Rafe he asks: "Rafael, beyelai, what will be your instructions?"

He places his hand on Rafe's shoulder.

"We're going to kill Mik'hael", Rafe growls, finally acknowledging and turning to Domiel.

"As you command, Rafael", Domiel mumbles, taking a half a step back. "Now?"

Bless, although confused, this large fearless angel is ready to follow Rafe's orders, no matter how dumb or suicidal they might be. I like him already.

"Of course we will", I gush as I take a few fast steps towards both men. Although in his agony Rafe is ready to press a "red nuclear button", I'm not ready to sacrifice myself or others to his grief.

"We'll make him pay. Everyone who failed Uriel will pay, but not just yet."

Domiel's confused gaze shuttles between me and Rafe, so I turn to the angel, and dropping my voice, begin to list: "We have lost most of Uriel's army. They took off and left after an old geezer made a scene. Chamuel is dead. This man here", I nudge my head towards Rafe, "assisted with it, and I think some of them got spooked after watching Chamuel die, among other reasons", I add. "So whatever we decide to do, we need take a minute, take a breath, regroup and think."

Domiel nods.

"How many stayed?" he asks.

"I don't know. A handful, maybe a dozen at a push. One of them is Tza..Tza..". I help myself with my fingers, trying to remember the young angel's name.

"Tzadkiel?"

"Yeah." I nod.

"I thought he'd stick around", Domiel nods to himself. "What about his father and brother?"

"They both went. His old man is the one who was very vocal about refusing to serve me."

Domiel nods, his gaze directed inwards.

"If they've left, they most certainly went to Mik'hael and if I know that crazy *sahu* at all, he has made enough of a rousing speech, persuading others to follow."

"To Mik'hael? All of them? Are you sure?"

It is one thing to lose an army, and another thing entirely for my army to join my enemy. I thought it might have been the case, but I said it half-heartedly, hoping to be proven wrong.

Domiel drops his gaze before answering me.

"Positive. He said that a human, holding Uriel's essence is an abomination – the first sign of Apocalypse, which every true angel must fight until his last breath, to rid the Sarukh of this curse."

Brilliant!

This is not that different from what he spat into my face, but in the quiet of this room, surrounded by a few, who chose to stand beside me, hearing that I was judged on *who* I am, rather on what I've done, hurts. Maybe because they'd judged me for something that I can't change about myself – I was born human, was born this way – or maybe because they made their decision before speaking to me.

Since it all began, my birth was thrown into my face countless times.

Who said it's all peaceful and cute up in Heaven?

Here you are: the angelic prejudice at its loudest and the best.

Domiel raises his brooding gaze to me.

"What else?"

Domiel takes a deep breath before jumping off that diving board, and utters: "And he said that the righteous angels of Sarukh have only one true beyelai now: Mik'hael. Uniting under his banner, they should fight to extinguish the mistake and *shaqaat*", he drops his gaze, "abomination delivered to us by Ophanims."

I can practically hear the old angel's voice when Domiel tells me this.

I smile, nodding my head.

"Okay."

"The abomination that was sent to test and temp us! The spawn of Devil!" My mother's crazy eyes and contorted face rises in my mind. Her hate and fear of me.

I close my eyes and laugh. I laugh louder, throwing my head back.

The craziness is bubbling, calling to come out.

"Okay", I say, "okay. We seem to have a consensus. I am an abomination. Everyone agrees. Well, I shouldn't disappoint them, should I? It's bad enough they didn't get what they've prayed for and now *I* won't deliver? We can't have that, can we?" I ask Domiel, smiling.

He gives me an odd look in return.

I laugh.

I walk over to the bed and look at the peaceful face of my sweet Jess then I lift my head up to the dome of universe above.

"The abomination must live up to her reputation, and if the abomination needs to annihilate it all? She'd better deliver it and get it done."

I keep my smile in place, forcing for my lips to stretch, knowing that the second I stop, I wouldn't be able to restrain the flood of tears and sorrow.

I want to cry; run away from them, hide and cry, but I force it out, refilling the empty canister with hate and anger, which would burn longer and hotter, and which will keep me safe.

Rejected again. Not godly enough for ones and not human enough for others.

"What are the two of you are still doing here?" I ask the large male, narrowing my gaze to him and stalking closer. "Shouldn't you scatter too? Join Mik'hael with the rest of them, to fight the bad scary human girl together? Because clearly it takes hundreds of you", I jam my finger into his metal breastplate, "to fight one girl. Bloody pathetic! Hundreds of angels against one of me, hundreds immortal angels against one girl, who isn't even a real angel according to your lot."

But it means they're scared of me, scared enough to run away, looking for another owner to take me down.

This thought pleases me, pulling at my lips, cheering me up. This thought gives me the hope that there must be plenty of something inside of me to make the difference, to make them run.

"We owe our lives to Uriel", the angel says, scanning my face, his face is calm as he relays this matter of fact message. "I owe my life to Uriel. I would be serving Baza right now if she hadn't given a shelter to me and my brother, smuggling us in and with it violating Dingir-Ki laws, and earning herself another hearing at the Dingir-Ki council. I would never betray her, no matter the shell of her Qal."

I want to slap him for the "shell" comment that I've heard already once from Uriel, which I didn't like then, but instead, I stand as my narrowed and suspecting gaze dances over his face.

"They have pledged themselves to Uriel", I say. "Them", I wave my hand, "at one point or another swore to follow Uriel, no matter what. They swore to stand by her, protecting her life at the cost of their own, and look how that has turned out: one had opened the door to the enemy that sliced her throat, and the rest stood by, idly, watching as the life left her."

I take a step closer to him.

"Why would I trust any of your proclamations?" I huff.

He looks down at me.

"Guess, you have no choice but to trust us", he answers, giving me a lopsided scowl. "Not many angels left in here to screw you over."

"Hmm, the angel knows some lingo?" I nod to him. "Impressive. But you're right, the less backstabbing morons I'd have to deal with, the better I'd sleep."

I give the angel a once over, before I walk to Rafe.

Rafe stands, looking out of the window. But when I join him and look out into the vastness of the pure blue sky as far as eye can see, searching for what he is looking at, I can't see anything, but a motionless wall of blue.

"Rafe", I call him.

He doesn't answer.

"Rafe", I call louder, tugging at his sleeve and slowly, he turns to look at me and I cry out and take a step back.

I am shocked by the sight of his eyes. The whites of his eyes are deep-red in colour, and I can no longer find the hazelnut coloured pupils of his, which are must still be swimming in that sea of blood. His bloodied eyes are outlined by thick, black circles of something that looks like an eyeliner, and further outwards the rims of meat-raw red circles of muscles, absent of the skin, encircles his eyes.

It's as if he burnt his eyes, somehow; as if they were burnt from within. A busy network of spidery black veins runs underneath his skin in every direction away from his eyes, covering his entire face in that gruesome black artwork of veins.

The blood-red whites of his eyes which swallow his pupils in the bloody sea...

Again! His eyes...like in Hinnom.

The memory of bloodied trails that bloody tears left behind, as they ran down his face, out of the bloodied whites of his eyes, rise in my mind.

"Domiel", I call in a strangled whisper, over my shoulder to the large angel, while keeping my gaze firmly on Rafe's face. The blood hasn't spilled from his eyes yet.

"Domiel", I call louder, clearing my throat, "can you please come here for a moment?"

The large man crosses the amphitheatre of the room, his steps booming on the marble floor, while I shuffle closer to Rafe.

Rafe's face, marred by the black veins, looks freaky: the bloodied eyes against that face are the eyes of a devil, a monster, an alien. I take Rafe's hands into mine. I need to remind myself that it's Rafe in front of me.

"How are you, Rafe?" I coo. "How do you feel, buddy? It's nice be back home, isn't it?"

The sugar is dripping off my tongue. But either he can't hear me or doesn't register a word of what I'm saying.

"He needs to die", Rafe says suddenly and clearly, raising his head and his unseeing gaze to me.

"Uriel will never be safe as long as he lives. He will come for her, no matter the vessel. He will come for that human girl too, and he will slaughter her just as he did to Uriel, and the human will do nothing to stop him. She is not as strong as Uriel was. She will not stand a chance against him. Every shell, every vessel is damned, until he extinguishes the qal, sending it through Udhad, shredding it into nought..."

Domiel is next to me, and judging by his sharp intake of air, Rafe's eyes are not good news.

"He strikes last, always strikes last, that's why he's still standing, all powerful", Rafe mumbles, staring at me.

"What's this? What's happening to him?" I whisper to Domiel.

"I don't know", he mumbles. "Did Sura leave with others, or is she here?"

"Who is Sura?"

"Dumah", he turns and barks at his brother by the door, "find Sura or whoever you can in the revivification sanctorum."

Dumah walks out, leaving the door wide open.

"Nobody asks where's An now", Rafe continues, "everyone has accepted Mik'hael's story about his mother's seclusion, but has anyone seen her since? Where did she go? All-seeing and all-powerful, how could she allow her daughter to be murdered? How could she stand by and do nothing? How could she have forsaken the balance she fought for so long? How could she have left all of her "children"? Including the ones she was told to ignore?"

Domiel and I look at each other.

"Once, I've seen his eyes filled with blood, and the bloody tears were running out of them then, but that was in Hinnom –" I start, but am interrupted by Domiel.

"What was he doing in Hinnom? When?"

"When he took me there to hide me from Baza and Mik'hael, and to teach me about the essence..." I mumble, "the fire had seared his two wings back then and his eyes began to bleed..."

The memory of that place is still vivid in my mind: the heat, the smell... and the guilt I felt when the fiery pillar shot up, searing his wings off. I feel guilty, for that day and for so many days since...

"I've never seen anything like this", Domiel says. "These black veins under his skin... I don't remember ever seeing them, yet somehow it feels as if I have..."

Suddenly Rafe leans in towards us.

"Unless she is dead too, murdered by a treacherous hand of her beloved son, just as Uriel had. The mother that is old and stubborn is a burden to a son. A tyrannical son is a mother's curse. He will end his mother if it might open the door to his most coveted dream, and with An gone, Uriel is the last obstacle in Mik'hael's way."

Rafe turns, swinging his empty gaze across the room.

"No one had seen her. No one had seen An in three GA."

He turns his head to Domiel and hotly whispers: "Have you seen An?"

Domiel shakes his head and stutters: "N-no."

"And I don't feel her Qal anywhere", Rafe continues his rumblings. "There's no manifestation of her la'atzu. Sarukh is empty of her qal and thoughts. Her la'atzu doesn't ring in the Khe-shedu. An is gone. Even Udhad is empty of her. Mik'hael is the only one who claims have seen her."

Rafe's blind gaze darts to me.

"Do you know what it means, Ariel?"

I'm startled by the sudden lucidity of his thoughts.

"What?" I rasp.

"You are next. He *will* finish what he'd started."

I gulp.

CHAPTER 8

The erratic beating of two pairs of wings cuts off just outside the open door and two bodies, one heavy and one lighter, land on the floor.

A second later, the large Dumah's frame appears and walks through door, followed closely by a slim and small female angel.

The female angel is old, looking close to 70-s in human years. Her beautifully proportioned face carries a few wrinkles and her white, thigh-long hair streams down around her. Her thin lips are pressed tight and her back is straight, as she scans the room with a disapproving and accessing gaze. Only the flexing of a cane in her hands to warn off the indolent students is missing to complete her pissy attitude of a feared school headmistress.

I note that she is the first angel I've met in this visit, who doesn't wear any silver armour. Her tunic and trousers are pastel light blue and absent of silver embroidery. Two powdery lilac wings are folded behind her back, protruding slightly above her shoulders.

Dumah and the "mistress" cross the room, striding towards us.

I come closer to Rafe, rising on my toes, stroking his hands in mine.

"Shh, Rafe, shh. Please don't say anything else, please. Shh", I rush, whispering in his ear.

I don't want anyone else to hear his words. I feel an underlying danger buzzing off his words as if they can start something if they are true, or start something if they aren't.

But something else is there. These words smell of blasphemy, and I fear that they might be the last words my remaining followers will hear, before abandoning me for good.

"My name is Amitiel", the old female announces and nods her head to me. She walks past me, and suddenly I feel a wave of cold air and the smell of winter.

She barges past Domiel to stand in front of Rafe, and taking a cue, Domiel and I both take a few steps back.

The old angel takes Rafe's face into her hands, gently turning it side to side.

"How long has he been like this?" she asks all business-like, non-flustered by the horrific look of his face.

"I don't know", I mumble, "I just found him like this."

"All of you", she barks, turning and glaring at us, "go and stand there."

Her hand flies, pointing towards the door, and I expect the clicking of her fingers, which doesn't come. "I need space."

As obedient students should, with heads drawn remorsefully down, three of us plod to stand by the door. It feels as if we were sent into the "naughty corner".

She turns Rafe's head from side to side. She walks around him, inspecting his wings, taking extra time to study his growing stumps.

"We call her Amy", Domiel leans over and whispers in my ear, "but she doesn't like it."

A naughty smile plays on his lips and I smile back, and then look at his brother, who's grinning as well. It feels like a school, where the three of us, kicked out of a class for rowdy behaviour, are waiting for a mistress and sentencing.

Sobering, I crook my finger at Domiel, telling him to lean down, and when he does, I whisper in his ear: "What Rafe said... earlier", I jerk my head towards Rafe, "can you please keep it to yourself?"

Instantly, Domiel sobers too.

"Do you think it's true?" he whispers back, his eyes dance over my face.

"But it's impossible", he rushes in, "not only that can't be done, but he is her son. The millennial Qal bond, bloodline, her sacrifice..." he mumbles. It sounds like he's trying to convince himself rather than me.

Bloodline. Ha! Blood relatives, mate, are the ones who can do the most damage.

But I don't tell him that.

I'm thinking what I'm going to do if Rafe is right. And if he's right in this, he's right in the last point he'd made: Mik'hael will come for me to kill me.

Rage pops in her head, adding: *"If he'd managed to get rid of his own mother, what do you think he'd do to a human imposter, pretending to be his sister?"*

But I ignore her nagging, as right now I can do absolutely nothing with this little titbit.

"So much for a quiet heavenly life and trying to take it easy for a spell", I sigh to myself.

"It's not his essence inside him, is it?"

I'm startled and pulled back from my thoughts, to find an expectant pair of eyes on me.

"It's not his essence inside him, is it?" the female angel repeats, calling across the room, glaring at me.

I shake my head "no".

She mumbles something to herself, but I can't make out a word.

"You", Amitiel calls across the room, pointing her finger at Dumah, "either of you. Bring me zall–anzig."

She takes Rafe's hand and leads him inside the circle of the columns, until he stands under the rotunda dome.

Dumah walks towards them, waddling under the weight of the... *black sphere.*

Again I watch the brightening of the sphere, the swim of the golden flakes within, the ray of light connecting Rafe's chest with the centre of brightened sphere, only this time I watch from a distance.

But when it comes to the ray of light to shine from the universe of the dome above, connecting with the sphere, the air above remains dark.

I raise my eyes upwards and so does Amitiel, waiting, but nothing happens under our eager gazes.

There's no silver ray shining from the universe into the sphere and out into Rafe. There are no silver flakes of the universe in the sphere, only a few golden specks that were left from healing me earlier, which are swimming from the sphere into him.

Amitiel spits to the ground and mumbles incoherent curses.

"You", she barks, pointing her finger at me, "come."

She is bossy and scary.

Gingerly, I plod towards her, stopping within the circle of the columns, but still a decent distance away.

Now, it's a party within the circle of the dome above: Jess on the bed, Rafe, the white-haired witch, Dumah and me, not far away. Domiel is the only one who's left out from our quaint gathering.

Dumah still holds the globe next to Rafe's chest.

"This", she says, pointing her thin finger at the sphere, "will keep him going for a while. For reasons unknown to me, he doesn't draw the energy from the universe. It's your job to replenish the sphere: to harvest the *gizin-ugdu* and fill the sphere regularly, letting your Qal in too, so the both of them can marry, enrich the fluid of life, and then regenerate and provide energy to him. Do you understand me?"

The old woman lets go of Rafe's hand and walks over to me.

Standing so close to her, I can feel the chill coming off her and when her light blue, almost glacier-white eyes look at me, I can see a fine layer of frost covering her pupils.

"If you want him to live, you do as I say until I discover the reason and the solution. Do you understand what you need to do?" she pushes.

She speaks to me as if I'm dumb.

"Yes, I understand", I bristle.

"I hope you're stronger than you look", she adds with a huff.

"Hold it until all gizin-ugdu are gone", she calls to Dumah over her shoulder.

With a last glance at the bed and Rafe on it, she turns to walk away. Her hair rise, following her motion, and I cry out when a strand of her hair brushes my hand.

I drop my gaze and watch an angry looking, red long mark blossoming on my skin.

"It's just frost bite. Don't be such a wuss", she dismisses with a wave of her hand.

With a few short yet clipped strides, she reaches the door and Domiel next to it.

"I will be back soon. Find her something dingir to wear so at least she looks the part", she instructs him.

With another fleeting glance, she walks out of the room and the next second, the beating of her wings fade into the distance.

CHAPTER 9

Dumah holds the sphere for a few minutes longer, until the golden light is extinguished and the sphere freezes into the solid emptiness of a black hole.

A few heartbeats later, Rafe turns his head, scanning with a confused gaze Dumah next to him, me and Domiel by the door.

"When did the two of you get here?"

His gaze drops to the sphere in Dumah's hands.

"What are you doing with it?"

He snatches the black ball out of Dumah's hold and walks to the wardrobe by the door to place it back there, giving Dumah a scowl along the way.

"We have arrived as soon as we heard, my beyelai", Domiel says, touching his four fingers to his forehead, bowing to Rafe.

"Chamuel had sent us to Apkallu, supposedly provide support to you, but as soon as we heard that you're here, facing the insurrection, we came back. Please forgive us, my beyelai, for not being here when Uriel and Uras needed us."

Domiel bends his knee and bows his head to Rafe, while still holding his fingers to his forehead.

"That's alright, my brother", Rafe answers, scooping Domiel's large shoulders and pulling him to his feet and embracing him. "You're here now."

Brother?.. Interesting...

Uras confuses me. The constant, unending and lethal power struggle under the mill of a gossip machine, with an unhealthy dose of long lost relatives, of sons, accused of killing their mothers and then having a crack at a sister. All of it feels real, yet illusory at the same time.

"Beyelai, can I please suggest to send Dumah to get you and..." he stops, his heavy gaze on me.

I begin to wonder if he has forgotten my name, when he speaks.

"Uriel..." another pause as he stares at me, then gives me a short nod, "fresh clothes and whatever else Uriel might require."

Rafe gives an absentminded nod and Domiel turns to me, waiting for my instructions.

"Please, call me Ariel", I mumble.

With him calling me Uriel, as opposed to "abomination", I take it as an acceptance of me as one of their own, accepting me for what I am.

He gives another nod.

My throat closes up at this unexpected display of loyalty and acceptance, and something tickles at my nose and my throat.

"Thank you, Domiel. That would be wonderful", I say, keeping my head down, being careful not to show my emotions, preventing myself from jumping up and hugging him tight, promising that I will not fail him or his brother.

Dumah's heavy footsteps take to the door, followed by the disappearing pounding of his wings.

"Domiel, please ask everyone who's remained to gather in Council's Chamber in one *bêru*", Rafe says, without turning away from watching the endless azure blue outside the window.

CHAPTER 10

The large long table, carved out of a solid piece of a grey porous stone, occupies most of the space in a white, oblong room with no ceiling. The light breeze dances between the pillars and the arched openings, which serve as windows.

The table is tightly packed with all that is left of Uriel's army, followers and worshipers. These twenty-odd angels is all that I have left, and judging by some scared, sheepish glances, not all of them are fighters.

I flew to this room escorted by a silent Dumah. At this point I began to wonder if he'd ever speak, as every question I asked would be met with a nod or shake of the head.

I flew following another angel and it was a new and fresh experience: to fly within a building, above the same corridors I used to walk only a few days ago, and watch the maze of them shift and change as I glide above.

It was a weird sensation to fly, to walk out of the room, open my wings and take into the sky after another angel, with the ease and normality of picking a pair of gloves by the door on a wintery morning, with an opening of my wings, accepting that I am one of them.

Before I left, Rafe told me that we'd meet the last remaining angels, that it would be a sort of initiation, where I'd be introducing myself to them, explaining what I am about, while boosting morale.

Rafe offered to speak to the angels on my behalf, but I declined. It was time for me to take full control over everything that's happening, and if I make a mistake, I want to be responsible for that. I want to be able to blame myself for once, to stop floating down the stream of someone else's decisions.

The both brothers, Domiel and Dumah, are here too, seated next to Rafe.

The "mistress" Amy with her white hair and pissy expression sits at the table too and so is young Tzadkiel with a sad and innocent face. Although he is still sealed in his armour, looking at me with a resigned expression, I wish he had given his armour to Amy. I think she would've done more damage and achieved more with it than he ever would.

There are three old male angels in dark tunics, three young females with wide-opened eyes and innocent expressions over their faces, and a few males, which are the only ones remotely looking like fighters.

If I were to take all females out of the equation, I have brothers, a hand full of fighters around the table and Tzadkiel, plus me and Rafe. And that's it. That is all against Mik'hael and Baza.

Even if I add the four females to the total in a hope that they know how to handle a weapon, it's still not an army, it's a gang at a push.

I am dressed in the angelic clothing Dumah has found for me, but my attempt to look the part, had failed miserably.

With Dumah's few runs back and forth, I've eventually sealed myself into some deep blue trousers and a pastel, almost white, tunic, virgin of any embroidery. After trying Uriel's lush silk, purple clothing, covered from collar to hem in splendid silver and gold stitching, I've resigned myself to the fact that I don't fit into it. Uriel's womanly shapes are not the match for my flat lanky frame, and after trying the heap of clothing that Dumah had to bring a few times over, I began to miss the excellently stocked wardrobe at Baza's place.

With the help of Domiel's chatter, I was updated on the symbolism of angelic embroidery and the meaning behind the colours of the angelic clothing. The higher the one's rank in the celestial hierarchy, the darker is the shade of the tunic, and with every new accomplishment the embroidery sprouts denser over one's clothing. The silver embroidery for angels is like inking within gangs, the higher the status and longer the kill list, the denser one's skin was decorated.

Now standing in front of the angels who still believed in me, or Uriel to be precise, and wearing mismatched clothing, looking nothing like a glorious Uriel would, but more like a patchwork ragdoll, I feel inadequate and nervous.

I'm not a visual representation of fearless Uriel, and I know it. The mismatched clothing of two different casts, one of the lowliest, I look nothing like The Bringer of something and Harbinger of Doom should look. I don't inspire fear or awe. I don't inspire confidence or following. Again I need to try harder. Again I need to jump higher than any of them could, to achieve the same outcome. But what's new in that?

I nervously tug at the hem of my white tunic as every face in the room is directed at me. Every pair of eyes is zoomed on me, reading my every move, ready to hear my every word, interpreting my every breath.

I stand at the head of the table with Rafe to my right, who unlike me looks breath-taking in his purple angelic clothing. His trousers and tunic are of a simple cut, yet covered in heavy silver and golden embroidery: flowers, leaves and vines blossom over his sleeves, intertwined with something that looks like ancient writing symbols, while the sun and moon are stitched over his shoulders.

Sunlight catches on his embroidery, shooting a million tiny bright rays off him. With his back straight and with his chin up, he looks regal and fearless, just as an ancient God should.

I lift my head up to the sky of the usual azure blue.

"Are you sure you don't want me to talk?" Rafe whispers in my ear, turning his back to the angels at the table.

I shake my head and bring my gaze down.

"No, I've got this."

Time to be a big girl.

I clear my throat.

"Thank you for staying", I start, "thank you for being here. Thank you for believing in me. I can imagine it was hard for you to accept the transition, but I'm grateful that you did."

My hopeful gaze collides with guarded stares of the angels in front of me and I swallow.

I take a breath and grab the side of the table, steadying myself. The grey stone of the table is rough and the rough edge cuts into my palm, but surprisingly, this human sensation soothes me, calming my nerves, reminding me of everything I've been through.

And I'll get through this one.

I straighten my back and raise my chin.

"We're all here because of Uriel", I call to the angels, louder and steadier this time. "She has gifted you freedom, even life to some. She's provided you with the safety of Uras and the company of likeminded –", I pause, tripping on my next word "people", catching myself in time.

"Angels", I finish.

"All of you made Uras your home. It became your safe harbour and it is certainly my safe place. None of us have anywhere else to go. Uras is our home", I call to them, founding my equilibrium, "home, which is crumbling under our feet. Our home is under threat! It's under threat from every angle. More forces than ever before want to break us, to knock us down, to dissolve our home, turning it into rubble. Our home needs us, more than ever. We need to protect Uras in Uriel's honour and everything she believes in. But even more so, we need to protect it for ourselves and our future!"

While I was waiting for the delivery of my clothing, Rafe has imparted a brief, yet very valuable, angelic history lesson, which not only has shared the story of angelic history, but gave me an idea.

"Following An's infirmity after the loss of part of her essence, and her later reclusion, Mik'hael came sick with rage", Rafe said. "He wanted to deliver his justice to the humankind – the ones he blamed for his mother's suffering. But An had forbidden him from doing so by sealing him into the oath.

"Enraged by his powerless position, blinded by his need for vengeance, by the forced restriction of his mother, unable to do to humankind what he thought was only fitting and deserving, Mik'hael directed his obsessive belligerence on his own domain. He took out his rage on his dwellers and followers.

"Swiftly and within a few days, Mik'hael had exiled all of his "uncomfortable" angels: angels of free-will and free-thinking, truth-tellers, soothsayers, the ones who were born from different Gods or came from different civilizations. He called it the "Cleansing of Sarukh". He called it a "needed weeding of traitors for the wars to come". Dozens upon dozens of angels were cast away. But words came to Uras that hundreds of hundreds were cast.

"Alter that, he permanently sealed the borders, locking in everyone who agreed to stay with him, everyone to whom he granted the residence. No one has heard from them in millennia.

"Some of the exiled came to Uriel and were offered sanctuary, but that's only a very few. Many others, although they have asked, were declined the refuge by Uriel. But there were many more, who after their ordeal with Mik'hael, didn't want to deal with Anukians again. Maybe fearing to be rejected for the second time or maybe nursing loathing and hate, they went to the only entity as powerful and great as Mik'hael and Uriel. They went to Baza.

"Baza didn't turn anyone away, as you remember he's not very scrupulous guy. For GA, he welcomed renegades, shysters and monsters with open arms. There were perverts and murderers amongst those angels, but also angels of arts, love, knowledge, free spirit and free will. One of those angels cast away by Mik'hael and accepted by Baza, you've met before. She is an angel of determination in mankind. She was cast away, one of the first for her association with humans."

"Who is it?"

"Tabbris. Tabby as you know her, the angel and guardian of self-determination. She's one of the younger guardians, created by An especially for humankind to encourage them to further their discoveries."

Tabby. A little girl with an atrocious sense of style, so loving and trusting, yet brutally thrown into a vipers' nest of Baza's place... Cute little Tabby...

"To this day, no one knows the scale of the exodus Mik'hael had caused", Rafe continued. "Since then, the number of angels residing with Baza of their own free will remains unknown. Arllu no longer holds only the angels who sold their qals to the Lord of Ki. Now Arllu is a place for uncomfortable angels too. With one move of Mik'hael's, Arllu has expanded drastically..."

And just like that, I knew who I need to see and where I need to go looking for soldiers and followers.

I pause, scanning the table of the last followers in front of me.

"It's only a matter of time before Mik'hael comes to our door, bringing his army in tow, just like Baza did earlier. But unlike Baza, Mik'hael has no business convincing me with alliance and he wouldn't offer refuge to any of you. He will come to kill me, to kill all of you. As far as he concerned, we all deserve to die."

I pause again. The angels are silent, not arguing with my assessment of the situation. It's nice to be right once in a while.

"He will come with his army, with his followers. He will pound his fist on the door. He will demand our blood, all of our blood, every single last one of you", I call to the council of the remaining angels. "Mik'hael would come to see our blood stream down Uras' corridors, down the steps, and then he would level Uras, leaving no stone unturned. He will kill us for many of our sins, real and imaginary, but he will kill us for Uriel's sins... *and his own!*"

"Ariel, what are you saying?" Rafe's hot whisper brushes my face as he leans in, but I ignore him, as I take a side step away from him.

"He will come calling. He will throw the entire strength of his army at us, and if we want to survive, we need to grow. We need grow our numbers, growing with it our strength. Our strength and survival *is* in numbers."

As I speak, I walk around the large table, behind each seat, and as I finish the prelude, I stop across from Rafe, next to pissy Amitel, listening to the held breaths of the angels, who are waiting for my next words. They know that something big is about to come, and I'm not going to disappoint them.

"I will go to Arllu", I say into a breathless silence, "and will bring refugees of Mik'hael's regime here, into Uras."

"Ariel..." Rafe's voice rumbles in warning, but I ignore him.

"I will offer sanctuary to everyone who'd ask for it. I will fill our ranks and we will grow. We'll get stronger, and with it our chances for survival will grow. I'll give us a chance to fight and live."

My last two sentences are drowning in the explosion of gasping and chatter, exclamations of approval and disbelief, cursing and mumblings, which are questioning my mental abilities.

Ignoring them all, I scan my gaze over the crowd, before I pin it on Rafe, who is glaring at me, and holding his heavy gaze, I yell above the rumbling: "I'll do what Uriel has failed to do. I will welcome everyone who needs help. I will do the opposite to what Mik'hael has done. I will turn Uras into a sanctuary for anyone who needs it. Uras will be an accepting place that welcomes everyone with open arms, and while doing it, I will protect my home at any cost. I'm going to protect my family", I turn away from Rafe, addressing the angels at the table, "and you are my family."

The shocked silence has smothered the stunned room. With the last of my speech, the earlier chatter has gone, as the angels' petrified gazes scream at me in a confused panic, at the fear of losing another leader to madness.

"I will turn Uras into the place Uriel has failed to make it. It will be a progressive place in Heaven to offset Mik'hael's craziness, and I will save us all in the process of doing so."

I walk around the table, past the stunned angels and every head that turns to me and walk out of the room, followed by the swish of my bottom wings on the stone floor.

But behind my back the room is coming back to life.

CHAPTER 11

"You should've not made this pledge without consulting me first", Rafe roars, striding towards me the moment I walk through the door.

He beat me to the room because I got lost coming back.

I must've taken a couple of wrong turns before getting completely lost, unable even to retrace my steps. I've tried to take to the sky, but from this height Uras looked even more confusing, like a 3D map of a lost city. Corridors upon corridors, halls large and small, the stairs, and after circling a few different areas for a while I landed in a nearby hall. Thank god, I've bumped into one of the younger females from the earlier meeting at the Council Chamber and she's agreed to escort me back.

Once her initial shyness evaporated and I agreed to answer her first tentatively asked question, she has relaxed enough to begin to fire an unrelenting line of questions at me about the "human world", my "very adventurous travel through Arllu and Apkallu" and "battles", which I apparently have won against Baza and his lizards in phenomenal numbers. With pauses only to draw breath, she was *telling me* about my great achievements, stopping now and again to verify details of my conquests. According to her, I was a weathered warrior and a true archangel, who's already defeated her enemies.

I didn't argue with her favourable picture of me. If I fail in what I plan, she'd be disappointed in me just like everyone else in Uras.

When I asked her name and what sort of angel she is, she turned deep red and mumbled: "My name is Akriel, my beyelai. I aid those with infertility."

In spite of her title and the sphere of her influence, she has turned out to be as innocent and naïve as she's appeared. But it's not the worst feeling in the world to have my own, personal cheerleader, even if she is slightly misguided in my achievements.

But I'm back with the one who is always "here for me" to point out my failings and mistakes.

In a few large strides Rafe is in front of me.

"You can't offer sanctuary to everyone!" Rafe roars to my face. "Some angels are not allowed here for a reason! There's a larger justification as to why Uriel didn't want them here in the first place, and now you've declared to offer refuge to *all* of them within our walls. *All!*"

He throws his head up to the ceiling and roars some more.

I have to say, I'm getting increasingly tired of his dramatic demands. I stand, ambushed, by the door, watching his loud and roaring overreaction, patiently waiting for him to end his outburst.

It's nice for a change not to be the one who's causing a scene. I wonder if I'm growing up or my head's getting better...

"You don't know what kind of dark sheep you're inviting in. Some are not even sheep. They're wolves."

He turns and glares at me and adds: "Perverted, treacherous, murderous wolves. The scum of Sarukh, and you are opening our doors to them."

I fold my arms and don't say a word, watching *his* rage morphing *his* face.

He screams some more for a few more minutes, leaning into me, then suddenly turning and walking away, only to run back and hang above me, while his eyes bulge and his spittle fly.

But I don't listen. There's nothing more to say. There's nothing he can say for me to change my mind or for me to back down on my promise. But if screaming helps him to feel better, I'm here for him and happy to provide the community service.

"I thought it was how we go about things nowadays. Make decisions by ourselves and do what we please. Killing whoever we want, offer the sanctuary to whomever we want..."

"Argh." Rafe spins away from me again. His frustrated hands are in his hair and the wind has gone from his sails.

Shuffling backwards, Domiel and Dumah skirt along a wall, backwards, towards the open door and disappear through it, slamming it shut behind. I hadn't noticed them before. They've witnessed Rafe's hysterics and my indifference.

"You will not do it", Rafe says, snapping his gaze to me. It is an order. It's final and not open for discussion.

He gives me the order, expecting me to obey it, and just as I'm about to laugh, softly explaining his misguided expectations, Rafe, clearly in his deluded attempt to soothe the sting, drops: "You're just a human, new to our world so I shouldn't have expected you to know what you're doing and what implications there might be to your poorly informed and rash decisions –"

"Excuse me?" I growl low, as anger strangles and vibrates my throat. I raise my eyebrows at him. "You did not just bring it up... again..."

Rage re-laces her boxing gloves, while rolling her eyes at me. She demands to know if "getting better" was ever an option, but mainly, was it worth being nice to others?

A very familiar vibration rocks the floor of the building. The room suddenly has gone dark as if someone has flicked a light switch, allowing deep dusky shadows into the room.

"Just a human?" I demand, repeating his words and taking a step closer to him. "Are you for real, man? What else am I "just"? Just a girl? Just a mistake? Just an... animal?"

I scream the last question.

"Go on", I growl, dropping my voice, "don't stop. Here's your perfect chance to share all your crappy grievances *again*. Tell me again how inferior I am to you, to *all* of you! I haven't heard that in a whole, what?.. five minutes? Go on, and don't forget your usual song about the greatness of your beloved Uriel. Don't leave anything out", I yell. "Make me feel it all again. Remind me. Make me feel it *all*!"

My hands ball by my sides and the room vibrates some more.

"But how about some wee irony, mate. It was me who gave you the essence, giving *you* life. So as far as I'm concerned, *I am* the freaking life-giving archangel now", I roar, as I throw my hands up in the air as if to praise a God, "and not you", I spit out, emphasising each word.

Rafe's expression is changing under my gaze from angry to annoyed, to confused.

I hate him so much right now. But I stamp down on my hysteria, on my hate, on every hurtful word I have swimming in my head, which demands to come out, to relieve the pressure in my head and punch a hole in his heart.

I clamp my mouth shut so tight that my jaw begins to hurt.

I breathe through my nose, careful not to open my mouth, glaring at him for a few long seconds, before I turn and walk away, taking a seat on the bed next to Jess.

It takes me a few minutes to calm down my heart and my Rage, who's not a happy bunny, demanding to know who's that softie she's speaking to and where Ariel went, and why is that guy not rolling on the floor, holding a key part of his body.

I stroke Jess' soft hair, my stroking rhythm flows into a rhythm of my heartbeat.

"Will she be like that much longer?" I ask Rafe, without turning to him.

A surprised pause at the unexpected question holds for a spell, before he rustles: "I don't know."

"Get a load of that", I huff, "the divine archangel who doesn't know something. I thought you were all knowing."

He doesn't answer and after another spell of silence, I turn to face him.

"What did I say about the lecturing?" I ask Rafe. "We have agreed that I am part of it and I have my own opinions and ideas, which you are supposed to listen to and respect. I am aware how wise and all-knowing you are, but have you thought that maybe I have a good idea too? Have you thought that maybe you're in this position exactly because of the way you do your business? Maybe shaking things up is exactly what's needed in your heavenly hierarchy? And maybe your Ofa-things knew exactly what they were doing by bringing me into the loop?"

"Opha-nims", he corrects me absent-mindedly, hopefully thinking on what I have just said.

"Stop it!" I bark, turning to look at him.

"Stop it. Stop correcting me. Stop treating me like I am an idiot. Stop treating me like I'm below you, like I'm dumb, unworthy. Stop it. Stop it all! If you want us to get along, and to last past today, you have to lay off me and quit talking to me like that."

I turn away and stroke Jess' cheek.

"The point is", I add, "give me some credit."

"*For the faith we walk, not by sight*", I recite one of my mother's favourite preachings.

I get up off the bed and walk back towards him.

"You need to start trusting me, and you must stop spitting out the word "human" as if it's something shameful. I will never be ashamed of it. I am proud to be human. Being human has made me who I am. And you will stop this, unless you want us to fall out, do you get me? I am not going to repeat it, ever again."

He is quiet. His deep heavy gaze under drawn eyebrows is glued to me, searching my face, my eyes, looking for whatever he hopes to find there, or maybe looking for excuse to not apologise. Quite frankly, I don't need his apology.

I need his promise that it was the last time I've heard it from him, because I wouldn't be able to promise that nothing would happen to him if he does it again. I won't be able to restrain my Rage.

As he glares at me without saying a word, I continue: "I want to write some sort of constitution for us to live by, a code of conduct of sorts that would govern everyone's behaviour in Uras."

A memory of the custody processing officer with his offer of "The code of conduct" comes to mind, bringing with it memories of Scouser.

I shiver, but I push to continue: "A constitution by which Uras and its every resident would live. Do you have such a document?"

Rafe shakes his head.

"I think with the latest walk-outs, with all underlying resentment and with potential new arrivals of a few very shady characters, we'd need one. One, in which all the expectations will be outlined: the behaviour, loyalty, the punishments and *hearings* for treason", I say, pointedly looking at him, "so there will be no impromptu executions, but rather public hearings, courts with judges and all. I want everyone to know that they will be safe here, yet if something happens, they will be judged, judged harshly, yet openly. I will not tolerate treason any more than you would, but we'll make it work. I will not run Uras like Mik'hael runs his place."

I try to gauge Rafe's reaction, but his face is closed off to any expressions.

At least he didn't say "no" yet...

"I would expect every new arrival to sign this document", I continue, "every current Uras resident, and I was hoping that you'd help me to write this document. You know, since you know the angelic way of life, the lingo, so you can include all the important aspects?"

"That would not nullify the fact that you have invited the exiled ones into Uras", Rafe bristles, but the righteous indignation in his voice has subsided significantly. "The remaining residents might not be happy. We might lose the last of them –"

I raise my hand, interrupting him.

"Rafe, look around", I say, spreading my arms, "we're already in deep shit. We're out of moves. Uras is out of moves. That's it! A few angels is all that is left of Uras, and right now we're just sitting ducks within these walls, just waiting to be shot. We have no alternative. We have no choice. We need more soldiers if we want to have a fighting chance."

Rafe looks at me and I feel that he's unconvinced.

"Look, Rafe", I try again, "there are only two outcomes here: we either survive Mik'hael's or Baza's assaults or we die trying. If we die, do you really care who fought next to you for their lives? I don't. In fact, if they're fighting next to me, I know that they're with me. And man, they will take the risk too. If I ask them to fight with us, ask them to be ready to lay their lives for us and Uras, the salvation and the chance to come back to Heaven would be the least we should offer them. That would be worth dying for.

"But if we survive, then we'll have a fresh, brand-spanking-new set of rules, under which this place would be run. We will have a chance to establish a new order, one that would suit most of us, one that would benefit all of us, the order which gives second chances, a safe shelter, gives freedom and brotherhood."

As he keeps quiet, I add: "Don't you think that everyone deserves the second chance? I sure do."

"Ariel."

A voice calls softly.

"Ariel?" It calls, ringing louder with panic.

Jess' voice is coming from the centre of the room, from the bed, and instantly the sweet joy, weaved with love, floods me, when I turn my head and I see my Jess, sitting on the bed, with her large hazelnut eyes on me.

"Jessie-boo", I call and a relieved laugh bubbles in my throat. It's sweet and tastes so delicious that I want more.

I rush to the bed.

"I'm here, Jessie-boo, I'm here. Ariel is here", I call to her, as I run, laughing with joy, my voice bounces within the grey shadows of the dim room.

But before I reach the bed and can scoop my little sister in my arms and give her the tightest of hugs, a wide beam of white light, as wide at the rotunda dome itself, pierces the air, illuminating the bed, shining like a searchlight on my sister.

"Ariel?" Jess whispers in a shaky voice.

She throws her head up, trying to look at the bright light, but slams her eyes shut, unable to take the brightness of the beam.

The next second she screams. Loud, from the top of her lungs, with pain she's experiencing. My Jess screams and howls, calling for her sister.

I run the last few steps towards the beam. I run with all the power I have.

I'm almost here. I can see the silvery specks, which are like dust dancing in the beam of the searchlight.

I reach out with my arms, ready to scoop my sister and save her from whatever causes her pain, when my hands fold and crack, colliding with a solid wall, and I scream, joining my sister.

Carried forward by my feet, my body slams into the clear wall, as my widespread arms hug the smooth yet *solid* form of the light.

I bounce back, falling backwards, landing on my arse.

The pain of impact rings in my head together with Jess' agonising screams.

I get up and run towards the bed, ramming into a solid shaft of light.

"No!" I roar.

I'm bouncing off the light, skidding across the polished floor.

I crawl to the wall of light, which encases the bed within its walls.

"Jess!" I roar as I punch at the white wall.

I clamber up. I scream and I kick the wall. But it's futile, as if I am human again, trying to punch a marble column.

I pound at the wall of light.

I roar.

I scream. I cry.

I claw at the ray, while Jess screams, howling, as she is being tortured inside.

Suddenly, Jess' little body rises a foot above the bed within the wide column of the searchlight. Through the hazy light of the beam, I watch her body lift higher, before it starts to twist and turn, spinning violently, Jess' limbs are flopping.

"Jess!"

I rip both of my swords out of their sheaths from the belt around my waist.

I throw my swords at the column of light, as I slice and stab at the beam, but my angelic swords vibrate in my hands, unable to make a dent. My swords don't sink in. They don't make a scratch, don't make a hindrance in this wall of light, and I can't break through it.

"Jess!" I roar, watching her violently spinning body.

My sister's cries grow exhausted and quiet, before her voice falls completely silent as her small body spinning within the beam.

"Jess!"

My wrists vibrate with the incessant resistance of the light. My wrists and arms begin to hurt but I stab at the light over and over again, while calling my sister's name.

Somewhere behind me, Rafe's voice screams something in a rolling and guttural language, but I don't pay attention to him. I don't listen to him, while pounding at the column.

The heavy slam of the door booms behind my back and two deep voices cry out in surprise, and as Rafe says something. They answer to him and Rafe says something, but I don't care who they are or what they want. I don't hear anything of what they say. I don't listen, busy stabbing, slashing at the solid beam, needing to get my sister back.

I raise my gaze up to Jess' floating body and my hand freezes mid-air in another erratic stab, as my mind ploughs through empty field of logic, refusing to accept, to understand or process the impossibility of horror that my eyes are seeing.

Through the silver-flaked veil of the light, I watch my sister's body morphing, bending and "running" as if it's a liquid on a polished surface of a table.

The scream rings in my ears and in my head as the floor sways from side to side, while it vibrates.

My knees buckle underneath me and my hands open, as I watch my sister's little body stretch for the entire height of the beam, and I scream.

I crawl closer. I claw at the beam's base, but I can't see much, as my tears corrode my vision and my head is full of pounding noise, and submerged in a scent of exotic fruits.

With the back of my fists, I pound at the wall of light, but my angelic strength doesn't even vibrate it.

I look up at the amorphous globule, which is floating, re-shaping, suspended mid-air within the light.

The dark shapeless blob of mercury no longer looks like my sister. It's no longer looks like anything. It's a large, brownish droplet of rain, falling in slow motion from the sky.

CHAPTER 12

My throat is raw, burning from my earlier screams, and an invisible mallet pounds at my head, at my ribs and heart.

I open my eyes to the warm sunlight and the smell of exotic fruits.

"I hate these fruits" is the first thought that pops into my head, before the memory of my sister and everything I've seen comes rushing back, testing my sanity.

I jump up.

Or so I think, as I painfully roll to the side, scraping myself off the floor. I rise, swinging on all fours and scan the area.

I'm in the same circle room with pillars and with the rotunda dome of the universe for a ceiling. I am within the outer circle of pillars.

The wide beam above the bed is gone and its absence brings the airy relief and a hope of a bad dream. I smile at the dome ceiling for a moment, before my gaze travels to the bed.

But the journey of my gaze is blocked by the wall of bodies surrounding the bed. They all have their backs to me: Rafe with his growing purple stumps, the large muscular backs of the brothers, Amy's slim back with her white hair spilling down it and the three old men from the Council Chambers in their dark blue clothing.

Their backs are bent and their attention is occupied by whatever is on the bed, as they speak to each other in hushed voices.

Bed... Jess...

I rise up.

I swing on my feet, coming towards the circle of the bodies, but the closer I get, the higher my panic spikes, my fear, urgency, doubt, confusion.

"Jess", I push past the hot pebbles lodged in my throat.

Every back snaps straight, every head turn towards me and every gaze locks on me.

There are a few shocked eyes, a few confused faces. Despair swims in Rafe's eyes, while pity floats in Amy's, the detachment of surgeons' covers the old men's faces, and anguish beats in Dumah's darting gaze.

"Jess" I croak, staggering towards the closed circle.

"Ariel."

Rafe takes a step forward, blocking my way. He reaches to hold my body, turning me to face him, calling for my attention. His strong hold presses my body to his. He holds my shoulders, my back. He holds me tight.

"Ariel. Ariel, look at me", he calls to me, and his voice is so gentle yet *scared*, unlike I've ever heard him before, that I raise my gaze to him and what I see there, whips in my urgency.

I twist my shoulders out of his grip, but his hold grows stronger. I look up at him, and with the last ounce of strength left in me, I push at his chest, shoving him away and the grip of his hands finally slips.

I stumble the last steps, almost tripping over my wings, reaching Domiel and Dumah, who without a word take a step back, away from the bed, letting me inside the circle.

Past the dark purple drapes of the bed posts, on the purple covers of the bed, sits a small furry creature with large, black, leathery wings behind its back.

The creature is a size of an average teddy bear toy and looks just as soft. Its entire body is covered in a short brown fur and its front legs are longer than the back ones.

The same brown fur covers the creature's entire face, apart from a pink piglet's leathery snout which stands out against the dark face. The four large fangs protrude from the animal's half-open mouth: two from the top, where canines should be, and two from the bottom. The creature has two pointy ears topped with a cluster of long hair, and one of the ears has flopped, swinging with the turning of the creature's head.

The beast has a pair of beautiful, hazelnut eyes, which are looking up at me with the intensity, intelligence and... recognition, as the creature is waiting to be recognised.

"What's going on?" I ask the group, turning my head to the left then to the right, from one angel to the next, scanning their faces.

"What is this? Who brought it here? Where's Jess?"

I wait for the reply but their shifting gazes, uncomfortable glances and the silence is the all answer I get.

"Rafe?" I call, spinning to face him. "What's going on? Where's my sister?"

But the longer I talk, demanding answers, the more agitated grows the creature on the bed, and answering my panicked voice rises its whimper.

The furry beast whimpers in a soft young voice, as its front legs shuffle over the cover. The thing tries to get up, but after wobbling on its four uneven legs, petrified, it plonks back down.

The silence of everyone in the room and the sad whimpers of the ghastly creature spike my panic.

"Rafe!" I roar, as I march toward him, past the brothers, "Where's Jess?!"

Behind my back the creature stops its cries, gulps and suddenly begins to howl: a long, excruciating howl of a coyote.

"Ariel, you need to know something", Rafe begins, "there's something I need to tell you but please understand that it's not the end of the world, weirder things happen every day... Our souls are universal and reside in many different life forms..." Rafe mumbles, while looking at his feet, looking lost. His voice is weak and pathetic, all earlier pomp and attitude are washed away.

I grab the fists-full of his purple tunic over his chest.

I rise on my toes to face him.

"I swear to God if any of you did something to her, if she's hurt..." I can't finish the sentence. I'm shaking.

I can't finish my threat because I can't breathe. It feels as if my lungs are squashed in a vice.

"Where is she?" I hiss, giving him a shake.

"I'm not kidding", I rumble low. "Where is she?"

"Where is she?" I scream.

Without meeting my gaze, Rafe raises his hand, pointing his finger somewhere behind me.

I turn around, but all that I can see is the angels around the bed and the creature on it. But I don't see Jess.

"Where is she? I can't see her... Where is she?!" I howl, as I spin back to him, then back to follow his outstretched hand, while the creature howls with me.

"There", he says. "The *adar* on the bed. That adar is Jess"

"What? What the hell are you talking about?"

I spin to look at the hideous creature of the size of a puppy and not of a twelve-year-old child.

The creature is an animal and doesn't have any resemblance with a human. It is a mutation experiment between a hairy pig, a bat, a hyena and a bear: a cross-species breading experiment that went wrong.

"Is this your idea of a joke? Well, it's a very sick joke, and I'm not amused. Where is Jess?" I ask Rafe in a hysteria-woven voice as I spin back to him.

"It's not funny. Do you hear me? Not funny! Where is she? What have you done with her?" I scream and cry.

Oh my god, where is she?

What have they done to her?

What have I done?

I don't know it yet and I don't know how, but I know it's my fault. My gut tells me.

Everything is always my fault and this one is not an exception.

I have brought her here. I couldn't leave her behind but instead I brought her here, in the place where they loathe humans.

I thought I was protecting her...

I spin away from him.

"What have you done with her?" I roar at the glorious angels around the bed. But their silence is all that I get.

I glance back at Rafe then turn back to the angels.

"You don't need her. You don't need to keep her. She's of no use to you", I gush at the silence. "I'm here. You can have me instead."

My gaze dances from face to face: the cold, closed off faces of old males, the stunned faces of brothers and the thoughtful face of Amy.

"Please, give her back to me, please. I beg you. I'll do anything you want. Do you want me on my knees?"

I drop to my knees and, as one, the angels take a step back away from me.

"I am on my knees. I am begging. Do you want to kill me? Is it my life or Uriel's essence you're after? Have it. Have me! You can do anything you want to me but please give me my sister back. Please. Please. I beg of you."

I shuffle on my knees to Amy.

"Please, please", I whisper, gazing at her.

"I am here. Take me instead."

I bow my head and stay like this for a moment but there's no answer to my pleas nor is there a cold steel touching my heck.

I raise my gaze to them, but I can't see them anymore through the thick film of my tears.

"What do you want?" I whisper. "I will do anything you want, just give me my sister back. You want me gone? I'll go. I will do anything you want me to do. Anything! Please, please. I beg of you. Please..."

I hold my head in my hands, covering my face. I think my head is about to explode.

"Just give her to me, please", I mumble. "Please. She's a child, just a child. She's suffered enough. She's suffered plenty, all of her life. She doesn't need anymore. Please don't hurt her."

I begin to rock.

"Have me. I can do anything you want but please don't hurt her. I'll do anything you want... I'll do anything you want...Please... Don't hurt... Anything you want..."

The forgotten words and pleas bring the dark memories. The kneeling and begging bring with them the taste of my past, a past that I've worked so hard to bury and hide under the blossoming garden of my life that I've built, a garden built over the graveyard of my horrific scars.

The begging is too familiar. It's too raw.

It has the same words I've used before.

The words have the same taste of earth, metal, blood and mildew.

CHAPTER 13

A soft hand lays on top of my rocking head. It stays there, following my rocking motions.

"Ariel!A-r-i-e-l!"

My sister's petrified young voice comes through, rising in my mind. It's distant and fading.

"Ariel", my sister cries, calling for me.

Confused yet hopeful, I tentatively raise my head up but my gaze, corroded by tears is obstructed by the vision a pure white angelic tunic, absent of any embroidery.

"Ariel", distant and muffled Jess' voice cries in my head.

I spin my head, but the hand on the top doesn't leave.

"That's your sister's talking to you", Amy says from above. "Open your mind and let her in. Let her speak to you and speak to her in turn. She is scared as well."

My gaze climbs up the white angelic tunic cased over a slim body, white long hair, reaching Amy's regal face.

"Answer her", Amy demands.

"Ariel, Ariel."

"Jess? Jess?" I spin my head.

"Where are you?" I call.

"Ariel, I'm here", Jess' scared childish voice screams into my mind.

"I'm here, on the bed. Why can't you see me? Who are these people? Where are we? Where's mum?"

I turn my head and look at the creature on the bed, who stares at me with its wet hazelnut eyes.

I gulp.

"*Ariel, I'm so scared. I want to go home*", Jess begins to cry in my head and the creature begins to howl.

"How?.. What?.." I croak.

I turn my head and my gaze reaches out to Amy.

"Keep your mind and connection open, and go and settle your kin. Her cries give me a headache", Amy bristles.

She removes her hand and then points to the bed.

"Jess", I whisper as I turn to the bed.

"Jess", I call louder.

The creature breaks its long, one-note howl, snaps her gaze to me and does a little short puppy-like whimpering.

"Jessie-boo", I call, crawling on my knees towards the bed, "Jessie."

The creature tries to rise on its legs and move closer to the edge of the bed, towards me, but it wobbles for a second before scared, it settles back.

"*Ariel, I can't move*", Jess' voice cries in my head. "*Why can't I move?*"

I'm next to the bed now.

On my knees, I look straight at the creature's face. I look into its eyes, looking for an answer or confirmation. Dare I call it Jess? But how is possible?

"Jess?" I call to the creature. I need to be convinced over and over that it's not my imagination.

"Keep the median open", Amy calls behind my back, "she can't answer you any other way."

"*Ariel.*"

Wobbling, the creature shuffles forward a bit more. Its pink leathery snout is next to my nose.

"*Ariel?*" Jess whimpers and so does the creature, and unable to push with logic further, or maybe just afraid of rejecting Jess if it is her, I scoop the furry creature into my arms, hugging it close.

"*Ariel? Why are we here? Who are these people? Can we go home?*"

The creature's wet snout brushes my neck, tickling behind my ear. Its fur is wet under its eyes.

I stroke the creature's – *Jess'?* – soft fur, its large, black leathery bat wings.

I turn around to look at Amy, to Rafe behind her.

"Someone needs to start talking", I croak.

Amy glares at the angels around me and one by one they bow their heads at her, Rafe, me, and after giving another fleeting glance at the furry bundle in my arms, they disappear through the door.

"Do you want to give your sister to Domiel?" Amy asks, nodding her head at the furry ghastly teddy bear in my arms, then at the brothers, who are still here.

"No!" I cut her off.

I don't know what's going on here or if I'm losing my mind, or if it's some sick joke or a trick, but as long as there's even a suspicion that it's Jess, she's not going to leave my sight.

The brothers bow out too.

Rafe speaks first.

"Ariel, please, please, you need to understand that I've never meant for any of this to happen. I would've never risked it if I'd known...if I'd even suspected..." he begins to say, sliding into mumbling.

"Rafael, *Beyelai Sar*, it would be better if I'd explained it to *kingu*", Amy interrupts Rafe.

She strides forward and stops in front of me. She reaches out and strokes the top of the creature's head with her finger.

The creature lifts her head at me, and when the wet hazelnut eyes meet my gaze, Jess' voice stammers inside my head: *"Who is she? What does she want?"*

But before I have a chance to answer, Amy begins speaking.

"I haven't seen any adar for fifteen *GA*", she says, looking at the fur ball in my hands. "The star of Ninasu had birthed them at the same moment when following An's will the universe was created. As you can see, they're as old as the universe, and not far from An herself. They were the fearless tribe, revered across one land and feared across others, and in their numbers they were known to bring down civilizations."

I want to scream at Amy, demanding to know what this history lesson has to do with my sister, but I'm afraid to hear the confirmation to what I think I might already know, so instead I say: "You want me to believe that this is my sister, and that's absolutely impossible. You're talking about some old dead creatures, who have nothing in common with my sister. Nothing."

"Before I continue, you need to understand that Rafael didn't know that it could happen, that any of it might be possible. Tell you the truth, even now, after seeing her in your arms, I doubted it myself, but it must be the only plausible explanation for what has happened."

"What does he have to do with it?" I grumble low, and although I'm asking Amy, I'm looking at Rafe, who looks at me with the saddest of expressions.

"Ariel, I swear to An–", he begins, but Amy raises her hand at him and he falls silent.

"I haven't seen adar for fifteen GA, because they're extinct. Following wars, The Great Hunt, extermination, every one of them had perished, and to make sure that their blood-thirsty souls didn't come back to bestow the vengeance on the Hunters, their bodies were drown in Hinnom and their souls banished into the Abyss of Udhad."

She stops speaking, gazing at me, making sure that I'm keeping up and still with her.

Yes, I am: so far, so good.

"Bringing a human into an Arllu is easy", Amy says, "all you have to do is to strip them of their soul. But Sarukh was never intended for perishable souls. It wasn't created for humans, so to bring human into Uras, Rafe gave your sister a *še* of his soul", she says.

I nod.

I know that. Rafe has told me and I have agreed to it.

"The problem, I think, has occurred because of *how* he has acquired his new essence", she continues, "or more precise, *where* it has been before coming into him."

She stops speaking, holding my gaze. Maybe she wants me to figure this one on my own or maybe this pause is for extra dramatism, or maybe she holds out for a congratulatory pat on a back from me, I don't know, but I keep quiet too, waiting to see where's she going with it and to hear the end of her speech.

I'm not in the mood for any of those games, so after refusing to bite, followed by a short glaring contest, she sighs and continues.

"Rafe has told me that you've called upon Uriel from Udhad for assistance. That was a mistake. The rules of life dictate that everything that dies should be allowed to finish the journey to be reborn or extinguished, whichever one it might be, but you've intervened. You've brought into this world something that had already crossed and was resting. You've brought back something that had no business to be with the living.

"I'm confident that the transference of your essence into Rafe, and Uriel's presence during transference while she came from Udhad was the starting point of everything that we currently have: Rafe's inability to draw the healing light from the universe and your sister's transformation."

I glance at Rafe, measuring his reaction to Amy's words. Not only does he know about his inability to regenerate, but he knows that it was my fault.

But he doesn't look shocked at these revelations. His steady gaze is directed into the distance, his indifference betraying someone who was briefed on these points prior to this little speech.

"You've connected Apkallu and Udhad. You've brought almost dissolved Udhadian life into the world of living and placed a tainted by Udhad essence into an angel, and then to exacerbate this, you have transferred the piece of that essence into a human, thus creating adar. You have done something that hasn't been done before, and I'd guess for a good reason."

My mind is struggling with processing what Amy says.

I understand every word. I understand the sentences, but when it comes to take in the meaning, the whole speech of hers, my mind refuses to push through the last yard.

"*Ariel? What is this woman saying? Who's adar?*" Jess shaky voice stammers.

"Hold on, baby", I say to the furry creature and give it a stroke behind an ear.

"Are you sure?" I ask Amy in a rough whisper. "Are you sure about it? Maybe you're wrong?"

She shakes her head.

"Of course I could be wrong, as we're witnessing a new transformation, something that hasn't been done before and there is no conclusive evidence, but the longer I observe the transformation, following the timeline, the triggers, taking into consideration all and every factor, the more I'm convinced of the cause of these issues. Remember when I told you where adars' qals were banished? Remember where they went?"

"Rafe?" I whisper, turning to him.

My pleading gaze is on him and I'm so desperate for him to tell me that Amy's wrong. I never wanted anything more in my life. I've never wished for anything else so badly.

"Rafe, what do you think? This can't be possibly right. She's made a mistake. She said herself that she hasn't seen these in ages so she's just guessing. How could it be right?" I plead with him in a hot rush. "How could she be right?"

I spin to face Amy and I feel my lips lifting up, baring my teeth.

"Just because you say that what's happened doesn't mean that you're right", I growl at her and my anger vibrates in my chest and in my throat.

"You said yourself this is something new. You've never seen it before, and besides why should I trust you that this", I nudge my head towards the creature, "is my sister? Just because you said so? I don't know you. I've only just met you. Maybe Jess is not here at all, maybe she's already dead."

"*Ariel?*" Jess' voice cries in my mind.

She must be wrong. I can't be responsible. That can't be my fault, not again.

Oh god, please, not again.

The heavy burden of self-loathing and guilt began to squeeze my chest. The loathing, hate and rage that earlier began to flower towards Rafe, have turned the full bloom, now directed at me.

All of it because I've refused to allow Rafe to die, and dragged his girlfriend back from the hell hole of hers, infecting everyone concerned.

Amy and Rafe's gazes are on me, his: pitied and apologetic, and hers: annoyed, steely and resentful.

It can't be my fault again.

"*Ariel?*"Jess calls to me but I ignore her this time.

"Who is she, anyway? What is she doing here? How can we trust her? How can *I* trust her?" I demand at Rafe.

Amy needs to, *must*, be wrong. I can't be responsible for hurting my sweet Jess.

"Ariel", Rafe say as he takes a step closer to me. "Amitiel is one of the eldest angels. She was born not that long after An. She is very knowledgeable. She was an archangel before Mik'hael banished her and on top of everything else, she's an angel of truth. It is physically impossible for her to utter a lie."

I glance at the silent Amy.

"As much as it's hard to accept this news, I trust her to speak the truth, and in this instance, I would trust her judgement and her knowledge too", Rafe says.

"*Ariel?*" Jess' stricken with panic voice calls.

What have I done?!

"*What have you done?*" Shocked Rage mouthed at me.

"Okay, she is not lying and that's fine, but it doesn't mean that she is right with everything else. She could be mistaken", I gush. "Just a simple mistake. Maybe this is not Jess after all, maybe that's not her, and whatever has happened, and even if it's her, maybe it's not my fault."

"If she thinks that this is the origin of our situation", Rafe interrupts, "I trust her on this."

Rafe's gaze is on me and so is Amy's. Neither of them add anything else, waiting for a penny to drop.

"Hold her."

I shove Jess' new body at Rafe, and once he catches her in his arms, I walk towards the door.

"Ariel?" Rafe's confused voice calls behind my back.

"*Ariel?*" Jess' hysterical cry echoes there too, demanding for my return.

But I run the last few steps through and out of the door, and once I'm out from under the enclosed ceiling of the room, I open my wings wide and soar into the trouble free, bottomless sky above.

CHAPTER 14

"*A* riel!" roars Rafe.

"*Ariel!*" Jess cries.

I clap my hands over my ears but this childish gesture can't stop the screams, roars and cries from penetrating into my head.

I'm rising up and so is my panic.

The weight of guilt presses heavy on me.

My mind is busy, vibrating from Rafe's howling demands, from Jess' screams of abandonment, her cries and the snippets of random conversations between random people or angels.

Amy's instruction to open my mind to Jess' voice has now opened the flood gates into other's minds and conversations, and in the open of the blue sky, I'm drowning in it.

My head is exploding and my heart is breaking.

Jess' cries bring to the forefront the sour taste of my own abandonment. Her cries are the echo of mine from years ago, her pain and rejection mirror mine, and within the cacophony of noises and demanding feelings, I can't make a decision.

I don't know what to do.

My fault again...

What am I going to do now? What am I going to do?

Jess' cries, Rafe's calls and angelic chatter ring in my head, suffocating me. I can't hear the wind or the beating of my wings above them. It leaves me no space to think.

I throw my head up and I scream.

I howl, like the monster that I am, like the animal that I've become.

I roar like the fearing archangel that they tell me I am.

"Give me a minute. God damn you all! Shut up and give me a minute!" I roar into the abyss of the open sky, and the voices in my head drop silent.

The chatter has stopped. The open radio channel in my head buzzes with a weak static of everyone holding their breath.

I take in a shaky breath of mine.

"Jess. I'll be back, sweetie."

"Rafe, go away!"

I'm scared of what I've done this time.

I'm in too deep. I have made that decision for Jess. I thought I was protecting her by bringing her here. I thought I was ensuring her safety, guarding her future but I've made things worse, so much worse.

I don't understand the magic of their essences or the laws of existence of angelic worlds. I don't understand the rules of their lethal games. The final goals of their desire for global domination evade me, probably because I'm not interested in it. I don't understand any of it, and in it is my weakness.

I don't think like them. I don't operate like them. Having the essence of one of them and wings are clearly not enough to be like them. Their priorities and mine are worlds apart, so why did I think I could do it? Why did I think that Jess and I would be safe in here?

I'm out of my depth in this world, yet I went ahead and I've made a call, and now I'm running blindfolded through dark rooms and corridors, while trying to find my way out of the deadly maze and stay alive.

I've trusted many of them. I've trusted Sam. I've trusted Rafe. Briefly, I've even trusted Baza.

To survive in these confusing worlds, I had no choice but to look for guidance, search for support and more often than not, I've taken their explanations at face value. I've trusted their pledges. I've relied upon their leading.

I was naïve then and I fear I might be naïve still. I fear that even now, I might be played.

I don't know who is lying to me and who isn't, and to make things worse, I'm not sure *if* anyone's lying, or if there was a mistake, simply a wrong call was made.

What Amy had said, could she be lying? To me, to Rafe, or to both of us? Or maybe Rafe is lying to cover for her, spurring the bullshit about her inability to say a lie. Wouldn't it be what a liar says? But why would they lie to me? What would they gain from that?

But I know that just because I can't see the reason, doesn't mean that the reason is not there. It's hard to look for something that you don't know is there or without knowing how it looks.

Could Amy be mistaken in her assessment? Maybe that cross-breeding experiment is not my sister after all? Or if it is her, maybe she is not like that because of the shard of the essence, but just the way she has crossed the threshold, or maybe without any reason.

Although Amy is adamant that she's right, but it doesn't mean that she is. Many people for centuries were saying that Earth is flat, but look where that theory is now. Maybe Amy is not lying but rather has made a mistake, a wrong judgement, and there's not an ulterior motive or deeper game behind her actions and words.

My head is spinning.

Every decision I've made so far was the wrong one. I've trusted the wrong people, the wrong angels. I've made plenty of wrong calls. Yet again I need to make another decision and I can only pray that this one will be the right one.

I'm so lost and alone.

Every decision is mine to make, every bitter pill is mine to swallow, every repercussion is mine to receive. There's no instruction or map to help me navigate this dark path full of monsters and old blood-thirsty worlds, the worlds where actions in one would echo in another.

The worlds which are linked, balancing one another.

Tied up and balanced... balanced... the balance.

Rafe's words from the cave about the balance of angelic forces and powers come in, the importance with which this balance was guarded and preserved by him and others; the balance in everything. The balance of scales which demands that nothing happens without echoing elsewhere in return, where every action is offset by a sentencing and every arrival is offset by a departure.

So maybe Amy wasn't that wrong after all.

Amy said that Rafe's arrival to life has brought something else with him. But what has it brought and what has it taken? Will something else be taken from me, and if so, when? What other loss is coming my way?

With her declaration, Amy had tied Rafe's and Jess' lives.

She had dusted off those scales, placing both of their lives onto each side, balancing the scales perfectly. But were their *lives* placed on the scales or rather *an existence*, their appearance in this world? Could it be the tie and the balance?

I'm confused. Nothing makes sense and my head is spinning.

But there's something else that nags at me.

A weak voice whispers something at me from the depths of my mind that I am desperate to drown.

It is Rage's voice. I can recognise it. It's her cautious whispers.

She tells me of another possibility, another game, another route of how things could've played. She warns me of another betrayal, and the thought of this one makes my stomach churn.

I struggle to say it in my head.

I struggle to form the sentence and acknowledge it, as if once I've said it, it might become the truth. It could become a possibility, and if that ever becomes truth, it would be the worst betrayal to date. Everything that has happened to me before, in this world and in mine, will fade into insignificance against this betrayal.

Rage whispers, mouthing the words to me.

My ears are closed to her, but I can read her lips.

I know I need to form the words. I need to say them, to taste them on my tongue, as this is the only way to feel truth or lies in them.

Saying and acknowledging them is the only way forward, the only way to fix everything.

Beating my wings, I take in a breath.

I exhale and then I take another.

What if Rafe knew all along what he was doing? What if he knew what the shard of his essence would do to a human? What if he knew what it would do to my sister? What if he gave her a piece of his essence on purpose *to turn her into that monster?*

I've said it and instantly I now want to throw up.

If he knew...

I can't finish this sentence. The implications are enormous.

The betrayal here would be by far graver than the little stunt Baza had pulled. If that's the truth, I've made a huge mistake by giving him half of my essence. I've weakened myself, placing my powers and trust in him to keep me and my sister safe. I've armed my enemy and stepped closer to the blade.

"The major screwed up" wouldn't even begin to cover it.

My wings slap the air around me, but there's no air in my lungs and I can't force any of it in. I begin to hyperventilate.

I want to punch something, to kick. I want to scream.

My hands curl as they rip the empty air. I thrash in the air, and finding no relief, I throw my head upwards and scream.

But the vast blue sky swallows my screams. It swallows me together with my misery. It feels as if the sky taunts me, taunts a weak human who bit off more than she can chew, now choking on that bite.

The sky is imperial and silent. It's regal and unmoving.

It wasn't made for gullible girls. It was made for ruthless angels.

That can't be the truth. It simply can't.

I reason with my Rage.

Why would he do that?

"*Ha!*" Rage huffs a dry laugh. "*For millions of reasons, some of which we can guess and some might be too obscure for us to see. If not for anything else but to screw with your head. Look what it's doing to you. Look at yourself!*"

Rage eyes are narrowed at me and her lips are pressed tight with disgust. The witness of all of my highs and lows, she was never as disappointed in me as she is now.

I know what Rage wants from me. I know she is waiting for me to stop rolling on the ground and crying. She wants me to get up, dust myself off and stand up to him, to fight him as I fought everyone before him.

But I don't want to stop my self-loathing. I'm not ready to get up and march.

I am afraid.

I am the most scared I have been for a while. I am as scared as I was on that first night I spent sleeping on the bench in the park that winter, when my mother kicked me out.

And just like then, the same thought pops into my head and begins to spin on a loop: *"Why me? Why me? Why always me?"*

Rage watches my thrashing with narrowed, heavy eye-lined eyes and folded arms.

"If I am right", she whispers, *"you've left your sister with your enemy. What else is he doing to do to her?"*

My eyes fly open and I exhale. These words bring me back like a slap.

On my wide-open wings, I bank and complete the hundred and eighty degrees turn, heading back to Uras, which is now a barely visible dot miles below me.

I have to make sure that this is the last lesson Rage will teach me. I will make sure that Rage is wrong, and if she's right, it will be the last betrayal she'd throw in my face.

But for now, I'm going to do the same as always: I'm going to survive and protect what is mine.

Later, I will fix everything. One way or another, my mistakes will be fixed.

CHAPTER 15

With my rapid descent, Uras grows towards me.

Sprawled wide beneath me, Uras is not a single building or a castle with a turret or two. It's a white island of white buildings on a background of purest blue. It's an uneven landscape of low and tall white buildings, nestled densely in a tight circle within a tall, protective wall. From this height and from this distance Uras is a perfect and idyllic image, a Heaven reimagined and brought to life in its pure, untainted glory.

Uras is a town, a small city, surrounded by a tall white wall, which carries four tall white towers, erected at the four sides around the city, facing west, east, south and north. It's a picture perfect medieval town with a few small squares, narrow streets, short buildings and a few towers. It's white, perfectly white without a splash of any other colour.

Slightly left to the centre within the white settlement, stands the tallest white castle, which dwarfs every other building of the settlement. The castle is made of a handful of tall and big towers, with three slightly shorter towers adjoin to the base of it. The light is glisteningand reflecting off the silver onion roofs of the towers.

The buildings of Uras expand, rushing forward with my descent.The walls of the buildings shine with polished stones. The network of a few narrow, shaded streets cut the white island across in different directions, pushing buildings apart. The quiet cobblestone streets of an empty town are laid with white stones too.

Everything is pure white underneath me, romantic and magical. If I hadn't met Mia, Chamuel and others prior to this flight, I could've been fooled thinking that this place is Heaven.

I turn, adjusting the trajectory of my dive and begin to spiral towards the tall tower in the centre. Descending, I circle the largest and tallest tower of the white castle.

I fly past the slim mast, the onion-shaped roof dressed in blinding silver.

I spiral lower until the carved out emptiness of the wide tall arches break the solidity of the stone wall.

I stop the descent, allowing my wings to hold me level with the carved-out arches of the windows, finally beginning to trust my wings.

Once I'm ready, the wings hold the rhythm for a bit longer, then tilting me forward and folding behind my back, thrusting me with my head forward into the arched window.

I dive head forward into the room, sliding on my stomach over the rough surface of a stone table, before the friction of its surface brings my flight to a stop.

I am spread like a starfish on top of the Council Chamber's table. The room which I left a couple of hours ago is now empty and quiet.

This time I know where I am and where I'm going, so it doesn't take long to get back to the room with the universe for a ceiling.

The soft muffled whimpering of a small animal comes from behind the closed door, drowned by the rising chatter of rumbling voices and arguments.

I throw the door open and instantly all noise stops.

I stride past Domiel and Dumah, towards Amy and Rafe, who holds the morbid-looking creature that is my sister.

I scoop her out of his arms, hugging her close, striding further away from everyone, towards the farthest side of the circle room.

"Jessie-boo, I'm here now."

"Ariel, I'm scared", she cries, "I can't move. I feel so weird, like not me, and I feel smaller, or maybe everything around me is bigger. Where were you? Where did you go? I was scared."

She whimpers.

"Where are we, Ariel? Can you see the wings behind these people's backs? Are they angels, as you said?"

Her words are unsure and rushed at the beginning, turning confused and panicked the longer she speaks.

Here we go...

I breathe out my panic – it's not the time for it.

"You have nothing to worry about, Jessie-boo. Everything is fine. I am here and you are with me, and you remember what I've told you? "Nothing is going to happen to you while I'm around".

I stroke her furry face.

"Jess, they are angels, just like me and just like I told you in the woods. I've brought you to their place where they, and now us, live. You see, Rafe is here too."

I turn to look at Rafe and the animal's furry face turns too.

Back in the woods I wished that I had told her lies, told her that my wings and glowing was her dream. It would've saved a lot of pain for both of us. But now, holding an animal instead of my sister, I'm left with no choice but to deliver the honesty.

"There are many different worlds around us, not just the world we can see. Things exist in different forms in our world around us, and as they cross over from one world to next, they morph."

"Like souls?" Jess asks, armed with knowledge from our mother's teaching.

"Like souls."

I stroke her furry head.

"The things and people change their shape as they move across the border of these worlds. Our bodies are just shells: very fluid, changeable shells. We are like water: we're snow in one world, vapour in the next and solid ice in the other. But the change in the shell doesn't change who we are, just as the four wings behind my back doesn't change who I am and doesn't change my love for you."

I smile at the animal.

"This world is different. Not everyone can come here, and only the special girls are invited. But when they come here, crossing into this world, they change, changing their shell for something else, for something new and exciting, and it has happened to you.

"But you're still Jess. You are still you and I am me. It's nothing to worry or to be scared about, baby. I promise. In fact, it's something to celebrate. We are having the adventure of our lives. You and I, we are living this adventure together, and it will be fun."

The smile is plastered over my lips as I'm spinning the yarn about how good this change is, but the truth is, I am afraid.

But this is not all. I don't trust Amy. I need to know if the monster in front of me is really my sister.

"Jessie-boo, I've got you, forever and ever", I say and stretch my neck, reaching my face towards the furry face with large ugly incisors and open mouth full of dark teeth.

My eyes are trained on her pink snout. Only Jess would know what I'm looking for. If it's really Jess inside this animal, I would know now.

The little animal reaches its face towards me and for a second my heart drops as I feel the animal's rotten breath on my lips, as if it's about to kiss me.

My heart stops and sinks.

It's not Jess. They lied to me.

But then the animal shuffles closer in my arms and its pink snout touches my nose then slides it side to side and side again, brushing my nose like Jess used to, and the held breath leaves me.

The realisation is bitter-sweet. The relief of having my sister back, knowing where she is and that she is alright is sweet, bursting its light bubbles in my head. But the final confirmation of Amy's words hangs heavy at the pit of my stomach, reminding me that she is like that because of me.

I scoop the little animal, hugging it close to my chest, before raising it above my head and start spinning with it, spinning *with Jess* as I used to.

"Baby girl", I gush, "it's going to be fine. Everything's going to be fine. I'll figure it out. I promise. I promise it will be okay. Remember, in the end, everything's gonna be okay, and if it's not okay, then it's not the end."

I pull Jess closer, showering her furry face, her pink snout and open mouth full of sharp teeth with kisses. My lips brush over her four dark fangs.

"We're going to start with it right now."

I stride to Domiel and Dumah.

"Guys, I need your help with something. I'm sick of getting lost and keep asking for directions. Can you please get me a map of Uras, please? This place is bound to have a map."

They look at each other then glance at Rafe and Amy behind my back.

Dumah touches his forehead with his four fingers, bows low, much lower than before, then turns and leaves the room to do my bidding.

"Amitiel", I turn and address the old woman, "I was told you only can say the truth, so... Do you like me?"

Her eyes narrow into studious slits before she answers.

"Yes, at the most I like you. You're adequate enough."

"Wow. Be careful with compliments! You don't want me to get big-headed", I huff.

"And what about my ability to take over as Uriel? What are your thoughts on that?" I push.

She purses her lips together, trying to hold the words back but it doesn't last before her mouth opens and she says: "You're not equipped for this role. You lack knowledge and maturity."

"Then why didn't you leave with everyone else, if I'm such a crap leader?"

"Uras is my home. Uras is my family, the only family which would understand and accept my birth traits."

"Fair enough. And finally, do you think Jess'..." I pause and then add, "*situation* can be reversed?"

Her gaze falls to the furry Jess in my arms, then darts to Rafe, and I can see that she's withholding something from me when she answers, not looking into my eyes: "It can be reversed."

Someone's hiding something from me. Not to worry, darling, I think I've figured it already by myself.

I keep the smile on my lips and my neck moving with agreeable nods.

"Thank you, Amitiel. I appreciate your honesty."

She gives me a small bow without meeting my gaze.

Dumah struts through the open door with a tube of a scroll under his arm.

"Here's the map of Uras, beyelai", Domiel says, taking the scroll from his brother and unrolling it on the table by the wall.

He puts two black statuesque carvings on the two ends of the large scroll of white glowing paper to stop it from closing.

The map is a blueprint of this place.

The weird and symbolic hieroglyphs twist and bend along the top of the document, probably advising that this indeed is the map of Uras. The rudimentary drawings of a sun, a wing, maybe a bird's or maybe an angel's, a tree and, what I'd assume to be the representation of wind, running down the left side of the document. The right side is busy with small, intertwined hieroglyphs. These intertwined hieroglyphs are all of the same size, like writing, they sit on straight lines, filling the left side, telling readers something I don't understand.

A fat large seal glows at the bottom centre of the document with purple-silver light.

I raise my finger to it. It feels cold and metallic to the touch.

My finger slides down the "paper" of the scroll.

But it's not paper. It's a very thin, finely worked leather, and keeping in mind the blood-thirsty nature of these creatures, I pull my finger away, wondering *whose* skin might have been used to make the scroll.

Everything is mapped and marked on the scroll. There are squares and rectangles of rooms and halls, their names are written inside the shapes in small, busy hieroglyphs. The busy network of halls, corridors and passageways connecting the rooms is outlined in blue shining ink. Some passageways are marked with a fainter, broken line of dots, while some are drawn in wavy lines.

"What's with the corridors' marking? Why are some marked with thick solid lines, while others are with dots and with wavy lines?"

"The solid lines indicate the corridors which could be walked or flown down", Domiel answers, leaning next to me. "They are visible and accessible to everyone. The dotted lines indicate the passageways, which can only be accessed by air. Some rooms can only be accessed by angels, or anything that flies, see?"

He points to the large square which has two corridors, connecting it to other rooms and halls. Both corridors are marked by dotted lines.

"So if you don't have wings, you can't get there?"

"Correct."

"Okay, and what about the corridors with wavy lines?" I ask, pointing at one.

"These are the access passages open only to the master, or masters", he says, darting his gaze towards Rafe, "of Uras, or for anyone who was granted permission by the owner to use them. They're invisible and inaccessible to anyone, but you."

Not bad. My personal secret passages.

I feel like Indiana Jones. But the excitement doesn't last long.

"What about the writing?" I ask Domiel. "Any chance to translate it?"

He coughs and darts another glance to the side where Rafe and Amitiel stand.

"Why do you keep looking at them?"

Domiel shifts, dropping his gaze.

"That's your– *Uriel's*, writing. I thought you'd be able to read it", he mumbles, telling it to his feet.

The embarrassment and anger come suddenly, washing over like a frigid wave. I grind my teeth, breathing through my nose, trying to control and subdue it. How many more times will I be made to feel inferior? Will I ever catch up to Uriel's *greatness*?

"Of course", I push out, while keeping the rigid smile on.

Rafe's steps resonate closer and soon I feel him next to me, but before he can say anything, Amitel pushes past him, brushing my skin with her frost and wintery scent.

Domiel bows out, taking large steps towards the door where his brother still stands.

With his departure, the smell hasn't changed and I realise that neither of the brothers have a unique scent, like Rafe, Sam or Amy have.

But my thought of that curiosity is pulled away by the sound of Amy's voice.

"Look at the hieroglyphs", she says next to me.

"I *am* looking."

"No, *Kingu*, look. Really look, look closer."

I don't know what she wants from me. But to placate her, I stare at the writing within the large rectangular towards the middle that I've chosen, where the four hieroglyphs like snakes curl over each other inside the shape.

I stare at it and my eyes begin to fill with tears, as my vision zooms in and out, blurring.

"I still ca–", I begin, about to complain, telling Amy that I can't see anything, when the entangled snakes come to life under my watery, fuzzy vision, beginning to move, straightening, coming apart, eventually re-arranging themselves into a "Grand Hall".

"Oh", I breathe out.

"I think you never truly opened your mind to who you are", Amy bristles. "It's Uriel's language. It's the language of her ancestors and it's your language too. You know it. You were born with that knowledge just like the energy of the essence does. For a while this language was spoken in Apkallu and humans called it Sumer. But that was before gods were forgotten and division was cast on Apkallu and Sarukh."

Barely listening to Amy's complaining, my gaze jumps to another word within a smaller square.

"Council's chambers" it reads.

My gaze darts to the next.

The whole map comes alive with words and meaning, and I almost feel the squares on the paper rise upwards like 3D, as I can see Uras for the first time in its full glory and for what it really is.

The hieroglyphs at the top and to the left borders of the map come alive as well. The rudimentary drawings blossom under my gaze, opening their meanings to me.

I snap my back upright, spinning on the spot.

I want to find more writings, more hieroglyphs. I want to read more of them. I want to try my new power, flex my newfound muscles. I want to feel that power of knowledge and understanding of this place seep into me, and finally, for the first time since it all began, I want to open it wide, absorbing it, feeling as one with this place, feeling like I could be *the one*, because finally I would be able to understand the history and customs of this place.

Armed with knowledge, I will be able to make better decisions. I will stop looking like the stupid and incompetent one. Maybe they even have angelic history books I'd be able to borrow and read. I would finally speak their language. I will understand them and they will finally understand me, and hopefully, accept me.

CHAPTER 16

I clear my throat and every head in the room turns to me.

"Can you please excuse us", I address Domiel and Dumah by the door, then turn my head to Amitiel. "I need to have a word with Rafael."

With a different degree of obedience and respect shown in their bows and glances, all three leave the room, closing the door behind.

"Ariel, I am so incredibly sorry for what happened to Jess..." Rafe begins, but I close my eyes and raise my hand, silencing him.

"No, Rafe", I grumble as I shake my head, "not now."

Jess is still in my arms but she fell asleep a few minutes ago. Not only do I not want her to hear this conversation, which definitely would upset her, but I'm not ready to talk to him about it. I know he will be asking for forgiveness which I can't give.

The decision that I made earlier is gnawing at me, questioning my resolve, demanding to know if there are other ways out, and if I've made the right call.

But I can't be swayed, not now.

I can't. I won't be. I will not allow myself to be weak. I need to put my sister first and fix the mistake I've made.

I clear my throat, searching for the strength, which will camouflage my shaky guilt and will smooth my voice.

"I just wanted to let you know that I'm sticking to my earlier plan. The first thing tomorrow morning..." I pause for a moment, looking around the permanently light-flooded room, "or whenever it's physically possible once certain preparations are complete, I intend to leave Uras and go to Arllu, looking for soldiers and followers, to build my army as I've announced to the Council."

"What?" Rafe's eyes fly open.

It's not something he'd expected.

"I had hoped you'd come to your senses. With everything that's going on, with the dangers that could come from this trip...With your sister..."

He trails off, gesturing at sleeping, softly whistling Jess, and the suspicion steals my breath, when Rage makes her appearance and with shocked eyes and raised eyebrows the little cow mouths at me: *"Not on purpose?"*

She leaves her question hanging in the air like smoke from a wildfire.

Breathe in and breathe out.

A breath in and a breath out.

I tell myself that even this is irrelevant now. I've made my decision, on purpose or not. I know what I need to do and I know how to do it. The rest is just details. No one will sway me from my path, not Rage or Rafe, and my decision about Rafe will not be changed either.

The dues must be paid.

"Nothing's changed", I say, glaring at him, stroking Jess' floppy leathery wings. "I'm going to get myself an army and in the process I'm going to figure this one out too."

I nod my head at Jess' body.

"I'll find a way. But I need to survive first in order to help her. I need to survive for mine and her sake, and for that I need an army. If I'm dead, she'll never be fixed."

He opens his mouth to say something, but I raise my hand, interrupting him.

"It's my turn to make decisions. I'm happy to hear your advice but don't expect me to follow it. I am taking Jess with me, as there's no way I'm going to leave her like that on her own. I will ask Domiel and Dumah to come with me. I have a feeling they will be good at this infiltrating the enemy camp kinda thing. Besides, they can fight.

"But you're free to stay behind and heal yourself. I won't demand your attendance. I'm sure Amy would take good care of you. Besides, staying here you'd be able to protect Uras for us if Mik'hael or Baza turn up here."

I walk towards the window, rocking Jess' new furry body in my arms. It's as if she's small again and I'm looking after her while mum and dad are at church.

In two large strides, Rafe is behind my back.

"If you're adamant on your decision to go to Arllu, I'm coming with you", he growls at my back.

He said exactly what I expected to hear.

"Do whatever you want, and if it's okay with you, I'd like to rest."

And without giving him another glance, I walk to the four-posted bed and climb in, hugging Jess' furry body to my right side, both of us curl up within a cocoon of my large purple wings.

***

I dream of Hinnom, of the lakes of fire which are spread wide below me, with not a slither of land in sight.

It's hot in Hinnom and sweat rolls off my face and my back.

I fly above the unending lakes. I'm tired and my wings push the hot air with desperation, calling on me to get somewhere, somewhere important where I need to be but I don't know where it is. All that I know is that I'm losing precious time.

I drop my gaze to the lake below which is bubbling, brewing like a hot pot on a stove. I try to rise up but my wings are too tired.

The hot lava bubbles below and suddenly, a tall pillar of fire shoots upwards from the depth of the lake, reaching high.

It sears my wing and I scream.

I beat harder with my wings, trying to get away, to get higher, when another fiery pillar bursts up, ripping at the same wing, and I scream again.

It rips at me once more, and riding that nightmare wave, I scream and jolt up awake.

I'm groggy from my dream but the pain in my wing sobers me fast.

I look down.

The bed underneath me is painted dark red and sloshes with blood. I draw my gaze to my right wing and cry out at the sight of my furry Jess tearing at my wing, at my purple feathers and... eating them.

My sister is eating my wing.

"Jess, no! No-o-o! Jess, no."

Screaming, I roll to the side, pushing Jess' body off me and off the bed.

Jess rolls off, on the way down yanking a few more feathers that were already in her mouth. Her body hits the floor with a thud, and the next second, loud and hurt wail rings inside the room.

Our cries lace together: mine are agonising and pained and hers, upset and disappointed. Our cries bounce around the room, echoing off the dome above.

I push with my arm, trying to get off the bed as well, but my arm gives way and I fall back onto my wing, into the sloshy and bloody mess of the bed, roaring in pain.

Somewhere to the right, the door bursts open and a bunch of footsteps rush into the room. Some of them stop abruptly by the door, while some rush forward, and I hear someone's gasps.

The two sets of footsteps are more decisive and they march across the room, stopping by the side of my bed.

I turn my head to see Amy and Rafe, towering above me.

Dumah hurries towards the bed too, with a cleaver in one hand and the sword in the other. But I'm not interested in who he's planning to fight, as I'm busy, trying to remember how to breathe.

"I thought it might happen." Amy's pissy and unfazed voice comments into the stunned silence.

Pocket-sized witch!

I want to say it out loud but the pain is too much for me.

"Domiel, please take her to North Tower", Rafe instructs somewhere above me.

Who?

Me?

Jess?

Not Jess.

I push and roll to my side to tell them "no", but the pain from the movement brings out another scream, which drowns my words.

More hushed words, more movement, followed by a slam of a closing door.

I'm yanked by my arms to sit up in the bed and the familiar smooth globe shape is shoved onto my lap.

I scream and writhe in agony, when answering the light from the sphere, a thick ray of the white light bursts from the universe, lightening the dark globe and the air around, as a fresh wave of pain shoots up my wing.

Suffering from blood loss, my body feels cold, while my wings burn as if on fire. It feels as if Jess is next to me and still going at my wing, pulling the feathers out one by one, but this time with a slow, methodical and torturous precision, as if the feathers are the petals on a daisy when she counts: "Loves me, loves me not".

And then, suddenly, the pulling and the pain stop.

"That will do for now. The rest of her body will heal itself."

Tired and weary, I flop backwards under the accompaniment of a revolting "splat" of the bloody slosh and open my eyes to the dark and ancient universe above me, but the ray of light is no longer coming from it.

CHAPTER 17

I rise up on my arms. I'm in discomfort but not in agony.

"Where is she?" I ask in a coarse and quiet whisper. I've lost my voice.

Rafe and Amy are the only ones in the quiet room.

"Dumah and Domiel have placed her into oubliette within the North Tower", Rafe answers.

"What's "oubliette"?" I croak.

"The holding cell, in case if she attacks anyone else", he says.

"What the hell?" I wheeze. "You've locked her up? In a cage like an animal? Are you nuts?"

My throat is strained and sore, and unfortunately, doesn't produce the noise reflecting the outrage burning inside me.

I swing my legs out of the bed and stand up but the blood loss has made me dizzy too. Everything spins around me and the air is sticky with the iron smell of blood.

"Take me to her, now", I croak, glaring at Amy.

"Adar are dangerous. They've brought down civilizations of... *angels*", she says, emphasising the last word, stretching out syllables. "Angels are their food source."

But as I silently glare at her, she expands: "Mik'hael is the one who led the Great Hunt and extinguished them. They are the only natural enemy of angels. Adar *eat* angels. Angels are their food source, along with a few other creatures. Adar must be banished from Uras for everyone's safety."

I've heard enough. I take a weak step closer to the woman. My face is an inch away from hers.

"The adar", I mimic her, "is my sister", I bark.

"So if you think I'll lock her up or "banish" her", I spit out, while doing the "bunny rabbits" with my fingers, "you had better find yourself another place to stay, because she's not going anywhere", I roar the last words.

I am livid.

"She will stay with me, no matter where I am. She will be protected by me, and she will not be locked up. Is that clear?"

I stumble out of the room.

I don't need their help and thanks to the earlier studying of the map, I find the North Tower with ease.

I hear Jess' animal howling the moment I pull at the heavy wooden door of the tower. As fast as my body allows me, I take the stairs down and through another set of doors, while Jess' cries grow louder. The animal's howling rips the air while her calls to me stab at my mind.

In the dark basement with a low ceiling, Dumah sits cross-legged on the stone floor in front of the metal grid that covers the pit below.

He rocks himself while humming a soft tune towards the pit. His voice is placating and soothing, but his hands that rest on his knees, digging into his flesh and his white knuckles betray his emotions.

At the sound of my footsteps, he raises his face and I see a glimpse of a pained mask of a tortured expression, before it slips, replaced with a look of shock at the sight of my blood-soaked clothing and hair.

I only can imagine how I look, but I don't care.

"Open it", I bark, pointing at the grid lid in the floor.

"*Ariel*", Jess screams into my mind.

Without a word, he reaches and lifts the round metal lid over the pit, and I could swear, I see an expression of relief washing over his face.

The heavy metal lid scrapes and booms when it flops on the stone floor.

I glance into the shallow pit that is dug out like a bowl, before I awkwardly clamber and then slide into it.

Jess' furry body sits on the floor in the middle of the pit.

"I'm here, Jessie-boo, I'm here."

I scoop her in my arms.

I don't know what magic is at work here, but she is larger and heavier now.

If before she was of a size of a very young puppy, then now the puppy has grown to the weight and size of a mature Labrador dog.

I squeeze her tight and her long front legs reach to me, flopping over my shoulder. Her soft snout kisses my neck and her black bat wings surround me.

"Everything's fine. Everything's fine. I'm not gonna leave you. I'm here, Jessie-boo, I'm here", I whisper as I hold her, stroking her furry back and leather wings.

We stay like this for a while. I'm petting her while she's whimpering.

When her soft sobs and hiccups die down, I lift her above my head, and courtesy of my developed angelic strength, push her out of the pit, climbing after her.

The dungeon room is empty and Dumah has gone.

I pick up Jess' furry body, and taking the same route in reverse, I walk out of the depth of the Tower.

When I push through the last door, I'm greeted by the sunlight, the obligatory overbearing smell of fruits and... a tight circle of angels.

I hate these fruits, but now I begin to hate the angels too.

The circle is the same crowd that had surrounded my bed before, minus Rafe and both brothers. Amy stands at the forefront like the initiator of this intervention, or as a leader of a village mob.

"What now?" I bark.

I am not to be pissed about with right now.

I put Jess down next to me. Sitting down, her head reaches to my waist, so I put my hand out and stroke her head between her tall hyena's ears.

"Adar cannot stay in Uras", Amy says. Her steely voice demands as her gaze rakes my clothing, rigid with dried, cracking blood.

Only now I notice the bared weapons in their hands.

Clearly that's the way of the angelic warfare, to ambush and gang up on a single person. There seems to be no honour in the angelic ways to handle disputes, only scheming and backstabbing.

Rage skips circles around me, humming something cheerful and upbeat, reminding me that teaching a lesson to this snooty bunch is well overdue.

The group is not big, and for a fleeting second a smile comes over my lips as a temptation to deliver a lesson to these angels, a similar to the one I taught the lizards outside my mother's caravan park, coaxes me.

But before my smile and decision can anchor, Rafe's commanding voice cries from above.

"Sheath your swords!"

He descends and comes to stand next to me.

I glance at him.

Rage mouths: *Not on purpose? Look who's the hero now?*

I don't care what he wants, what the rest of them want.

I have the plan and no one will sway me from my road. No one will convince me to abandon it, and if these posers with their angelic toothpicks think they can scare me into turning my back on my own sister, they have another thing coming.

"Amitiel, although I appreciate your disquietude, it would've been more prudent to voice your concerns and grievances with Uriel through the discussion, to engage the Council and follow the protocol that was established specifically for these instances..."

But she shakes her head at him and he falls silent.

"We are no longer in that position, Rafael. The new changes that have befallen upon Uras had called for the adoption of a martial law. Most of the Uras is gone, and that", she turns, gesturing to the small mob, "is all that's left of once large community."

She takes a step closer to him, gazing into his eyes and speaking softly.

"Rafael, you know how dangerous the adar is. You know what they can do, what they're capable of. And look at her", she says, gesturing at me. "She is too young to understand what she's playing with."

"Amy", I say, making the point addressing her by the nickname I know she hates. "*She* has a name and it is Ariel, "Uriel" if you want or "Your Royal Highness" if it tickles your fancy. Feel free to drop to your knees if the mood takes you, I won't object."

I am pleased with the deadpan tone of my sarcasm.

"But I have a bit of a friendly advice for you, darling", I say as I come closer to her. "Don't ever address me in a third person again or speak about me as if I'm not here unless you want your "truthful" head to leave your shoulders once and for all."

The furry Jess growls and, with a cautious glance, Amy takes a step away from me.

"Amitiel", Rafe says, snaking between myself and Amy, "we need to remember that this adar is Ariel's kin, and the banishment would not be a feasible solution..."

"It's dangerous", one of the old men at the front of the crowd cries.

"How 'bout I'll make it easier for everyone?" I call to the mob, stepping around Rafe.

"As promised, in a few hours I'll leave Uras. I'll leave your white-walled, smoothy-drenched insane asylum the way I found it: sterile, stuck-up, backwards and dysfunctional – just the way you like it. You can have it back", I call to them, spreading my arms wide. "You can have all of it back. Hell, throw a party while I'm gone, have fun. If you're lucky enough, I might not even come back. Wouldn't you be pleased?"

I smile scanning the thin crowd.

"Of course, Mik'hael will come knocking soon, but I'm sure you have a solution for that eventuality too."

I dismissively wave my hand at them.

"You don't need to worry about adar anymore", I add for Amy's benefit, "she won't be your problem for much longer. I'm taking her with me. But meanwhile..." I stop, pausing before I hiss, "get out of my sight. All of you! Scatter, before I let her finish her dinner."

I turn around, taking a step back to my sister, noticing Domiel and Dumah standing like a convoy to both sides of her, and as I'm about to run at them, protecting my sister, they step aside, letting me come close to her, and when I pick her up and walk away, leaving the mob and Rafe behind, both brothers follow.

"What are you two doing?" I ask, glaring at both of them in turn. "Told to escort the prisoners?" I huff.

But Domiel meets my gaze with an open gaze of his.

"I've told you, we've promised our lives and loyalty to Uriel, and that's exactly what we're doing. We're following and protecting Uriel."

But that doesn't answer my question. Too many people, and angels, tried to screw me over, citing my inadequacy as a reason for having their way, and that's the trump card Rafe utilises the most.

I turn to Dumah, who gives me a short nod of confirmation of his brother's words.

"Whatever", I mumble.

I open my wings and with a push at the white-stoned ground with my foot, I soar into the sky with large Jess in my arms, Domiel and Dumah flanking me.

"Aren't you afraid that they'd seal Uras off to you after you'll leave?" Domiel calls to me after a few seconds of silent flight, straining his voice over the gushing beating of our wings.

"If I'll find myself an army, the army that will take Uras back for me, one way or another, or I will level this place to the ground trying. And if I don't find an army, Uras will be as useful as a chocolate fireguard to me. This pitiful crew and these walls won't stop Mik'hael."

CHAPTER 18

A nother preparation for another expedition into Hell begins, but in all honesty, sometimes it feels as if I've never left Hell, although it's a Hell of my own.

If the frequency of my visits into Arllu holds, Baza will start charging me admission and will issue me with a "frequent flyer" card. I wonder if he'd stamp it at every visit, and after how many visits would I be able to claim my free coffee?

The packing didn't take as long as I thought, and thanks to the brothers, the preparation was by far better organised than my first expedition.

Domiel has brought me a fresh set of clothing – all virgin white this time – and Dumah has raided Uras' arsenal, piling an impressive collection of swords, cleavers, metal balls with spikes on chains, a few crossbows with a set of arrows and a bunch of small knives in a metal pile on the floor of the rotunda room. He has brought a few mystery pouches as well, which he showed Domiel and then tied them to a thick leather belt encircling his waist.

Once I've sealed myself into a new all white ensemble, looking more romantic and angelic, yet medieval than ever, Domiel and Dumah changed too. They are now sporting an all-black get-up of military grade jackets, trousers and boots, with rigid frames of shiny protective vests over their chests, looking very modern and hi-tech. A brave duo of wicked mercenaries, ready to destabilise another small, oil-rich nation. Their yellow wings are incongruously jolly backdrop for their faces and attire.

But in spite of the foreboding uniform, both brothers began to grow on me.

They both possess solid characters behind their steely appearances, yet with it holding an open brutal honesty that I appreciated the most. When they pledged themselves to me, they meant it. I don't feel a hidden agenda from either of them. They're "straight shooters" and I admire and like them for that.

Dumah constantly remains silent. I have never heard him say a word, leaving all communications to his brother, but a few times I caught him smiling at the "monster" Jess, when he'd walk past her, and for that I liked him even more.

The furry Jess now sits on the floor next to the weaponry pile, eyeing the preparations with interest, now and again asking questions into my mind. I was pleased to hear calmer tones in her voice, although I was growing concerned at the glances she would dart at Domiel's and Dumah's backs, and I could swear I saw her swallow.

Earlier, I tried to convince Rafe on the prudence of him staying behind, in Uras.

As much as his burned wings have almost grown back, perfectly mirroring the healthy two, his inability to draw the light from the universe meant that if something was to happen to him out there, or should he die, there would be no way to fix him.

But after a very short barking match and a few seconds of back and forth, Rafe announced that he is coming with me and that "that is the end of it", and if it makes me feel any better, I am free to fill the black sphere to the brim with gold and silver healing specks and to bring it with us, into Arllu, and "fine", he will carry it.

As much as the thought of trekking miles on end with extra weight, through Arllu, didn't appeal to me, I decided that to have my own, personal, resurrection equipment might not be such a bad idea after all.

My plan was to drop straight inside the Baza's glistening skyscraper, to land inside it just as I've landed twice in the halls of Uras. I envisaged dropping on Baza's unexpected head right in the middle of his dining hall, during one of his ostentatious dinners, but Domiel, always so careful not to offend, softly "reminded" me that without an "invitation" we wouldn't be able to drop into his dominion, however the thin barrier of the Gates will open with ease to Uriel.

When I asked why nobody else is using the passage or why Baza hasn't sealed it off, Domiel shrugged his shoulders, rightly asking, who in their right mind would go into Hell willingly?

I had to admit that he had a point.

Between Butcher, lizards and the "grey" army, I'd imagine Baza feels safe enough in his piece of a hellish Eden not needing to seal the thin barrier of the Gates, maybe leaving his options open. Besides, didn't he mention something about the Gates and the lizards' infiltration onto Earth? Wasn't there a connection? I wondered if they use the Gates for that too.

The one chunky positive did come up with the prospect of this trip.

Since Amy's instructions to open my mind up to my sister's, I had inadvertently opened my mind to every angel in Uras, to their every conversation, to their chatter, a leisurely chit-chat or heated arguments, often about "new Uriel".

Although, their conversations were hushed, pushed to the back of my mind and playing in the background like store music. The chattering was a constant, bubbling in my head, as annoying as a whistle of a boiling kettle. The kettle was whistling, and nobody had come to take it off.

But according to Rafe, my mental radio will stop working in Arllu. I wouldn't be able to hear other angels' thoughts and nobody would be able to speak to me, into my mind, not even Jess. "Sarukh's powers don't work in Arllu", he said.

But I was okay with that.

Finally, I will get some peace and quiet in my head, even at the cost of suffering the Hell again.

Rafe came into the room only once, to check on the preparation and to confirm that he was coming with me, but after his earlier refusal to listen and stay behind, I just waved him off, busy sliding a few small knives into the external sheaths at the wide black leather belt that Domiel had given me.

The wide belt circled my waist like a corset. Stitched from layers of rigid black leather and once strapped and buckled around my waist, the belt's width went from under my breasts all the way to my hip bone.

The little portable armoury of the belt boasted the two sheath pockets at the bottom to house each of my small swords in addition to the sheaths for knives at the centre of the belt itself. As well as this, there were two small pockets and additional numerous hoops to hold weapons sewn into the body of the corset, into which I've stuffed my knives.

I wanted to quiz Amy before my departure, testing her inability to lie to see if she'd hold her loyalty to me, if I'll be allowed back into Uras, if Uras will be mine on my return, but instead, I just waved my hand at this idea as well. As I said to Domiel, if I have an army, I'll take Uras back, and if I don't find my numbers, then Uras will not remain a safe haven for much longer before falling too.

When the five of us left the Uriel's tower, there was no farewell parade in our honour on the streets of Uras, children and women didn't line up both sides of a street, cheering us on, waving flags and showering us with flowers.

We are leaving Uras to the ringing, deafening silence of the angels, hiding behind the closed shutters.

Uras is empty and quiet. The once-busy city of hundreds, was reduced to two dozen residents, and even the remaining few are about to exhale a relief at our departure.

So be it.

It's not like their farewell handkerchiefs' waving would've helped me in any way.

My "Hell party" is quiet too. There's nothing more has left to say, the plan was discussed and agreed. The brothers are quiet and solemn, and sometimes I'd catch Dumah's loving gaze stroking the medieval white buildings of his city.

I wonder if he thinks that he'll ever come back to this place, his home. I wonder if he regrets coming with me, but I don't ask.

This city is not mine. I don't belong in it and the residents don't want me in it. By leaving, I'm doing everyone a favour.

"Ready?" Rafe asks, scanning our faces.

His voice bounces off in the empty small square of white polished stone. The carved white doors and windows on the one storey buildings around the square are shut. The taller white towers, crowned with silver roofs, wink in the distance, past the low buildings, and when I spin on the spot, I can see the four tall, large towers in four directions around Uras, dwarfing the city's buildings.

The light on the white of the buildings is blinding, but still, and only the breeze and constant scent of fruits are roaming the city.

Rafe is sealed in the same black tactical gear as he was in our first expedition, matching the brothers' get-up perfectly, black combat boots, trousers with pockets of ammunition' belts strapped to his thigh, the black high-tech plastic armour over his black jacket. The wide belt around his waist houses two large, curved knives, leather pockets, a metal ball with spikes on a chain with a wooden handle and a small axe. His two large swords are behind his back, their hilts rise behind his each shoulder, and the leather harnesses crisscross his chest.

Even with my heavily weaponised belt, I'm packing the least in our small group.

Domiel and Dumah nod.

I nod too, hugging the even more grown, furry Jess to my chest. She grows with every minute like yeast dough.

Jess' furry head is big as mine now. Her four protruding canines are as long as my hand and when I hold her, I can feel tight knots of the lean muscles rolling under her skin.

After losing half of my wing to her, I have to admit, *I am* scared of her, but I force myself to hug her closer, stroking her body covered in the brown fur, placing a light kiss on her pink snout.

"Where we left off?" Rafe asks me.

I nod.

Rafe steps closer and so do the brothers. We form a circle. I feel someone's hands on my waist.

My wings open wide, touching someone else's wings, sending zaps of energy to dance over my spine. My body jolts and I close my eyes, at the last second reminding myself where I need to be.

The pull, the drag and suddenly, I feel the burn of hot air on my face, in my nose and my throat when it slides into my lungs.

But the hot air, stripped of oxygen, doesn't fill my lungs, instead bringing the familiar stench of the rotting dump and with it, the familiar nausea reflex.

To prevent vomiting, I clamp my mouth shut and open my eyes to my new surroundings.

CHAPTER 19

aza's hellhole begins to feel familiar, almost homely.

B The charred low desert brush and the twisted fingers of dead, broken trees, the cracked red soil and barren to the horizon landscape of lifeless Mars, none of it has changed.

The notorious wind billows through the land, raising a perpetual veil of dirt and dust, rolling the brushwood along the red cracked soil.

I forgot how bad this place smells. I yank up a thin piece of fabric I've ripped of the bottom of old tunic and tied up around my neck – another home-made mask in another attempt to stop the swallowing of Hell's dust during yet another expedition.

Sometimes, like now, I begin to wonder if I invite all of the crap on myself, if my troubles are of my own making, but I stop these thoughts, as dwelling on it won't change the thing.

My wings wrap and cling to my back as a disturbing sense of déjà vu strokes its chilling fingers over my spine.

As one, Rafe, Domiel and Duma yank their black scarves to cover their faces, and with the bottom halves of their faces hidden, they look even more sinister.

Jess is the only one unfazed by the wind, heat or smell. She climbs out of my arms and once her paws touch the red soil, she begins prancing on the spot like a show dog, testing the feel of the soil under her paws, and after a few more seconds, she squeals and takes off running.

"Jess", I yell after her.

But I am ignored, as she yaps and howls when she pounces on the moving dust over the ground. She chases the rolling brushwood, only for the next second to abandon it and to sprint into the distance after something else.

She runs back to me, spinning circles around our group once, twice, three times, making me dizzy, her muscly legs pushing her forward with an impressive speed.

Her bat wings, now grown and bigger, flap behind her back, and when a sudden gust of wind would come, her wings would open a tad wider and her body would lift off the ground for a second or two, and Jess would squeal in delight, her voice ringing silver bells of excitement above the boring plane.

Suddenly she is agile, lithe and comfortable in her new skin. It's as if this place gave her that energy.

I turn around and look behind me.

The opening of the Gates shimmers with a thin inter-dimensional movement of a veil, which morphs the picture of the landscape. The area of the Gates passage shimmers and glistens, rippling slightly, but apart from it, it looks unremarkable and barely noticeable, and if I didn't know of the existence of the Gates, I would never have found it here.

Rafe spins on the spot for a moment, scanning the empty landscape from under his capped hand, before without a word, raising his hand above his head and waving it towards a prosaic part of the horizon, which looks like the entire horizon around us.

He sets off towards the chosen direction and we follow.

I'm still wearing my old plimsolls.

With Uras fashion favouring dainty moccasins, made of the thinnest leather with no sole to speak of, their shoes wouldn't have lasted an hour of walking through the crushed rock and sand of the Hell. But of course, given the chosen mode of angelic transportation in Heaven, comfortable or sensible footwear would be low on their list of priorities.

Back in Uras, I have asked Domiel for the tactical gear for myself, along with their military grade boots, but was told that they don't have any of it in my sizes, which has made me wonder if my sizes are particular small in the angelic world or if they have something against women wearing military-grade gear. Maybe angels don't expect females to join the fighting and these kinds of expeditions. This is, if that's the case, another bone for me to pick when I get back to Uras; if I get back...

Our little caravan sets on its route, following Rafe's lead and slowly, our formation shifts, adjusting to our strengths, weaknesses and overall attitude towards this merry little outing, with Rafe leading the way, me in the middle and both brothers behind, bringing up the rear. Jess, like an excited puppy, spins circles around the group, running ahead and then back to us, measuring unending circles with bounds of her energy.

I called after her a few times, but soon gave up, as my nagging was ignored and clearly was spoiling her fun.

After a few hours of trekking through the moving wall of dust, the empty horizon begins to fill, bringing with it a change to the song of the wind.

I had been expecting this moment since I uttered the word "Arllu".

I knew it would come. I knew what I would see here and a cold shiver touches my sweat-drenched spine.

The noise came earlier than I expected and it's much closer to the Gates than when we left Hell last time.

The wind no longer sings with a whistle of air and the brushing of the sand grains, the rolling dust, it now weaves percussion tones into an orchestra, as the wind and dust brush over and collide with metal.

The dot in the distance grows towards us with every new step and I tense up.

Through the screen of dust, it morphs into a low building of shining metal, similar to the buildings I've seen before, similar to the building that I've walked around, the buildings that I knew were the forewarnings of the beaming white light.

The metal coating on that building is new and shiny, polished, not yet scuffed by the constantly billowing dust. When we come closer, I note the closed and locked doors of a vacant property that stands, waiting for its visitors, for whom I know, these sheds will be their final destination.

I swallow, beginning to question my intellectual capacity for deciding to come back here.

As we press forward, more buildings begin to appear, filling the air with a growing racket of the dust banging on the metal.

We snake past shiny, recently erected buildings. They interrupt the red, previously empty and uninhabited landscape, as if this part of Hell went through a rapid expansion or an intense housing development since I visited it last time. There are more sheds, more housing facilities now than I remembered seeing before.

The waves of tension begin to vibrate off Rafe and the brothers. Their unsheathed swords are raised higher.

"Jess", I yell into the wind, and once she comes, bouncing back, I add: "Stay near me. I need to see you at all times", I instruct her. With our telepathy connection severed, I hope she would understand me as now it's the only thread of communication left.

But either she can't understand me or ignores me, as she turns around, darting back into the distance, zooming past the low silver buildings, running circles around them, her black bat wings flapping behind her.

"Her flapping wings are like the flapping ears on a spaniel", I suddenly think.

It doesn't take long for the first human cries and moans to appear. They reach me, brought over by the wind.

At first, the cries are faint and weak. They dive in and out of the wind and cacophony of dust banging on the metal, dispersing and disappearing, when suddenly, they would solidify, emerging forward, out of the whistling wind, surprising me with their sudden clarity.

Being away from this place, sitting high in my ivory tower of Uras, I had forgotten how painful these cries are. I'd forgotten the feeling of agony when these human howls of suffering enter my soul, and as it turns out, I'm not ready for this.

I knew I'd find human suffering in here. I knew that my chances to avoid those humans were slim, but naively, I've forgotten the depth of cuts their pleas for mercy leave through my heart. I've forgotten the pain their cries, when their souls would be ripped from their bodies, would wring from me. I've forgotten how these humans cry with each bursting flash of that light. I've forgotten it all, naively hoping to grow out of that reaction, hoping to avoid it this time.

I know I will see naked humans and lizards next.

I force myself to breathe under my fabric mask. I force myself to find the sound measuring the bounces of Jess' paws on the soil in the shredding dissonance of all sounds and stick with them, find the calming beat in them, bringing it forward, while ignoring, blocking the sounds of human suffering.

I glance at Rafe's back. I turn and look at the brothers, but Rafe's back is stiff and silent and the brothers' faces, covered by their masks, release no emotion. Their eyes are calm and steely.

Rafe's and the brothers' strides remain strong and decisive: either none of them can hear and "feel" these cries or the screams of dying humans don't bother them.

With every step forward, the peaceful moments of silence grow shorter, thinner and weaker, and the landscape grows denser with buildings, until the silence is burned out completely by agony of the screams, like fog under the rising sun.

The beating of Jess' paws is no longer discernible in the sea of cries.

I try to close my eyes but I almost trip, so I open them again. I try to count my steps in a desperate attempt to drown the screams and to take the burning heat of tears out of my eyes.

And then I see a bright flash. I trip and I stop.

CHAPTER 20

I strain my eyes, searching for the bright flash on the red horizon, wanting to find it yet hoping not to see it ever again, when through the curtain of the red dust, the piercing white light bursts and with its lasting flash I begin to sing.

At first it's a humming of a random pop tune, but as it fails to drown the cries and my engulfing panic at the sight of the light, my voice rises with the words of a chorus, matching the volume of the deathly screams.

I drop my gaze to the red ground and I cover my ears with my hands, as I continue screaming about "building the castles out of the rubble of his love" and "being more than he ever thought I was".

A hand touches my arm and I jump.

With his black mask drawn down, Rafe's mouth moves, saying something, and I drop my hands covering my ears.

"What's happening with you, Ariel?" Rafe asks. Or I think it's what he asks as I can barely make out his words over the human's screams and the whistling and the banging of the wind. I read his lips instead.

I'm afraid to stop singing and I'm afraid to move forward.

I remember the humans from the last time. I remember their naked bodies, their vacant eyes, the little bodies of the children. I remember the whimpering cries they made when a lizard's tongue would whip at them. I remember the pulsing of the glorious white light and the agonising, dying cries of humans with it.

I'm afraid if I move forward and stand next to the light, I might discern every single cry within that ocean of agony, every single plea in that unending cycle of misery and I will drown in it, never resurfacing myself.

"Cries?" I read Rafe's mouths.

I nod. Maybe trekking through the Hell wasn't such a good idea. Clearly, I have no memory for pain.

"Uriel was set to hear the cries of the wronged and the cries of the punished", the memory of Rafe's words come into my mind. "She was made to deliver the justice for the first ones and to draw her energy from the latters. You were made to hear these cries. Like a predator's hearing was tuned by the nature to the sounds of its prey, you were made to hear these people, but more than that, you were made to feel their pleas in your soul, as by feeling it your Qal could bestow its justice. You were born this way. You're tuned to their suffering. By hearing their calls you deliver the justice for the innocent and you feed on the punishing of the guilty."

"But back in Arllu, they were all punished. All of them were crying. How could I have made out who was wronged? They all sounded the same, one as desperate as next. How was I supposed to differentiate between their cries, and even if I had, what was I supposed to do then?"

"The judgement of the Uriel is the righteous one. It's high and it's final because it's true. I'm not saying you should've done anything in Arllu, all that I'm saying is that you're the judge and the saviour of their souls...and angels' Qals."

His words then brought back the memory of the dream from the cave. The memory of me, floating above a crumbling ancient city, while watching the destruction and death, earthquakes, tsunami and lizards, consuming people, while supervising the chaos below with a satisfaction of a job well done.

"How sick is this? Out of all people, I'm the one, who draws energy from someone else's suffering?" I thought at the time.

"You will never make it through if you don't block it." I read Rafe's slowly moving lips. "You need to close your mind to it. You hold no command over Arllu. Uriel can't punish or redeem anyone in here as it's not her domain. The judgement was delivered and you don't need harken to their pleas."

But I don't know how to block their screams or how to stop the flood of their desperation from entering my head and my heart, and now looking up into Rafe's warm, kind, hazelnut-brown eyes, the deeper guilt sets from what I might do. It comes over me and I want to howl with the wind, with the screams, fall to my knees and beg for *his* forgiveness.

I shouldn't be the one issuing the salvation. I should be *pleading* for it.

I grind my teeth and I nod.

I turn away from Rafe, starting down into the direction he has chosen for us, while changing my song, now screaming into the wind about how much "I like to move it, move it!", needing to cover my tears and my pain.

Sure enough, but sooner than I expected, Jess' furry body sprints back towards us, whimpering and howling to the wind like a coyote, while glancing behind her as if being chased.

The cloud of dust is thicker in the distance behind her, signalling the presence of dozens upon dozens feet marching, raising that dust cloud.

It could be only one of two scenarios. Either lizards are moving another group of humans, and it was Jess' first encounter with them, or Baza had sent his soldiers forward to meet us. Both scenarios are just as likely.

"Stay with us!" I bark at her.

I don't need to say it twice, as she darts behind my back, wedging herself between myself and Dumah.

Rafe is next to me now. Both his hands carry his long swords of white rippling fire and I draw one of mine.

We move closer. The light ahead flashes brighter, and after a few more yards across the cracked soil, a small group becomes clearer through the veil of dust.

It's a group of humans, surrounded by taller, lizard guards. Rafe and the brothers lower their white swords but don't sheath them. However, I decide to sheath mine.

Ahead of us, the bodies of the lizards around the perimeter of the group are at least a foot taller than the people within the circle. Their egg-shaped heads are slick, blind and hairless and each lizard drags a thick tail behind him.

The veil of dust is thinning the closer to the group we come, and the closer we come, the better I can see the naked people within the circle of the lizards.

This group is smaller than the group I saw on my first visit to this safari.

The group consists of just over a dozen of humans and three lizards.

Although the lizards are blind, there's something different about these ones.

These lizards are erratic and less organised. Reluctantly, they plod around the humans. Occasionally, their thick snake tongues whip out of their holes to discipline the humans, but more often than not, their tongues instead make a connection with another scaly skin and then a short squabble would erupt. Both lizards would whip at each other with their tongues, attacking the opponent with high-pitched shrills, forgetting about the "cattle".

There's no glistening of gold on their necks or on their wrists. The black whips don't hang off their waists and their loincloths are dirty and raggedy.

The obedience and the trance of the humans are the same, though.

This all-male group roams with vacant eyes within the circle, bumping into each other and whimpering, when lizards' tongues make contact with their skin, ripping off a chunk along the way.

We are about a yard away from the group. My head is exploding from human screams of other groups from miles away, from the weak whimpering of the males within this herd, and from the panicked cries of Jess, which progressed into a crazed howl of a scared and trapped animal.

I turn to my sister, kneeling in front of her. Her fur-covered face is above mine. She has grown from a size of a Labrador to a size of chunky, over-fed mastiff or a pony.

"Jess, you need to calm down, darling. These animals can't see us", I say, referring to the lizards as "animals", suddenly realising that this would apply to the human cattle too. There's nothing left of their humanity.

"The lizards can't see or harm us", I add.

I stroke her big head.

"The lizards are blind and the humans... Well, they chose to come here, to be here. You see, Jessie-boo, they made a bet. They gambled and they lost. They sold something that wasn't for sale and now they're here. I can't do anything for them, nobody can. Once here, these people will die here, and nobody would be able to do anything." I sigh.

"That's how this place works. These people decided to be here, they chose to come. But please, don't be scared. No one will harm you when I am around. Trust me, Jessie-boo."

Jess' soft eyes watch my face as I speak to her. I think she understands what I'm saying, at least I hope, and if she doesn't, I hope that my calm voice would sooth her.

I lean over and kiss her wet pink snout.

Dumah is next to my sister, his hand resting on her withers, softly playing with her fur.

Suddenly, a human voice cries out behind my back.

I turn in time to see another squabble erupting between the two lizards, escalating into an animal brawl, with flying hungry tongues, shrieking hissing and kicking of their back legs like kangaroos, and a naked, scrawny old man,who is caught in the middle of their quarrel.

The two screeching blind animals whip their tongues, aiming at each other, but their anaconda tongues rarely catch the target of another scaly skin, as both lizards move with surprising agility, diving, ducking and swinging to the side.

But the human livestock in their zombie daze is less alert. The shrieking lizards dance around naked bodies, and while some naked humans manage to roam away, one old man is caught in the middle of this lizards' brawl.

He is in the centre of it.

The lizards dance, skirt around him, trying to get each other, and when lizards' tongues make a contact with his body with a wet towel slap, the old man screams.

The old man is locked in the circle of their moving bodies. He is their human shield, and slowly their anger towards each other subsides, as they realise the fun of a present play thing.

The lizards' game changes and the atmosphere shifts.

The lizards' screams grow less irate and furious, until it dies completely, replaced by the sharp barks of chatter and hisses that sound very much like a laughter. The lizards' tongues make contact with the old body every second now. Whereas before it was accidental, now it's with a calculated intention. It's for their reptile pleasure and joy.

The lizards take turn to whip their tongues at the old man, and prior to every tongue's flight, a small guttural bark would escape lizards' mouths, which I think is an announcement of where they aims to hit the old man.

The old man's body is riddled with scratches and chunks of missing skin and flesh. Looking at his branded torso, his head and his limbs, I'm surprised that he's still standing. The two large gashing wounds of missing flesh are bleeding at his right side and his back.

But he doesn't try to stem the flow of blood or to protect himself. There's no panic on his face. His arms hung lifelessly by his sides, and weak whimpers is all that show his distress.

The five of us are rooted to the ground, watching the gruesome show.

Jess sniffles next to me, which sounds like a hiccup. But maybe it's a cry.

In her animal form, I can't tell, but I can't take this viewing any longer and before I have a chance to form a clear decision in my mind, my hands find the handles of my familiar swords, freeing them from their sheaths, as I stride towards the group, towards the closest lizard.

The zombified old man is next to me and I can smell the metallic stench of his blood.

His blood, falling onto the red soil, tolls in my head with its every drop, spiking my madness and waking my mate Rage, who is pleased to be released. She hasn't been allowed to flex her muscles for a while. She hasn't tasted blood in a long time and she has a lot of suppressed crazy to burn.

Fuelled by her bellicose chants, I spring upwards on my last step, and my wings open behind me, bringing me to the height of the lizard in front of me.

Its scaly egg-shaped skull is an inch away from me.

The teeth around his tongue hole are grey and uneven, and the dribble that the creature secretes from its hole, holds a stench of decomposing flesh.

The creature freezes for a moment, aware yet unsure of a new presence in front of it, but by the time it senses the danger and opens its hole wider, ready to release the tongue and fight, my small sword draws a decisive line across the creature's throat.

The familiar, thick black mucus pulses from the lizard's slashed throat, covering the white rippling fire of my blade and running down creature's bare chest, but not before the lizard manages to open its mouth, producing a weak gulping short shrill of a dying animal.

A sudden pain slices at my top left wing, twisting it, yanking, and surprised by this pain, I scream and drop to the ground, landing on top of an already fallen lizard.

I twist, looking over my shoulder, behind my back, to see blood beginning to pool, coating bitten off and mangled feathers.

My gaze darts up the white pasty body of the naked old man above me, then jumping to the crowd of human cattle to my right, darting to the green lizard behind the old man, looking for the danger, trying to figure out, who assaulted me and where the danger lies, when my gaze jumps at the green slimy face of the standing lizard, noting a fleck of purple down hanging from the corner of his mouth.

I push at the slimy body underneath me, and I am about to roll and slide off the lizard's body, when the thick anaconda snake flies towards me.

I drop my head back in time, as I watch the snake tongue speeding above me, the small piranha teeth at the end of it clacking, looking for my head, and finding nothing, dropping into the feathers of my wing.

The piranha teeth dive into the soft tissues of my muscle and feathers, sinking in, tearing, as the lizard shakes its head.

In agony, I scream and I cry.

I throw my hand with my sword towards the snake tongue, stabbing at it, slicing erratically. My vision is eroded by my tears and my panic.

I roar. I turn and with another throw of my arm, I separate the snake-tongue from the lizard's body.

The teeth holding my wing relax, and the snake tongue falls off.

The lizard's long, one note screech rings in the windy air. I'm pleased that I've hurt it, but suddenly the lizard screams again, this time with straining and suffering. His scream rises, riding the higher note of fear and death.

I roll off the dead lizard, scrambling to my feet. I yank another sword out of my belt, swinging both in front of myself, as I sway.

I wipe at my eyes with the back of my hand, but I have to blink through the haze three, four times before my mind is able to process the picture of animal Jess, sitting on top of the lizard, ripping it apart with her large grey teeth and... *eating it*, the black blood of lizard flying.

I turn away and double over, needing to throw up. But I have nothing to bring, not even bile, as I haven't eaten for a while.

I drop to my knees.

I can hear an animal chewing and swallowing behind my back and the weak huffs of the dying lizard.

Careful not to turn, I clamber up. Once up, I cover my ears with my hands as I stagger around the bodies of the lizards I've killed, keeping my gaze on the red soil, plodding away, towards frozen to their spots Rafe, Domiel and Dumah.

Their mortified gazes are glued to the scene behind my back, relaying their shock, stupor and disgust. I don't need to add a commentary, they've seen everything.

I don't turn. I can't. I'm afraid to look.

I'm absolutely petrified of what I'll see, so I stand next to them, watching their faces, but as they continue to watch, unable to draw their gazes away, I stumble around them, walking behind them, then sliding to the ground behind their backs.

CHAPTER 21

The chewing sounds went for a while.

Once the shrieking of the dying lizard had seized, a short beating of leathery wings echoed behind my back, and then another chewing session had erupted.

I hid my head between my knees, keeping my hands firmly over my ears, but the sounds have still managed to slip through.

When the wave of noises has died and I was about to remove my hands off my ears and turn around, another sharp beating of wings had descended above the howling of the wind, followed by the hissing and the screams of another lizard.

Oh god.

A warm hand stroked the top of my head then pulled me to my feet, turning me, and I was cocooned by Rafe's warm body and his scent of ocean and fruits.

I thought about pushing him away but I didn't want to be alone, and I was afraid.

I sit on the ground, now in Rafe's warm embrace, listening to the whistling of the constant wind, interrupted only by the distant human cries, relieved that the chewing sounds have gone.

Domiel's and Rafe's voices mumble dimmed nonsense above my head, when I feel a light tug at my sleeve, then another light touch and I open my eyes to Rafe's face, with him kneeling in the dirt in front of me.

"Ariel, Ariel. She's fine", I hear a faint Rafe's voice, and he pulls at my arms. "She is asleep now."

But I shrug off his hold, pressing my hands tighter to my ears.

I don't want to take my hands off. In fact, I'd like nothing more but to close my eyes, my mind and go to sleep, waking up to it all being a horrible nightmare, which could easily be dissolved by sunlight and waking.

I am not ready to turn around. I'm afraid.

I'm *petrified* to see the creature behind me. I'm afraid to confront it. I'm afraid if this creature is no longer Jess, and most of all, I'm scared of being unable to pull Jess out of this nightmare, the nightmare of *my* making, if she is within that shell, trapped, alive and scared.

"Ariel, we need to keep moving", Rafe says above me, pulling harder at my arms.

"I don't care. I don't care, do you understand me? Can't you see what I've done? What *you've* done?" I scream, lifting my face to him.

"I should've left her behind, behind on Earth. Maybe she would've been alone but she would've been safe, she would've been *her*", I mumble.

I snap my gaze back to him.

"You should've told me. You should've warned me. You really expect me to buy that you didn't know? *You?* The top archangel and didn't know? You probably wanted it to happen. For something that I still don't know, for some perverted game of yours, you've planned it."

"Another game... Again blindsided, again at loss", I mumble, to myself rather than him.

"You have always demanded my trust in you, in your decisions", I gush, "but how am I supposed to trust you, any of you, scheming lying bastards! How do you expect me to trust *you*?"

"It is you who should be there." I jam my thumb behind me, where I left my sister.

"It shouldn't be her trapped in a monster's body, going crazy, it should be you. You should've been sent to Udhad."

I slam my mouth shut before I say something else I will regret. I drop my gaze, grinding my teeth, forcing my words back into my throat.

I can't say it all. Not yet.

I wipe my eyes and clumsily rise to my feet.

"Turn around. Don't be a wuss! Just turn around!" I demand of myself.

On laden legs, I turn.

The small herd of naked humans has dispersed, now roaming wider, some of them lumbering aimlessly further and further away.

I force myself to bring my gaze closer, to look at the red ground, at the dark brown and red puddle with islands of greenish-grey within, and a large brown furry pile amongst the bloody sea.

I swallow and, childishly, close my eyes.

I breathe, delaying looking at it all.

I'm weak and I know it.

Grinding my teeth and mumbling profanities, I open my eyes, looking straight at the massacre of my doing.

The chewed up and dismembered pieces of the lizards litter the ground. The blood that had spilled earlier, already had soaked into the hungry red soil, and on the top of this murderous mess, lies the furry creature – my Jess.

She has grown.

Her brown furry body is larger than it was before, bigger than a cow, maybe the size of a small elephant. Her head is big and her protruding canines are massive. The two black leathery bat wings of hers are four times bigger than mine and folded behind her back.

She is huge, and whatever "cute puppy", furry look she had going before, now it has gone.

Her large head rests on her long front legs, as she is nestled on the ground, rolled into a cosy ball like a cat.

The soft whistling snores escape her pink snout, and her legs move a little, and she whimpers as she sleeps.

I look at the slaughter around my sister and I don't know what to do.

The memory of her eating my wing is still fresh in my mind, and I'm scared of her. I'm afraid to come near. I'm afraid to be next to her.

But I'm more afraid of her waking up to this carnage and getting frightened. I still don't know how much of *her* is left in her.

I have to remind myself that this creature is my Jess, as I take cautious steps forward on my stiff legs.

I walk towards her. My plimsolls kick up dust, but three steps later, they begin to trudge as I tread through the bloody mud.

I'm in front of my sister now, and up so close she is even bigger and scarier. Her pink snout and canines are covered in dried blood and a lizard's claw is stuck in the hairs on her chin.

I push revolution spasms down my throat, repeatedly swallowing.

Reaching out, I stroke above her snout, patting the bridge of her hairy nose. I shuffle closer, stroking the soft fur between her long, pointy ears.

"Jess", I croak, but my voice is barely audible. I clear my throat.

"Jess, Jessie-boo. You need to wake up, sweetie. We need to keep going."

I stroke her, lightly tugging at her large eyelids and her ears.

The furry Jess yawns and opens one eye. Her animal-self yawns, louder this time, stretching its lean body and reaching the large front paws past me.

"You passed out, Jess. Probably the stress, strain, the lizards..." I say, waving it off, while stroking her soft head.

She opens both of her eyes, and I can swear I can see Jess and her sweet baby smile behind these eyes and the furry face.

Her sleepy gaze travels to the three angels in the distance behind my back. Her gaze returns to me, then dropping to the bloody mess under my feet, her eyes instantly wake up, scanning the bloody massacre, and her legs fold, bend, beating crazy, as she tries to rise, yet slipping on the mess.

She is scared and repulsed, and I heave a sigh of relief.

"Yeah, sorry about that, baby. It was me. I've made the mess. One animal had attacked me, then another jumped up and I had no choice but to kill those lizards. They were a nuisance. But you were great though. You've helped me so much: you were keeping the humans safe, keeping them away. You've helped me a lot, Jessie-boo. You saved my life, Jessie. You've saved your sister and all those humans, my little brave puppy."

I pull her furry face towards me and plant a loud wet kiss on her pink snout.

"Good girl. Well done, baby. Are you ready to go?"

I place another kiss on her snout and, ignoring the sloshing and the mess. I walk back to my mercenaries angels, listening to the rapid plodding of the large paws through the mud, following as fast as her large body allows her, and I am pleased about it. I can't contain my smile. My sister is still with me. She hasn't been taken over by that animal.

I glare at the angels.

"Let's go. What are we waiting for?" I ask, and turning around, I walk around the mess, setting back onto our path, towards our destination.

CHAPTER 22

"Why did you lie to her? Why haven't you told her the truth?" Rafe's low voice says as he keeps marching next to me.

"She'll figure it out soon enough", he adds, "when she is hungry and needs to eat."

I glance at him and turn my attention back to Jess, who is ahead of us, learning how to fly.

She bounces ahead of us until I can no longer see her past the veil of red dust, then suddenly, the pounding of her large feet would sound closer, rising, approaching us, followed by a spell of silence and I would see her large body carried above the ground on her enormous wings. She would drop to the ground in front of me, would give me an excited bark, then turn and run, repeating the process.

Dumah jogs half a mile ahead of us, keeping an eye on my little monster.

"Don't you think I know it?" I answer with another short glance at him, the next time Jess runs away from us. "I didn't want her to get scared. Not just yet... I'll tell her all of this later."

But I know that I'm lying to myself and Rafe, simply trying to postpone the inevitable. Maybe I'm hoping that whatever magic is at work here will dissolve and disappear by itself and I wouldn't need to have any further difficult conversations. Although with her rapid growth spurt, I doubt that magic would go away and my wishful thinking would materialise, I should be so lucky. But I am sick of being the bearer of bad news, so maybe not just yet.

The landscape has become busier and industrialised. The metal outer buildings grew upwards, replacing the earlier sheds with two storey, sturdier buildings. The metal on these buildings is duller and rougher, and some of them begin to look familiar.

That's good. It means we're getting closer.

But, unfortunately, with the denser arrival of the buildings came bigger herds.

The herds of humans appear more often now, larger, consisting of men and women, sometimes children, and guarding them lizards are the lizards I remember: the disciplined beasts with gold collars and wristbands, with black leather whips at their disposal, which they utilise often, keeping their tongues to themselves.

The earlier cries and whimpering of humans have turned into a tidal wave of a cacophony, which blankets the landscape in one, singular note of suffering, from which I can't discern a single voice. Their cries have entwined with the singing of wind and screeches of sand over metal.

But either I've turned numb to the human pleas, the intensity of it or one note of it had washed the sting out, almost as if taking the humanity out of it, merging and blending this pain with sounds of nature and landscape.

How did they say: "The death of one human is a tragedy but death of millions is statistics"?

When another wave of screams descends over the landscape, I stumble as my shoe catches on a rock, and to stop myself from falling, my wings burst open and I wince, as the top of my left wing sings in pain.

"What?" Rafe asks next to me, his eyebrows knitted with concern.

"Wing", I answer, breathing through my teeth and nudging my head behind my back.

"We have to stop. You need to rest and you need gizin-ugdu. The sphere", he adds to my confused glance.

"Domiel!" he calls.

"Rafe, stop it. We don't have time for it and stop arranging things for me, and stop arranging my care", I hiss.

"Domiel", I call, waving my hand to the angel. "It's fine. No need to come."

I spin back to Rafe.

"We need to keep moving. Every minute we spend here is one extra minute for Baza to find out that we have arrived. We are not invited, in case you forgot that. We don't have time for stopping, healing or sight-seeing. Besides, we'd better save the sphere for a life and death situation, which this is not. I can walk and we'll continue walking. I'll be fine."

"Ariel", he starts.

"No. That's the end of the conversation. Let's move it."

The number of "lighthouses" has increased over the landscape too.

If before, during my first visit to this joyous place, I came across only one processing plant, now during the same trek, I see a few bright white flickers on the horizon, one closer and two further away, and have trekked around one earlier.

The industrial development of Arllu is evident. I only wish I knew what had spurred this rapid growth.

We are next to the tall metal fence that encircles the original processing plant, from which the nightmare of that place had begun. I know that about a mile away, to the other side of that building, I will find the familiar fields of drying humans skins, and would hear skins creaking and flapping, as they swing on their poles.

"I need you, guys, to stay here".

I turn to Rafe, stopping a few feet away from the nearest herd. I try not to look at them, at their naked bodies, at their bleeding carved chests and their vacant faces.

Rafe stops with me and Domiel comes closer.

"I need to do something and I need to do it alone. Please wait for me here. Don't go further. I won't be long."

Rafe furrows his brow at me, glancing at my face, trying to read my intentions and is about to quiz me, when Domiel asks: "What about adar?"

"Her name is Jess", I correct Domiel, who drops his gaze and bows. "She's fine. If she wants to follow me she can, but I'll speak to her in a moment and ask her to stay with you. Just keep an eye on her, but she'll be fine."

"As you wish, Beyelai."

Domiel bows and jogs off to his brother, who weaves in and around the herds, following sprints of my sister.

"Jess", I call, cupping my mouth, yelling to her over the wind and cries. "Jessie-boo. Jessie, come here!"

When she turns her head, I give her a little wave.

She sprints to me but Dumah doesn't follow. He's listening to what his brother is telling him.

The creature the size of an elephant with a body of a hyena, covered in the brown fur of a bear, with a monstrous face that holds a pink snout and the large canines of a sabre-toothed tiger and enormous bat's wings ploughs through the crowd, scattering bodies like pins in a game of bowling, no longer running around obstacles but rather powering through them.

"Good girl, Jessie", I say, stroking her face and large head. "You stay here. Look after Rafe and Dumah. Do you like Dumah? Of course you do. He is nice. Look after them and Domiel too, make sure nothing happens to them. I will be back soon."

I lean towards her wet snout and place a light kiss on it.

"Stay here."

As if on cue, Rafe's hand flies towards me, stopping me in my tracks.

"Ariel."

"No", I stretch, as if warning off a dog who's about to pounce, keeping my voice low, yet commanding.

"No!" I repeat, holding his gaze. "You stay here and leave me to do what I need to do."

I shrug off his hold on my sleeve, walking away from them, towards the largest gathering of the naked bodies and scaly blind heads above the gold collars, toward the building of constantly burning white light, deeper into the ocean of screams and pain.

Once I'm pressed from every side by dirty and bleeding bodies, I begin to feel suffocated, and with a push at the ground, I fly to the sky, forcing my wings to lift me above the crowds, gliding while watching the moving waves of suffering.

Rafe may have chosen this particular road, but I knew where it would lead, I knew the scenery it would weave through and I knew that amongst this sea of misery I will find what I am looking for.

There's something else I need to do here, extra support I need to secure before I descend deeper into the depths of Baza's Hell. I have a few more things to do.

I have an extra agenda here and I'm not ready to share it with anyone. This agenda is the reason why I've sourced this crowd, why I came into the centre of this Hell.

CHAPTER 23

Three black clothing clad bodies and a large brown hill stand up against the red horizon like a sore thumb.

"Or four sore fingers", I giggle in my head.

The four of them have taken refuge by an old crumbling tree on the outskirts of the herds' roaming grounds.

I drop to the ground and finish the last few yards of the journey on foot.

"Okay, guys. Done", I call to them once closer.

The three angels have settled on the ground, talking to each other in hushed voices. Jess' large body lies to the side of the group, behind Dumah, as if looking for a shelter or protection, and a new sharp slither of jealousy stabs at me.

His hand strokes her large furry head, while she purrs, her hooded eyes heavy.

"Shall we continue, ladies?" I ask them, nudging my head towards our destination. "Or do you need a longer rest, to finish sharing gossip and lippie?"

I don't know why I'm annoyed again.

No. If I'm being honest with myself, I know.

I do know.

I want them to loathe me as much as I loathe myself.

I want to tell them what I'm about to do, every last bit of it, of what my plans are and how far I'm prepared to go, how much, and who, I am prepared to sacrifice. I want them to be outraged, shocked, appalled and disgusted. I want them to know the real me, so they'll run for the hills, screaming.

But I won't tell them, any of them, any of it. I have a lot to do. I have far to go and I need them if I want to make it there.

The angels rise to their feet to greet me, and orphaned by Dumah's hand Jess opens her eyes and yawns, stretching her back like a cat, before rising to her full height of a grown animal.

"We'll have to fly", I announce. "The herds are everywhere and it's tight. We'll be here forever if we continue on foot."

"Beyelai, we could be spotted", Domiel interjects, shaking his head. "It's many of us, plus adar. We'll be too noticeable if we take to the sky, and we'll lose the protection of herds."

"I know. We might be spotted. But this has gone long enough as it is, and I don't have any more time to kill. So we're going to open our big-girl's wings and flap them like we mean it, and while we flap, we'll pray that we get to Baza's place in one piece and before any alarms are raised."

The herds and the time are not the only reason for my impatience.

I already feel Rafe's narrowed gaze on me, assessing the change in me, wondering where I've been and what I've done, waiting to pounce with his relentless questions, and I could do without it.

"And Jessie-boo could do with some practice", I add, coming to my sister and stroking her muscly leg.

"She needs to learn how to use her beautiful wings", I coo.

Jess towers above me, exceeding the size of an elephant.

"You'd like to fly, baby girl, wouldn't you? I'll teach you. It's so easy."

Obeying my command, my four wings flash open and I wince at the pain heating up my left wing. I grind my teeth and to hide my pain, with one practiced kick at the ground, I jump up and I'm airborne in no time, beating my wings next to Jess and around her.

"Careful", Rafe growls, watching my shenanigans.

But I ignore him, concentrating on my sister and my pain.

I think I'm faster than the animal in Jess, or so I hope.

I fly around my sister, in front of her fur covered face with protruding grey teeth and fearsome pig snout. Like a butterfly, I fly around her, taunting, guiding, inviting.

I take myself a tad higher, before I bank on my wings, descending, dancing in front of my sister's eyes.

A string of drool rolls out of her mouth, hanging there for a moment, before it drops onto the red soil.

"Ariel", Rafe warns, his voice rolling low.

"Do you think you can catch me, baby girl? Sure about that? Let's see it then."

"Come and get me, Jess. Come and get me", I call in sing-a-sing voice.

I bank in front of her large head, on my way upwards noticing her large bared teeth behind her pulled back lips.

"Anytime when you're ready, ladies", I call to the astonished angels, who are watching my antics in disbelief.

"Come on. No better time than the present."

One by one they open their wings. Two pairs of pastel yellow wings of the brothers and the shimmery purple wings of Rafe fill the sky.

Left behind, on the ground, Jess follows the angels with her gaze, whimpering to the wind. Her gaze lingers longer on Dumah's body, before she begins to spin on the spot, jumping, trying to reach the suspended above bodies.

Her black leathery wings are open but they don't beat. At every jump, she would glide for a few seconds, riding windy streams, but every time she would fall down to the red soil with a great "thump".

"Come on, Jessie-boo. You have to do better if you want to catch me", I call down to her over the whistling wind and human cries.

"Ariel, I don't think this tactic is very prudent –"

Rafe begins with another lecture, suspended mid-air, when a set of grey teeth clacks an inch away from his purple feathers and he darts sideways barely avoiding my sister's hungry jaw.

I laugh.

I take it as Jess telling him to shut up.

Jess' wings beat a crazy jig of different tempos, as if unable to decide on the required speed, and failing to find one, her body plummets down and she wails.

"Come on. Don't be a wuss. If you want me, you better catch me. And stop crying, tears never fixed anything."

I swing down and bank once again.

"Come on, baby. I'm waiting for you, and Dumah is here too", I tempt her.

She turns her head to look at the large angel with yellow wings in the sky behind me.

She swallows her dismayed wail and dips her head to the ground. Her gaze zooms in on Dumah's form and her butt wags as she prepares herself to pounce.

Her powerful paws push at the ground and she leaps upwards.

"Come on, Jess, your wings, your wings. Move them. Don't forget your wings", I call, encouraging that leap, and sure enough, her heavy body holds mid-air as her wings begin to beat a rhythm, which slaps the air like the claps of a whip.

She holds her position and doesn't fall. Her taught body is strained, aimed upwards, and slowly she begins to rise, the beating of her wings bringing her higher.

"Well done, baby girl. Woo-hoo!" I call to her. "Come and get me."

I'm not going to sacrifice anyone to my sister, let alone the only angel who was kind to her, so I twist and dive in front of her, obstructing her view of Dumah, who's now flanked by his brother, with one last glance, begins to float away from us, following the direction of our quest.

"Come here, Jessie-boo. Let's fly after them."

My wings open wider and my body tilts as I begin to measure the air, following the disappearing in the veil of dust bodies of the two angels.

With a final glance, Rafe flies after them.

"Come on, girl", I call, glancing over my shoulder, finally hearing and seeing a confident rhythm in her wings, and saving my arse, I fold myself tighter, pushing at the speed of my flight, knowing that she's following me. My little sister is flying.

The opening and closing of her wings is slower than mine, the span of them is greater. To every three flaps of mine, her body replies with one, and she's catching up with me.

I had to admit to myself that after watching her drooling over me and after experiencing her scissor-sharp teeth first-hand, I'm concerned to lose too much distance between us, so I change the trajectory, diving towards the ground, gliding above the herds and lizards.

With a slight delay her body changes its path too, descending, following me.

But she hasn't got the knack of flying yet, and with that change of direction, she loses the control and pummels into the crowd of humans and lizards, scattering them, before tumbling head over arse and coming to a stop sprawled on the ground.

I dive after her.

"Jess! Jessie-boo, are you alright?"

I run towards her, jumping over sprawled bodies, and I lift her head. But before I can begin the mourning shrill of mine, she shakes her head like a dog, dislodging the pain, then narrows her gaze on me, giving me a short bark.

"Shall we do it again?" I ask, smiling at her.

I step backwards, inviting her for a chase. I turn, and pushing two nearby lizards out of my way, I take to the sky and with a low howl Jess follows, the beating of her wings is the confirmation of her presence.

I fly faster, keeping the distance between us, but her flight path behind me veers, diving in and rising up, and the next time I turn to look at her, I see the bottom half of a lizard hanging from her mouth.

After a few miles, the herds below begin to thin out, showing the red cracked soil beneath their feet, and a few miles after that, the billowing of the wind begins to subside, with it shifting and dispersing the constant veil of dust.

The light has changed too.

If before it was a murky orange hue of a dust storm, now it begins to shine with sunlight of a summer day on the backdrop of a freshly washed, crisp-blue sky, and in that open horizon I can see a glint of Baza's skyscraper, twinkling in the distance, surrounded by the green tint of his lawns.

CHAPTER 24

"Are you sure you want to do this? Is there anything I can say or do to make you change your mind?"

Rafe's constant nagging begins to get to me. Every time he questions my decision, I grow madder.

"Yes, I am sure, and no, nothing you can say would change my mind", I bristle without looking at him, as I pull out my short swords of rippling white fire out of their sheaths in my corset, one at a time, inspecting them, then sliding them back into my black leather corset, and tightening the buckles on the corset over my once white tunic.

Domiel offered me one of his long swords from his weaponry belt, but I declined the offer. If I've never used such a weapon and don't know how to handle it, what use would it be to me when I come to rely on it? Knowing my clumsiness, I might kill myself before slaying any enemies.

During the few hours that Dumah spent erecting a small green tent on the verge of the green lawn, Domiel and I spent in training.

He showed me a few new moves, emphasising each time that in every confrontation my strength would not be a physical power and reach, but the speed and agility, especially with the swords that are so short.

He tested and attacked me, and I was pleased with myself that I managed to deflect or escape each of his strikes.

But the moment a pleased smile took over my lips, he crouched, and swinging his leg in a smooth, sweeping motion, he kicked my legs from underneath me and I dropped to the ground like a sack of hammers.

"Don't lose your focus, Beyelai", he said, offering his hand. "And if I might suggest...don't gloat to your enemies even if you've won, Beyelai. Some of your followers might not take kindly to that."

Now, I am about to leave.

A few times I asked Rafe to stay behind, but he refused to listen to any of it, so I gave up asking.

"Very well", Rafe says, nodding. "How do you propose we'll get into Baza's sanctum? You're aware that it's closed off for us without a residential agreement, right?"

"I am aware, you've told me. I've made arrangements", I answer, and turning to him, I look at him and add, "Sam has agreed to help. He'll meet us there."

My declaration is met with a pause and a brooding silence, while Rafe's gaze pulls at mine.

"Samael?" he asks eventually.

"Yes." I nod. "Sam. He'll meet us."

"How does he know we're coming?"

Rafe's eyes are half-hooded and his seemingly calm voice betrays the familiar emotions witnessed, at which I'm not surprised.

"I spoke to him before we left."

"How?" he starts. "Ah... I see."

He clocks it. The only way I could've spoken to Sam, would've been utilising the angelic telepathy, and to have that line open, there must've been some prior arrangement...or a deeper connection.

"Very well", he repeats.

"Shall we?"

He swings his arm wide in the direction of the glass skyscraper, in his chivalrous gesture inviting me to lead the way.

Although there's a smile on his lips, it doesn't touch his eyes.

"You're always welcome to stay behind. I've told you that many times."

"What? And miss a reunion and my chance to see Samael again?" he calls in exaggerated excitement. "Never!"

"Then do whatever you want", I mumble.

I walk to Jess, who is lying on the ground, sprawled to the limit of her incredible length and the size of a small airplane.

I come closer, and hearing my footsteps, she opens one eye, nudging her head in my direction.

I stroke her large furry head, planting a kiss on the large pink snout.

Seeing her as the animal, witnessing her diet of blind, slimy lizards and unable to hear her voice, I begin to doubt if she can hear or understand me. I begin to wonder if the human child is in there.

But I must believe it.

"I'll be back soon. Ariel's not going to be long, sweetie", I coo as if to a pet or a baby. "Ariel will be back very soon, and in the meanwhile, you have to listen to Domiel and Dumah and do what they say. You behave, okay? Be a good girl for your sister, deal?"

I stroke her fur.

"Try not to eat too much, and if you'll be a good girl, Ariel will bring you a present. Would you like a present?"

I talk to her like when she was a tiny baby who couldn't understand words, and speaking to her like this upsets me, and before I dive deeper into this miserable pond of questioning and inevitable self-loathing, I turn and walk away, leaving her to get back to sleep.

"Dumah, please try to control Jess and her appetite. I'd rather she didn't eat many lizards. I will be needing them."

Rafe shoots me a quick glance, but I ignore him.

"Take care of her. She is very important to me."

Without a word, Dumah places his four fingers to his forehead and bows.

I'll take it as an agreement and acknowledgement.

"Beyelai, please don't worry about your kin. Her safety will remain of the greatest importance to us and we'll guard her with our lives against all dangers", says Domiel.

"Thank you."

And before I get emotional, I turn away from the three of them, stepping on the lush green grass of the lawn, starting my couple of miles long trek towards the glistening skyscraper.

"Can you trust him?" Rafe's low voice asks me after a few minutes.

I know who he's talking about. Clearly, he can't let go.

"Trust has very little to do with it", I answer, keeping my gaze ahead and my pace steady. "I need to get inside that building and he has a key. I don't trust him, or anyone for that matter. I'm going there, hoping and praying that he doesn't betray me, and right now, I trust him as much as you trusted Chamuel with your Uriel's safekeeping."

I turn my head and look at him.

Rafe doesn't say a word, doesn't reply or argue. We were both betrayed at some point or another, and he is the last one to reprimand me on reading and understanding people, or angels, and their intentions.

"This leap of faith I have to take, like I had to trust you."

I don't remind Rafe of Sam's appearance in the woods, and that we're currently alive because of him. I don't tell him of my gut instinct about Sam, and I most definitely, will never admit to him my feelings towards Sam.

CHAPTER 25

"Thank you for agreeing to help me", I say to Sam, leaving Rafe's name out of my gratitude or my plans. Mentioning his name would be detrimental to my cause, here, with Sam. Besides, whichever way I go, Rafe is not going to be a part of my plans for much longer.

"Anything for you, Mermaid", Sam answers, gifting me with one of his gorgeous smiles. "I wouldn't miss a chance to see you again, even if you look like a mess."

He swings his gaze over my once white tunic, now covered in dried black lizard's blood.

I do look like a mess but he looks as gorgeous as usual.

A thin-knit black jumper hugs his torso, showing off his wide shoulders and pecs. His long legs are dressed in grey jeans and a pair of black trainers finishing off his outfit. His four large white wings look glorious behind his back, especially against the backdrop of the dark colours of his clothing.

The soft breeze of Baza's artificial world gently moves his dark hair.

"But the accessories?" he continues, "very badass. Changed the stylist while in Uras?"

He nods his head at my belt full of weapons and his blue eyes twinkle.

I ignore his remarks, giving him a deadpan stare, so he sobers and continues: "The Mermaid is all grown-up, I see. Not the girl I met. With your rising powers and your control over Sarukh, which are coming in leaps and bounds as I've heard", he gestured over me, "I've figured I might be saving my behind by assisting fearless Uriel incarnate, the Great Ariel: The Harbinger of Doom, The Keeper of Gates, The Protector of Uriel's ways."

I roll my eyes at him when he finishes reciting the titles I've bestowed upon myself and bellowed at my now long-lost army.

His soft gaze is on me as a corner of his mouth lifts, bringing his magical dimple forward, as he takes the mickey of me.

"I see you know more than I've told you", I say.

"Yes. I know plenty, from many sources and in much juicy detail. The entire Arllu is abuzz about it, about your little revolutionary speech and movement, and the later disintegration of Chamuel by iksudaqataya upon the eyes of a surprised audience."

"As I've said before", I sigh, "you, angels, are just a bunch of gossip girls."

"Oh, come on. You can't hold it against us. It was dead boring in Dingir-Ki before you, and since your arrival... Well, it's the most excitement Dingir-Ki had seen for about twenty GA, and judging by your arrival into Arllu, it's not going to die down any time soon, my little mutineer. Always against the establishment I see."

He shakes his head.

"Besides, I can't believe you expect me to ignore any news concerning you."

I roll my eyes at his theatrical outrage, and changing the subject, I ask: "Did any of my old army come here?"

"Are you kidding? These old farts think they're the holiest in Sarukh. They'd never come to bend their knee to Baza. From what I've heard, most of them, if not all, went to Mik'hael. Your chances to stay alive are getting slimmer with every passing day, Mermaid. First you lost half of your essence", he glances at Rafe next to me, "now your army..."

"Which makes me appreciate your help even more", I interrupt him, not interested in getting into another lecture or a long speech. "Have you seen Tabby?"

He sobers.

"No." He shakes his head. "I haven't seen her since that day when she took you out for a walk in the park."

His gaze is on me, and in it I read: *"and when you convinced her to help you to escape."*

"Do you think she is still out there?" I ask him, jerking my head over my shoulder towards the depths of Arllu that I came from.

"I honestly don't know", he answers, concern touching his face and voice. "I don't see why she would be, but if Asmodeus had found you there, there's no reason why they wouldn't have found her too."

I'm afraid to ask the next question because I'm afraid of his answer. I know that question will sound dumb and naïve, but I have to ask, because deep down I'm hoping for good news.

"What would they do to her?"

Without a word he raises his eyebrow at me.

"Ariel, you're certainly not that stupid", his look says.

Yeah. I'm not.

"Sam, are you sure you're okay doing this? You see what happens to people around me..." I begin.

"Yeah, Mermaid, I see. You're one unlucky charm", he answers, smiling.

He comes closer, ignoring Rafe next to me, who's glaring at us with the least favourable of his looks.

"But I like the thrill and the excitement", Sam leans in and whispers.

He straightens up, and taking a step back, he continues: "I am helping you, because quite frankly, I don't think I have a choice if I want to see you alive for much longer. From what you've told me, to bring the new blood under your flag is the only move that is left for you, especially since you've halved your essence and powers."

He glances at Rafe. The second time he placed the blame at Rafe's door. Sam has decided who is at fault for everything that's happened to me.

"I think we've already established how I feel about you and your life", he adds simply, but his voice and his words are heavy with deep feeling and admission.

I drop my gaze and shuffle on the spot, before turning my gaze to Rafe, who's staring into the distance, pretending to see something incredibly interesting out there, while his jaw muscles work overtime, rolling under his skin.

"*Off we go again*", I sigh in my head.

Inwardly, I roll my eyes, moving the subject back onto a business trajectory.

"Have you spoken to Mik'hael's exiles?"

"I have arranged a soirée tonight at my quarters, and have invited every fallen angel I could reach within Arllu. I didn't tell them the reason for the gathering or of the fact that you'll be there, and of course, I haven't divulged into the topic you will bring up. Whatever you need to tell them, it would be better coming from you. Since their exile, a lot of them don't trust anyone in the Sarukh."

"Thank you, and thank you for arranging it."

"It's another chance to see you and the perfect excuse to give you a party. Fingers crossed, it will go better than the last one."

I think he is trying to joke, but after a quick glance at my face he mumbles: "Sorry, Mermaid. Shall we?"

He turns around, starting down the gravel path, leading through the green lawn of manicured grass, towards the glass and steel skyscraper of Baza's place, shining ahead like a shard of a diamond.

Rafe catches my arm and I grind to a halt.

"It was a mistake to come here", he whispers. "We can't trust him. We shouldn't even be here. It's too dangerous for you, for me, for all of us."

"We've already discussed it, Rafe, a number of times in fact, and I've noted your concerns. But as I told you before, I'm out of moves and he's the only one I can reach here. So if you don't mind, Rafe, let go of me. You're always welcome to return back to Domiel and Dumah, and wait with them, or return to Uras. I believe you can find the way back."

I shake his hand off my arm and follow Sam.

The artificial lifestyle Baza has created is still shining strong. The perfect emerald green grass of a golf course, the bright blue sky above with the soft breeze and sunshine, and the sparkling headquarters of the evil ahead are picture perfect, polished to the highest gloss of wealth and comfort.

Rafe's black ominous body next to me is like a shadow of doom against this glossy backdrop. Both of his swords are out of their sheaths, ready to drink the blood of any fallen he'd meet, and I wouldn't discount him aiming his swords at Sam's back.

Out of habit rather than fear, I keep one of my swords drawn out too.

Scanning my gaze over low rolls of emerald green lawns, I begin to wonder what is the purpose of this constantly empty golf course to Baza and his crew as we cross it without meeting a soul.

The larger the glass building ahead of us grows, the heavier the pull of dread is in the pit of my stomach. It brings the memories of my last dinner here, my past that was aired in front of everyone so blatantly, in a calculated manner, forcing reactions and shame out of me.

I've escaped this place once before, wanting to save my human-self, but now I've come back to the monsters within this building and to the monsters of my past, desperate to save my angelic-self, my new life and the life of my sister, and I wonder if it shows my increasing strength or my stupidity.

The movement of the gravel under my feet, its soft clanking, silent warm air without insects – all of it brings the memory of the first time I met Baza, and Tabby. Even now looking into the glazy distance, I could swear I could see her small body bouncing, skipping along the gravel path, and I could hear a little hum of her songs, and with it comes guilt, whispering in my mother's satisfied voice a reminder of a testament to her warnings of death to everyone, who comes near me.

And just like that, my thoughts of Tabby are replaced by the thoughts of my sister. I think of my sister, a monster, growing bitter and blood-thirstier with every new kill, who would never survive this world without me and who needs me to fix what I have done.

"Under the sky
Here I lie,
Under the sky
My sister and I
Trees above us and the bottomless sky..."

"Nobody'll save her but I", I mumble to myself, finishing the rhyme and changing its last line. This correction is a reflection of my thoughts and an echo of my determination.

Following Sam, we reach the building in complete silence.

He opens a large glass door and stands to the side, letting us in to the sparkling foyer.

"A bit garish, don't you think?" Rafe asks, the moment he takes in all the dazzle of the hall, announcing it loudly for Sam's benefit.

The angelic propaganda murals, the crystal chandeliers, the large mirrors in gold heavy frames, gold handles and buttons on the lift panel – I forgot how flashy, yet tacky, Baza's place was, probably blinded by the sparkling wealth back then, now seeing it through Rafe's eyes.

Yeah, maybe a tad garish.

But Sam ignores him, striding towards the lift doors and calling it.

The tiny space inside the cabin is tight with three bodies and tense emotions, which are ricocheting off everyone. Hate and resentment radiate off Rafe, reciprocated by the same resentment from Sam, yet mingled with... lust and joy, and taking into account that I can sense it, so everyone else probably could as well.

My face heats up and I drop my gaze to my feet.

"Where is everyone?" I ask, turning to Sam. "I thought we'd meet someone by now, especially walking through your park."

"Since your little coup in Uras, barely any malakhims are stationed here. Everyone is busy as Baza's preparing for war. He deployed a dozen malakhims to Apkallu to scout for resources and quick energy fixes. Last week alone, he started four inter-tribal wars in Africa and had organised a dozen of civil unrests on two continents. A few malakhims were dispatched to collect the long past-due payments from government officials, issuing an ultimatum: either you tighten the screws on your electorate so the ibnatums can collect extra souls, and faster, or welcome to Hell. You'd be surprised how reluctant the government officials are to come here."

He barks a bitter laugh.

I listen to Sam with an open mouth. It is one thing to "kinda" know what Baza is responsible for and is another to have a nice and detailed breakdown of all his deeds and little projects on Earth.

"This week he plans to start a few forest fires", Sam adds.

"Hold on, what do the forests' fires have to do with anything? How are the forests' fires going to help with a war, which is not even fought there?"

Sam huffs, rolling his eyes at my naivety.

"Forest fires equals", he begins, folding his fingers and starting the count on his list, "destruction to humans' homes and wildlife habitat; death to wild animals, which breaks the food chain, the smog covering the sun means no crops growth, which all would result in a food shortage, which then lead to wars and unrest. Mothers will be selling their souls for a measly handful of grains just to feed their children, and Baza's malakhims will be on the ground, ready to collect the offerings. Plus with increasing pollution to air, water, the government's officials would finally be able to fulfil their life-long dream and charge for clean water and air, by the sip and by the breath. The smog cover would melt the ice caps, leading to rising water level for survivors, with later displacements, resulting in unrests..." he says as he swings his heads as he lists the possibilities.

"I can go on for hours about Baza's benefits here."

"Wouldn't it take longer than a week to get to that point from forest fires?" I mumble past my frozen in shock lips.

"It could. But it might not. You see, it's all in the execution and in connectivity." He taps his nose.

"If one were to throw a natural disaster on top of already precarious economic position of a poor nation, or say a nation with a weak and fragile peace, but place it on a nation, which is located strategically within an important continent, then to top this already tense situation with every other hate, struggle, corruption that you might find or create and wars will begin to explode inside that nation, and soon, across that continent in no time, swiftly engulfing the whole of Apkallu. Besides, if he wins Sarukh's war, which he thinks is already in his pocket, the logistics and infantry would be in place for his immediate expansion, and the advance from this point would be seamless."

It feels as if the air in the cubicle has been sucked out. I can't breathe.

Baza's plans are horrendous, but not as scary as the fact that this "Sarukh war" Sam is referring to is *my* war, the war Baza plans to wage and win against me.

"He needs to win that war for Sarukh first", I bristle at Sam, but my voice is too scared, mousy and pathetic to be truly threatening.

I was prepared to fight for myself, for my life, for my sister, but the thought of the fate of seven billion people that I am bringing into it has never crossed my mind.

"You look a bit white. Are you alright?" Rafe asks next to me.

"Yeah, fine", I mumble, although I want to scream, telling him that nothing is alright, blame him and all of them, for never telling me the stakes of my new job appointment.

I look at Sam.

"Is there more?"

He gives me a "once over", taking in my pasty face, then nods.

"About a dozen malakhims were dispatched to supervise ibnatums and pulhu-nasu on Apkallu, to expedite the contractual agreements for souls' subjugating and harvesting, especially for overdue collections. He is opening new projects across the globe, bringing all new souls straight here. He even built extra processing plants by the Gates to increase the output and sustain the needs of the war."

I turn to Rafe.

"I told you there were more factories than I remember."

"How many *extra* exactly?" I ask Sam.

"Baza has tripled our earlier number."

The lift pings and the doors slide open.

I think we're on the floor where Sam's rooms were but I can't be certain as the halls in this building look the same.

Sam comes out, walking left down the hall, past one set of white double doors then the next, stopping at the third. He throws the doors open, letting us in, but before I can take a step through these doors, Rafe barges past me, shoving me to the side with his shoulder, taking a cautious step through the doors first, his sword at the ready.

"I would never endanger Ariel", Sam grumbles at Rafe's back.

"So you say", Rafe answers from within the room, walking past the open doors, his swords facing down yet at an angle, ready to fly at a moment notice.

"You can come in", Rafe pops his head out, addressing me and ignoring Sam completely. "It's clear."

"Thank you", I mumble, unsure whose side to pick, and wondering if I can pick neither.

CHAPTER 26

"We have some time to kill. Game anyone?" Sam asks, strolling past Rafe, who still stands in the middle of the room, glaring at his surroundings.

The room is set in a pompous theme of wealth and gold, and has a similar vibe to an exclusive and posh gentlemen's club.

The best way to describe the room is probably to call it a "drawing room" in a wealthy stately home.

The walls in the room are covered in muted yellow velour, which looks very much like gold. One wall is occupied by four tall, floor to ceiling windows, framed by pulled back, heavy golden drapes. One of the short walls of the rectangular room is swallowed by an enormous fireplace, sealed in black, veiny marble and the densely placed mirrors and paintings in golden frames dot the remaining two walls of the room.

The settees, armchairs and coffee tables are scattered around the room, creating pockets of conversational zones, which are lit with table lamps. Two heavy, crystal and gold chandeliers are suspended off the room's high ceiling.

"We have cards, Monopoly or if you prefer, Rafe, we have bingo. I've heard older angels favour this human pastime", Sam says as he walks towards the nearest golden settee and reclines on it, stretching his long legs, and folding them at the ankles.

Rafe spins towards Sam. His long swords whirl with him, flying in high arches, slicing at the nearby lamp.

In the resentful silence of the room, the two pieces of the murdered lamp roll off the table and on to the plush carpet with a muted clonk.

Grinding his teeth, Rafe glares at Sam, mumbling something under his breath, and I'm pretty sure it's not gratitude. Sealed in black, standing in the centre of the large pompous room, he looks ominous and menacing like Death coming to collect his dues.

"I think we'd be okay without games, Sam", I say, "or better still, shall we play the "Who can stay silent for longer" game?"

I walk over and take a seat on the settee across from Sam's.

"Do you still have all those clothes in your wardrobe? The ones that fit me?" I ask him, after a moment of uncomfortable silence.

"Yes. It's all there, just as you left it, Mermaid", Sam says low, unfolding his legs and leaning in towards me, resting his elbows on his knees. His voice is velvet and I can practically feel the warmth of his body.

I turn and glance at Rafe, who is less than pleased with this loaded exchange, and it's not like I can blame him.

"Um", I clear my throat. "I thought to change out of these clothes, that's all."

Sam reclines against the backrest of the settee.

"I would advise you against it, Ariel", he says. "The angels who would gather here later maybe were exiled, but they have a decent life here, to which they grew accustomed. They will be very cautious to throw it all to the wind, unless they believe in the cause and the leader."

"Look", I say, swiping my hand over my once white tunic, "I'm covered in lizards' goo."

"All the better", he answers. "With this, you look like a real warrior, a fearless leader who is not scared or afraid to get her hands dirty."

He smiles at me.

"I agree with him", Rafe pipes in from his side of the room. "You need to stay in your angelic clothing for now."

Then, after a moment of thought, he adds: "Have you decided what you're going to say to them?"

"I don't know."

I shrug my shoulders.

"Something about my destiny, my archangel's powers, being the Uriel and all that palaver. Basically, the speech following a theme of my earlier one in Uras, when you took it upon yourself to dismember Chamuel."

I turn to glare at Rafe.

"You didn't", Sam theatrically gasps from his seat and a slow smile blooms over his mouth, before morphing into a wide grin. "I thought you were mates."

But Rafe doesn't say a word, silently glaring at Sam in response.

All we seem to be doing is glaring at each other.

"What were those brown insects anyway?" I ask Rafe, changing the subject away from Chamuel and onto Rafe's favourite track of teaching me all things angelic. I know how much he enjoys sharing his "wisdom" with me.

Whatever pleases the baby as long as it doesn't cry...

"Iksuda Qataya", Rafe answers, stretching the syllables, as he strolls closer.

"Arllu burn my wings!" Sam exclaims, turning to Rafe, his face suddenly serious. "Everyone in Arllu has heard of Chamuel's fate, but the means of the punishment were very vague, just a rumour. Someone has suggested beheading, some said he is imprisoned in Uras, while some said he was absolved by the new lord of Uras."

He glances at me.

"No one has seen iksuda qataya for a few generations, since the Dark War..." Sam mumbles.

Then he shakes his head and smiles.

"I'd be banished in Udhad!" Sam cries, his excitement at the news tangible. "I can't believe you did it! Not only the balls it took to kill your own, but the way..."

He shakes his head, and then dropping his voice, he adds: "I've heard it's one of the most excruciating of deaths. Apparently, iksuda qataya eat a little bite at a time, while keeping their food alive, keeping it fresh and blood pumping for longer, leaving the blood vessels and nerves for last. Is it true?"

"Why don't I demonstrate it on you and you can tell me", Rafe growls low.

Unfazed, Sam throws his hands up, giving Rafe another smile.

"Friend, friends", he says with theatrical fear. "I'd better watch myself with a commander of iksuda qataya. But I have to say, suddenly, I like you, *gir*. Not shabby. Not shabby at all."

Rafe just growls at him in response.

"Well", I say, "if my advisory board is dead-set against me changing my clothing, can I at least have a pair of clean and comfortable shoes?"

"Running trainers would be best," I add, raising my eyebrows at Sam.

"Sure. One pair of trainers is coming up."

Sam gets up and strolls out, leaving me and Rafe alone in the vast and pompous gilded room.

This is my chance.

I clear my throat, taking a deep breath, preparing myself for what I'm about to say and for the following inevitable argument.

"Rafe", I start, "I need you to get back to Jess and the brothers."

"What? Why?" He spins towards me.

The light streams from the windows behind him and I can't see his face.

He takes two large steps towards me and I rise off my seat. I need to meet him standing, as I know the pushback I'm about to get.

I take a step forward too, meeting him in the middle of the room.

"I need you there", I say, looking up at him. "You will take care of Uras and everyone in there if anything happens to me. If anything happens here, or doesn't go the way I expect, you will be the leader that I won't get to be."

He opens his mouth to argue, but I raise my hand, interrupting him.

"If I don't come back, somebody needs to be there to protect the people who chose to stay with us. Remember, the ones, who swore to Uriel and who didn't ditch me in favour of Mik'hael?" I reason with him. "It's the least we can do for them. You have obligations to them too, just like I have. *"You have Uriel's essence and with it her responsibilities"*, I repeat to him the words he said to me, and I smile. "Not fun, is it? To be responsible for so many souls and to do only what you've been told?"

He huffs.

"Like you ever did what you were told."

I smile.

"That's fair, but currently it's you being judged. This is your chance to demonstrate to me how sensible leaders should act and how they should prioritise their people above their needs. You can show it to me, and maybe, eventually", I grin, "it will rub off...if I live long enough to learn it."

His head jerks up and his metallic gaze is on me, although the fear swims behind that metal.

"Just kidding", I say, raising my hands at him. "Gosh, overreacting much? I am coming back and when I do, you, from the height of your experience, will lecture me on the appropriate behaviour of responsible rulers, and by then you'd even have hands on experience, and give all of the "told you so" jobbie."

He says nothing.

"Come on", I say, coming closer and taking his hand in mine, "you know that I am right. The angels in Uras need our protection. Should anything happen here and I do not get an army, or something happens to me, it will be up to you to protect these angels from Mik'hael. Domiel, Dumah, the old woman who doesn't like me, the young, pretty girl, who chose to stay behind, that boy... What's his name? Who stood against his father..."

"Tzadkiel", Rafe mumbles.

"Him", I nod.

"Look how young and naïve he is, and he pledged himself to Uriel and Uras. Do you think he'd survive on his own? Young, inexperienced and so upstanding, with his young maximalism, believing in doing only the right thing? Do you think his father will take him back and will forgive him? I don't think so. His dad didn't strike me as a forgiving kind. And Jess..."

Rafe's gaze flies to me, but instantly drops, as if it's burned by mine.

He feels guilty about what has happened to her, and as much as I don't want to remind him of it, right now, bringing that guilt to the forefront, might be the only way to make him do what I need from him. I'm prepared to use it to get what I want, to keep everyone safe, including my sister, if I should die.

"You and I, we both hold Uriel's essence. If her essence dies, it will be the end of her. It will end the balance, as you said, and then, not only the worlds will change, yours and mine, but the planes of existence will be affected. Do you know what it would do? Does anyone?" I ask but Rafe doesn't answer.

"The fact that she was so adamant to keep the balance going, and so was her mother", I continue, "tells me that there must be a serious reason for that, and I'm not going down in history as the one who screwed up the worlds, mucked up the balance, killed everyone and then died, all because she was too stupid to handle it correctly. No way. Besides, if her essence extinguished into the both of us, it would mean that she died for nothing. Ophanims have put her essence inside me for nothing. Her sacrifice was for nothing. My life was for nothing. What has happened to Jess was for nothing too...

"You yourself said that we need to preserve this balance. Well, this is your part of the job. That's what you'd need to do. Even a non-angelic person like me, knows what's going to happen if Mik'hael left to govern your precious Heaven unopposed. I understand it and so does everyone else. That's why they've stayed.

"And you will be the one who will look after them, should anything happen to me."

I pause.

"If you're right about An and the fact that she's dead, then he will bring every single plane of existence under his thumb, and not just Heaven. Earth, Udhad... I don't know what else he might do, how far he would reach, but I'm sure you know it better than me."

Rafe is not arguing with me.

So I am right.

I wish he'd argue, telling me in his usual dismissive manner, what a ridiculous child I am and what crazy, made-up stories of an overactive imagination I'm spitting out, that I need to get a grip and stop this hysteria, but he doesn't say a word.

Shit.

I fall quiet.

I didn't expect his confirmative silence.

At the back of my mind always lived a hope that the situation isn't as bad as I think, and there's a way out of it, and I had hoped that Rafe would step in at the last minute with an announcement of an alternative way forward, which he figured out from the height of his wisdom, while I've spent all my time on useless running.

His silent confirmation and unwillingness to argue toll in my head with finality of funeral bells on a tower.

"Quite frankly", I say after a long silence, "I don't know what you can do if I don't get us an army. I don't know where you'll run. If I knew, I would've done it myself, instead of being here, but that's the beauty of it: it will be your mess to clean up, it will be your problem, not mine", I add and smile, trying to light up the mood.

But Rafe is not interested. He looks at me and doesn't say a word.

"You need to be there, and you know it", I say, keeping his gaze.

"Don't give me a hard time over this", I warn him.

"Okay", he says, "but only after the meeting. You'll need me here to convince them."

"Rafe", I interrupt. "You said it yourself, it might be a trap, and if it's a trap, you'll get caught with me, and then what? How would we get out of it then?"

His eyes flare up and his jaw sets.

"That's my final offer, Ariel. I will return to Domiel and Dumah and will do what you're asking of me, but only once I know that you're safe here."

And as I'm about to open my mouth to argue, he adds: "I'm not negotiating here."

The door swings open and Sam comes in, carrying a shoebox under his arm.

His smile weathers with every step he takes into the room, as he scans our faces.

"You, kids, are alright? A little fight? Couldn't decide who would be the banker in Monopoly?"

"We're absolutely fine", I answer, smiling. "No fight, no spat. We're all friends here. One big happy family."

I step towards him.

"What have you got there?" I nod at the box.

"I think you'll like them", Sam beams.

He places the black box on the settee and lifts the lid.

"What the hell, Sam? Were you picking those in the dark?"

"Bloody hell, way to stay inconspicuous and in muted colours", I mumble to myself.

A pair of acidic yellow trainers, laced with bright pink laces lie in the box. I know they are expensive, the padded writing on the black box speaks the volume, but what the hell is with the colour?

"Are you kidding me? Why yellow? I was kinda hoping for something muted, black or grey, white at a push, at least then it would've matched my tunic."

"You said running trainers", he answers, lost.

"For a parrot?"

"That was the only pair of running trainers in the closet", he mumbles, shrugging his shoulders, confused at my displeasure.

I grumble and roll my eyes, but I don't have much choice. As much as I'll feel like a clown, at least I will have clean, and most importantly, comfortable, footwear.

I take the trainers from the box, walk to the nearest settee and begin the swap.

With the fresh trainers on my feet, I feel better. I do a few jumps on the spot. The trainers are soft and cushioned, even if they look like duck's palmate.

"Thank you", I say and look up at Sam, smiling at him, and his responding smile is dazzling.

CHAPTER 27

Hours later the first tentative knock sounds at the door.

"Show time", Sam mouths to us from the door, just before he turns the handle.

"It's not too late to leave. We can go now", Rafe leans into me and whispers. "We'll leave this place, collect your sister and get back to Uras. We will think of something, I promise. We don't need him or his questionable chums."

Rafe's pleas are hot and urgent.

"No", I shake my head. "I've got nowhere else left to run."

Sam throws the doors open.

"Come on in, *Kud Anshar*, may your evening be a blessed one."

"Cacama", a chorus of voices answer in unison past the door.

A conversation begins immediately after, but slowly dies as each of them step through the door, and see me and Rafe.

The group of three female and two male angels is silent, warily eyeing Rafe, standing with his thumbs looped behind the black shiny vest, like an expectant executor, sealed in black, and me, although dressed in the latest celestial fashion, but covered in lizards' black blood.

"Please come on in."

Sam ushers in the small group and shuts the door.

"What is the meaning of this, Samael?" A female angel asks, turning to Sam. "Why are we here?"

Her gaze dances between the three of us.

She is studying me and I'm studying the five of them.

The five angels by the door are dressed in dove-grey tunics of a similar style to mine, only their tunics are spotlessly clean.

As if related, the skin of the five of them is dark, while the hair atop of their heads is pure, snow white, the shade of Sam's wings. Their hair is plaited in different styles and different fashions. One male has a long plait resting over his shoulder, while one has his plait pinned to the top of his head, while the females wear their hair in intricate braiding, pinned or dropped loose but just as gorgeous.

The white hair on the background of their dark, mahogany skin is not the only stark attribute of their features. The eyes of the five are identical: the same almond shape, the same white, colourless pupils of an albino, and to make the things even eerier, all five are blinking in unison with their female leader at the forefront, as if tuned to her, or sharing one nervous system and the one set of reflexes.

"Nanael", Sam begins, "I swear to you, no harm will come to you here. All that I am asking of you and your confrères is a *bêru* of your precious time. Please, stay. There are a few more malakhims coming, and once everyone's here, I will reveal the reason for your presence tonight. But all that I ask of you for now is to be patient and please, give me some time, and some of your trust. Have I betrayed you before?"

"There's always a first time for everything, Samael", the angel answers in a soft musical voice.

Sam smiles at her remark but continues: "And with your infinite wisdom, Nanael", he bows, "I know that you'd require to collect as much data as possible, before you'd risk of arriving at the final conclusion, which potentially could change the course of the history."

"History?" she asks. She turns her gaze to me, scanning my body head to toe, the four angels behind her mimicking her moves and glances perfectly, as if they are her mirror.

Freaky...

"Damiq", she nods. "Would you introduce us to your guests?"

"I will, Nanael", Sam bows, "but only once everyone's here."

She watches him for a moment as if weighing up her pros and cons on his offer, but eventually, Nanael touches her four fingers to her forehead, bows in agreement and walks towards the window, giving Rafe a side glance on her way. The four angels bow slightly at Sam, and carefully skirt around me and Rafe, following their leader, bringing with them a unified scent of baby powder.

I follow the departing party with my gaze, watching the four bright yellow wings, smaller than mine, folded behind each back.

That's one freaky quintuplets set, unless it's some sort of freaky magic, but then, why the males?

"*My trainers are a match to her wings, though. Sam should've given it to her. It would've finished her outfit perfectly*", I muse.

Rage in my head is gaping at them, mouth wide open. It's nice to keep her shocked and speechless once in a while, so I can have some peace and quiet.

The rest of the group joins Nanael by the window, and all five begin a hushed conversation among themselves in hot, quiet whispers, their yellow wings open and close agitatedly.

"Who are they?" I whisper to Rafe.

"Nanael used to watch over sciences before Mik'hael exiled her", Rafe answers in a matching whisper.

"So, she used the facility to clone herself?" I ask with a smile.

Rafe gives me a deadpan stare, ignoring my joke, and then he continues: "All of them were responsible for the sciences and knowledge. Harahel was responsible for the Grand Celestial library of Knowledge in Sarukh, Umabel, for the delivery of astronomy and physics to humankind, Barman and Sabathiel were guardian angels of intelligence, but once Mik'hael had started his "cleansing", he exiled them, burning the library behind them, locking in and simplifying the celestial knowledge."

"What? How can you "simplify the knowledge"?" I shrug my shoulders.

"Collective intelligence and wisdom were modified. Some information has been taken away, some wiped, changing the indigenous, angelic, traditional knowledge system. What an angel in Mik'hael's domain knew before is no longer what they'd know now. Their history was taken away from them, replaced by the indoctrinated information which feels real, wiping or shading the past."

"So basically, some sort of brainwashing went in there?"

"Basically."

A series of knocks dance over the door, producing an upbeat, a march-like tune.

"Come in, Kud Anshar. May your evening be a blessed one", Sam recites the familiar greeting, opening the door.

"Cacama", deep male voices boom in answer.

The crowd of large males, dressed in the modern clothing yet strictly of the black colour, fills the room, suddenly swallowing the space and stealing my breath, saturating the air of the room with a strong mixed scent of blooming flowers and heady spring blossom.

As the group before them, this one ceases the chatter, stopping past the doors, eyeing me and Rafe with open interest.

The nine men must be brothers.

They have the same caramel skin tone of the Hispanic descent and their hair is jet-black. The black sweaters, black buttoned up shirts, black polos stretch tight over their very large torsos. The five brothers are wider in the shoulders than Sam or Rafe, and much taller too, with the shortest of them easily scraping at the six feet mark.

The brothers' hair is the complete opposite to the hair of the first group. Their hair is jet-black and cut shorter, to a buzz cut on the top, with no intricate braiding or time spent on their appearances. Their faces are covered with stubble, each grown to a different degree, and some of them, including their leader, flaunt grown and neatly-trimmed beards.

The nine pairs of eyes that scrutinize me are dark brown in colour.

Some males sport four wings behind their backs, while others have only two, but irrelevant of the number, their wings are of an identical shade of cornflower blue, and their wings are the largest I've seen, almost as large as mine, Rafe's or Baza's.

"Who are your guests, Samael?"

One of them demands, jerking his head towards us, on the others' behalf. His voice confirms the Hispanic descent, carrying with it a weirdly familiar lull, which I can't seems to place.

"Why is this lass wearing Sarukh's garbs?"

Scottish?!

I wasn't prepared to hear that.

The male who spoke takes a few steps closer, looming over me, and I have to crane my head to look up at him. With him this close, I'm engulfed in a strong and suffocating scent of lilies.

"May your evening be a blessed one", I tell the male, copying the Sam's earlier response.

"Sarukh's vainglorious traducer speaks", he turns, announcing to his comrades and ignoring my greeting. His remark produces a few barks of laughter and a low rumble.

"Why are we here and why are *they* here?" he then demands, turning to Sam.

Sam comes closer to the large male, placing his hand on the male's shoulder.

"Sabrael, you need to hear what she has to say. It all will be revealed shortly, but you have to wait just a *geš* longer. I promise, friend, it will be in your interest to hear her out", he says softly.

"Samael", the male booms, "you know, I've never hidden my thoughts about Sarukh and its eejits. You, more than anyone, know my opinion on Mik'hael in particular and Sarukh in general, and above all, the reasoning for that. You've made a mistake by calling on us, mo charaid. Nothing she could say would change that nor do I want anything to do with Sarukh again..."

"I am not from Mik'hael. I have nothing to do with him", I interrupt the large male.

"Who are you then?" he turns to me, for the first time addressing me.

"Sabrael", Sam jumps in, answering the angel. He then spins to face the rest of them, "Zaazenach, Zabkiel, Tagas, Sabaoth, Tartys, Pronoia, Kafziel, Iaoel, please stay. Please give me a chance to explain, but I promise you need to hear her out."

Silence takes over the room for a moment, then unexpectedly, brings a faint mumble of males' voices in my head as if I'd caught a rogue transmission. The voices are mumbling, I think arguing, but surprised by the sudden telepathy wave, I can't make out a word, but I'm sure it's these nine angels.

I strain my mind to hear them, but the transmission dies as suddenly as it has begun. The nine large, burly males glare at each other, although none of them have opened their mouth.

"Damiq", Sabrael barks. "Aye. We'll wait."

The nine of them walk towards the farthest side of the room, picking up a spot with a cluster of four golden settees, the nine bodies falling on those, reclining into the soft cushions, and the springs of the sofas sings and cry their objections under the males' weight. A few seconds later, a guffaw rings from their side of the room.

CHAPTER 28

"Who are they?" I ask Sam, nudging my head towards the crowd of boisterous beautiful male angels.

So far, I like them the least out of the invited crowd.

"Tagas oversee, well, oversaw the singing angels battalion under Mik'hael's command. Zabkiel and Pronoia were guiding humankind. Kafziel had something to do with universe. Iaoel was the angel of visions. Sabrael had guarded the first Heaven and Sabaoth, Tartys and Zaazenach oversaw hours of night."

"I don't understand. Why are they here? I mean, here in Hell? Did they sell their souls to Baza?" I ask, catching the "too" just in time. But Sam knows what I've emitted and his gaze drops slightly.

"They were cast by Mik'hael during the "Cleansing"."

"I'm a bit confused", I admit. "I understand what Rafe said about the knowledge, but what singing angels battalion or hours of night have to do with Mik'hael's "cleansing of Sarukh"?"

Sam sighs.

"The purity Mik'hael had demanded from Sarukh went deeper than who you are or what you've done. It went down to one's bloodline, one's ancestors and what *they've* done."

"Their ancestors? What did they do?"

I turn to look at the large gorgeous males, imagining the gravity of the sin their ancestor must've committed for their descendants to be banished into Hell.

"They are brothers."

Sam nudges his head towards the men, confirming my earlier appraisal.

"Born millennia apart, they have one fallen ancestor in common, who was imprisoned in Arllu at the beginning of time, during An's reign."

"And?" I ask, stretching my neck, ready to catch juicy details. "That doesn't answer my question? What did that ancestor *do*?"

Rafe comes closer to us, listening to this conversation.

"Nobody knows," Sam answers, shrugging his shoulders.

"The records are long lost, or forgotten, and even brothers themselves were not told of the crime of their ancestor."

I'm deflated by not receiving a gossip I had hoped for, and confused by Mik'hael's ruling.

Unless there's more...

"But they were serving Mik'hael prior?"

"Yes."

"Diligently? Truly and without an issue?"

"I think so", Sam nods.

"And after years of service, they were cast aside, banished without an explanation?"

"Yes."

I glance at the large men.

I think there might be "not so hidden" hate and resentment towards Mik'hael I could use.

"That's a bit...heavy-handed, don't you think?" I huff. "Kicked out because of the crime your gran has committed, and even then not to be told of what she has done?"

I sigh.

"With that logic half of my estate would've never seen the outside of prison."

Another thought suddenly strikes me.

"Hold on, but how did they get into Heaven? Forgiven by the grace of "Great An"?"

I roll my eyes upwards and pull my lips, feigning the awe at the An's name.

"All nine had fought for their redemption", Sam answers, ignoring my face. "At some point, each one of them have pledged loyalty to Sarukh and fought the Old Lord of Arllu under Mik'hael's banner on a number of occasions. That's why they are so angry. They feel betrayed, and rightfully so."

I nod.

"Fought?" I repeat Sam's word, mulling on it. "I could definitely use good warriors, especially ones who have a bone to pick with Mik'hael."

Suddenly this black clothing clad bunch with bright blue wings looks very good to me.

"Why didn't they go to Uriel when Mik'hael had banished them?" Rafe interjects.

"After Mik'hael, they wanted nothing to do with Sarukh and it hasn't changed", Sam answers Rafe, and then turning to me, he adds: "If you want to convince them to join you, you have a lot of convincing to do."

I dismiss his words with a wave of my hand.

"That's fine. I'm not an angel, not in the sense of a heavenly acceptable angel breeding program, that is. I was told of it plenty, in fact I just came from that mass rally. I have a spotty and questionable past, and so do they. I think we have plenty in common to bond over drinks in a pub. I will convince them, or I'll die trying. By the end of this evening we will be best mates. With their backstory and centuries long fighting experience, especially against Mik'hael, I want them on my side!"

I turn and beam at Sam.

"These guys might be the best present I've ever received."

Just before Sam turns to get back to his post by the door, I grab him by his sleeve, indicating for him to lean closer, and when he does, I whisper: "By the way, what's with the Scottish lingo?"

I carefully nudge my head behind my back, towards the brothers.

Sam quietly laughs.

"Under Mik'hael's command, the brothers fought on Apkallu for centuries against the zealous pulhu-nasu and their Arllu Lords. Following turbulence of human history, they chased pulhu-nasu from continent to continent, and so they've picked up a few traits from locals, along with colloquialisms. I think they've been spending a lot of time in Scotland as of late."

Sam drops his voice.

"Tartys said that Scots know how to party."

Sam laughs and I nod.

He leaves me with Rafe, returning to his post.

The little group by the window had settled and quietened, although Nanael had progressed from occasional glances our way to full stare at me and Rafe. For a split second, I consider marching over to her and demand to know what's her problem, but with whatever ounce of politician I have in me, I just turn away, ignoring her.

The show must follow the script, delivering the big reveal.

The two timid knocks brush over the wood of the door.

Sam opens the door, repeating his earlier greeting word to word, letting in a group of gorgeous young female angels, dressed in floral, long and floating, yet fairly-modern dresses. With their loose waist-long hair, floral dresses, cherubic pink open faces and the slow elegance of their movement, they look as if they've stepped off the set of the latest haute couture perfume ad.

Seeing the already busy room, the young ladies freeze by the door, unsure if they should bolt through the still open door or proceed forward.

Their faces turn bright pink, matching the colour of their wings, and before they make a decision, leaving for good, I step forward.

"May your evening be a blessed one, ladies. My name is – "

Sam's urgent cough interrupts my introduction.

"I'll tell you, and everyone else present, my name in just a moment, and why Sam has asked you to join us. In meanwhile, I swear to An's guiding light that you have nothing to fear from me. Please come through and make yourselves comfortable."

I put my four fingers to my head and bow to them, before coming to stand next to Sam.

"An's guiding light?" he asks me with a corner of his mouth, watching four pretty angelic models with pink faces and pink wings, walk through the room, choosing the settee farthest from the band of warring brothers.

Rafe comes to stand next to us.

"Close enough", I wave Sam off, "they understood me and they stayed. Who are the modelling crew by the way, and why do we need them?"

"It's Sablo, Purah, Kabshiel and Hasdiel. They are the angels of benevolence, forgetfulness, graciousness and protection."

"Wait. Stop, don't tell me. Let me guess."

I put on my mind-reading, clairvoyant's face and close my eyes.

"I doubt that this bunch, who scared of their own reflections, would've committed a punishable by banishing into Hell crime", I announce to Sam and Rafe in a whisper. "I think they are further casualties of Mik'hael's "Cleansing" policy, just like the brothers. Am I right?"

I open my eyes to Sam, who smiles and nods.

"There's probably no space in Mik'hael's Heaven for grace, benevolence or scatterbrains?"

"Something like that", Sam laughs.

"How many are we waiting on?" Rafe interrupts.

"Nine more", Sam responds in an even tone, refusing this time to pick a fight. "But I'm not sure if all of them would want to get involved or if Ariel would want a few of them to be a part of the resistance."

"Very ominous. Why wouldn't I want some of them?"

Another knock interrupts us.

"You'll see", Sam answers over his shoulder before taking a step towards the door.

He opens the wide door under the accompaniment of his usual greeting and a few female and male voices begin the customary reply behind the open door, but fall silent one by one, as their eyes scan the room past the open door, landing on Rafe.

The jaw of the large bearded male angel drops and the two females that flank him struggle to keep their eyes in the sockets, before chaos erupts.

CHAPTER 29

The male rushes into the room, nudging Sam out of the way with his wide shoulder, his companions following after him.

"*Kien Sar*", the male mumbles, stopping a few steps away from Rafe, as if afraid that the sight of Rafe in front of him is a mirage, which could disappear any moment under the blistering sun.

He shuffles closer, mumbling something to himself before he speaks louder.

"*The Great Kingu... Lord...* What are you doing here?"

"Please, Yofiel", Rafe interrupts the male, the smile spreading over his face, and without a further word, Rafe closes the last of the distance between them and scoops the bearded angel in his tight embrace.

The four white wings on the mystery guest fly open. The emotions and the history of the friendship are obvious.

The rest of the company pushes through into the room and Sam shuts the door behind them.

Rafe and the angel pull apart, but not without extra clasps on the backs.

"Lord", the angel booms, shaking his head. "How did you come to be here?"

The newly-arrived party is five angels strong, including the bearded one. The angels are dressed in plain black angelic tunics and trousers, similar to mine, and like mine, their clothing is free of any, so customary for angels, embroidery.

The rest of the group by the door, two males and two females, shuffle closer.

Preoccupied by the new arrival and the scene of reuniting friends, I hadn't noticed the silence in the large golden room.

I can hear the ringing silence of held breaths and I turn, scanning the room.

The earlier-arrived parties have stopped their idle chatter, now paying close attention to this exchange, listening carefully. Sabrael and his brothers have abandoned their settees, and slowly and silently like predators, they have sauntered forward.

"Lord", the bearded male says, bending his knee to Rafe and bowing at the same time, touching his four fingers to his forehead.

It's hard to tell the male's age or determine his attractiveness, as most of his face is hidden beneath the large black beard, bushy black eyebrows and messy black hair, which streams to his shoulders, covering the sides of his face. However, his moves are lithe and sure when he bows and moves, so he must be fairly young.

The angel keeps his head bowed.

"I think he knows you", I mouth and bulge my eyes to Rafe, but his response to me is only a fleeting scowl.

"Okay", Sam calls to the angels around him that shuffle closer. "I think we're going to begin, because, quite frankly, I think it's only a matter of seconds before my dear friend Yofiel will announce to everyone present, the name of one of our guests."

Rafe, ignoring the audience around, claps the angel on his shoulders, pulling him up to his feet.

"It's good to see you, brother."

They hug again. But this hug is brief and fleeting, and they pull away soon, clasping each other's upper arms, Rafe's purple and Yofiel's white wings burst open around them.

My gaze travels to the bearded angel's companions.

The three of them, two females and one male, have pale, almost white skin. But unlike Nanael and her albinos, the skin of the faces of the new arrival shimmers with a luminescent glow of a pearl. It seems if I were to touch their cheeks, it would be cold and smooth under my skin like a pearl's lustrous body.

The almond shape of their eyes reminds me of Asia, and combined with the uniformly jet-black colour of their hair, with identical bluish hue, they look as if they're related and came from the same descent. The style of their braiding and plaits is the only difference between these angels.

One male angel in their group has a dark mahogany skin colour.

"You're the last one I would've expected to find here. Why are you here?" Rafe asks his bearded friend, as his gaze slides to the faces of angels behind Yofiel.

The smile dies on Rafe's lips as the realisation comes.

"Oh..." He utters, the understanding soothes wrinkles over his forehead. He lets go of his friend and comes to stand in front of Yofiel's companions.

"Rachiel, Sidqiel, Ophaniel", Rafe says, addressing the pearly-skinned ones.

Rafe drops to his knees in front of the two females and one young male and the audible gasps sweep across the room, and a few male voices of the brothers mumble behind my back.

"My gratitude will be forever with you for everything you have done for Uriel. For as long as the eternal light shines on Sarukh, I shall never forget your deed and I pledge my support to you and your kin for as long as my Qal shall breathe."

Another wave of gasps glides through, this time shocked and strangled, bringing with it a delayed bunch of crisp and familiar angelic profanities I've heard from Sam and Rafe before, this time delivered in Sabrael's voice.

The angels from the farthest corner of the room push closer.

"Uriel?!" Sabrael rumbles low in his throat.

But it's only low at first. When he growls Uriel's name again, his deep voice vibrates the walls. His brothers stand behind him in a tight wall of bodies.

"I knew that Sarukh garbs were not for nothing", Sabrael roars.

He pushes through the crowd, coming into Sam's face.

"What are they doing here? Who are they?" Sabrael demands of Sam.

But before Sam has a chance to answer, a soft female voice cuts in: "His name is Rafael."

Every head turns towards the voice.

The tips of the bright yellow wings move toward us, above the heads, until Nanael comes through to stand at the forefront of the crowd.

"His name is Rafael", she repeats, telling it to the murderous-looking Sabrael. "He is the commander of Anshaan Kataaru, Counsel to Uriel and... Uriel's Great Arcanum."

A rustle of female gasps, sharp intakes of air and low, muffled swearing of the brothers to my left, float through the room.

I turn my head, scanning the faces, trying to understand the emotions that have prompted this reaction.

Nanael turns to face Rafe and me.

"But what are you doing in Arllu, Rafael, and who is your consort? That's what I'd like to know."

"Why "consort"?" Rafe quietly asks, glaring at Nanael from underneath his drawn eyebrows.

"Because of both of your wings", she answers.

Within the tight space that the angelic mob has left me, Nanael takes a step towards me and, after scanning me, she adds: "Is she Uriel incarnate?"

The breathless silence suddenly explodes, replaced with soft cries and gasps, a hysterical laughter, a few male growls, a string of profanities in a few voices and some guttural exclamations, which could mean anything from "Yes! What a great news!" to "Hell, no!"

"Everybody! Everybody, please!" Sam calls over the wave of a loud chatter, which has suddenly engulfed twenty agitated angels. But Sam's voice drowns inside that wave.

"Now, you know who I am and who she is", Rafe roars to the crowd from the door, where he nudged himself. "Nobody's going to leave this room until you hear her out."

Someone barks something from the back, and a decisive stride of male's footsteps reach the door and Rafe in front of it.

"I said, no one!" Rafe roars.

"You have to stay", Sam calls above the commotion. "Please, Kafziel, stay and hear them out."

"You will not drag me into this! I want nothing to do with Sarukh's bitch."

"Don't you dare..."

"Show some respect..."

"Oi!" I yell over the commotion. But I'm ignored.

"O-o-o-i-i-i!" I wail.

The scuffle dies and so does the chatter.

"If you want to go, Kafziel, go! I'm not going to hold you! But before you leave, a word of warning. I'm coming for everyone who stays in Arllu. When the time comes, I will show no mercy to my enemies! Everyone who is not with me is against me, and everyone who's against me is going to die!" I hiss.

"Do you know what has happened to Chamuel? Of course you've heard. I did it to him. Me! He is the first of many, and I promise you, there will be many more."

I narrow my gaze on him.

"The time of the battle is coming! The time of choosing alliances is here. The time is now, and I'm offering you one. I am here out of respect to you, to every one of you, to everyone, who had suffered under Mik'hael's rule, who lost homes, friends, family, loved ones *because* of Mik'hael, who were betrayed by Mik'hael. I'm offering you a second chance and I'm offering you salvation. I'm offering you your home. I want to give you back the home that was taken from you. I'm offering you Sarukh."

I walk towards the door. The angels part in front of me, until I reach Rafe and Sam, blocking the door, and Kafziel next to them.

"And what I hope you'd find interesting, Kafziel, I'm offering you a chance to get even with Mik'hael."

"Child", he answers, looking down at me with the most patronising half-smile. "You can't offer something that isn't yours."

"I'm not a child, Kafziel. I am Uriel. Can you see this?"

I point at my filthy tunic, with the dried lizards' goo stark against the white purity of it.

"I fought my way here. I fought my way to the top of Uras. I have fought for my life every single day since I was born, and as you can see, I'm still fighting. Baza came at me with the force of his ibnatums and his army, but I'm still standing. The lizards came at me, hoping for easy prey, but they're the ones who are burning at the bottom of the earth. Chamuel wanted me killed, but he is the one who is dead right now. Have you heard the news? Uras is under my control and so is the entire essence of Uriel. I deliver vengeance and I deliver justice, just as Uriel once taught. I am most certainly not a child."

I turn to face the rest of the angels.

"I am Uriel and I offer everyone present salvation."

"A wee bairn declares herself against Baza and Mik'hael?" Sabrael barks a short laugh. "You are a funny one."

His smile suddenly evaporates when he adds with disdain: "I can still smell human on you."

Sabrael turns to Sam.

"I'll give you one thing, Samael, the entertainment today was top class."

"The *wee bairn* does, and did, declare herself against Baza and Mik'hael", I growl. "I've killed the assassin Mik'hael had sent."

Inwardly, I twinge at the first time in a while thought of Mia.

"I fought off Baza's advance and ambush, and I'm taking control of my lizards and my powers. Maybe once upon a time I was a wee bairn", I mimic his words, "but I'm not that girl anymore. Hear me out, Sabrael. Hear me first, before you'll make your call, for yourself and your brothers."

But as he takes another decisive step towards the door, I call after him: "Or are you afraid to get into trouble? Afraid to be spanked by Baza? Or maybe you are scared of me? Scared of a *wee* human girl?"

The silence, that I was fighting for so long, suddenly descends over the room, and the next second, his murderous face hangs above mine. His lips are drawn over his teeth, which screech as he grinds them to pulp.

"You little Sarukh –"

Don't think so.

Faster than his raging mind can see or process, my hands slide to my black armoury belt and fly out, armed with two small daggers, short like fruit knives, which stop only an inch away from both sides of Sabrael's neck, just under his over-working jaw.

The unison sharp intake of air echoes in the room.

Domiel had taught me a few tricks with my swords, but the survival on the streets had taught me all I needed to know, but mainly: once you draw a weapon, be ready to use it, and I was.

Both of my daggers stroke the soft skin of his neck.

"Don't force me into it", I say softly. "What's another dead angel in this world? Especially the banished one. I will win this one. You die, you live, each outcome is good for me, but not so much for you."

I'm face to face with him. I lean closer, when I say: "By the way, these knives are Hinnomian, *man*."

Barely noticeable, his skin turns paler and I'm pleased about it.

The silence hangs a few heartbeats longer.

"Maybe you're not that useless after all", he grumbles low, careful not to move his neck.

"I am not, I promise. Ready to finally listen?"

"Damiq. Aye. I'll listen to what Uriel incarnate has to say."

Carefully, while watching his eyes, I pull the daggers away from his neck.

I scan the room, only now noticing Sam and Rafe standing to left and right of me, *on the ground*, in a protective circle, their weapons drawn as they swing them in front of themselves, guarding off anyone who might have a stupid idea, while I... *float above the ground* on my wings, face to face with the tall Sabrael.

Through the silence of the room, I hear the approaching crystal laughter of female voices and a moment later, a light knock dances on the wood of the door. The female voices chirp behind it.

Sam pulls at the door, but the door opens only a fraction due to the bodies in front of it.

"Sorry we're late..." The familiar voice begins. "My, this is a bit tight. How intimate, Samael. Big party..."

Lis squeezes in, giggling, but her mouth slams shut the second her gaze falls on me. Her golden shimmery wings shoot open around her, but pressed by the bodies around, they don't get a chance to open, almost instantly folding back.

"What are you doing here?" Lis asks me.

She spins to Sam.

"Why is she here?"

The laughter of Lis' mates dies the second her sour voice begins with demands.

"I'm here to speak to everyone, including *you*, apparently."

I glare at Sam.

"Nanael, will you stay? Sabrael?"

Sam turns, asking the tight crowd, ignoring me and Lis.

"I'm ready to listen", says Yofiel.

"So are we", the two females and the male add, in front of whom Rafe had dropped to his knees earlier.

"Damiq."

"Damiq."

One by one, the voices chime in and the crowd begins to disperse, as the angels take seats on the settees in the centre, while Sabrael's brothers drag extra settees and armchairs into the centre.

In a suddenly empty area by the door, only the newcomers, Sam, Rafe and I are left.

Lis' body is sealed in a skin-tight golden, heavy beaded mini dress, matching her golden wings perfectly and offsetting the soft glow of her skin. Her long, wavy blonde hair is pinned to one side.

She looks gorgeous tonight, and next to her, I feel embarrassed of my once plain tunic, now covered in the mess of Arllu's life, inadequate to Lis' glamour in every sense.

She gives me her "once over", pursing her lips, thinking the same.

"Fine", Lis says, nodding at Sam.

But before she leaves, she turns to him and grants him a wide, startling glorious smile, then with a practiced move, she pulls her lips together as if taking a selfie, then giving Sam a smouldering gaze with her hooded eyes.

I feel hot under the collar, and these manoeuvres were not even directed at me.

"But they are for your benefit", Rage growls low.

Lis strides to a vacant settee, bringing with her a thick and sticky cloud of a sweet scent, her friends, two females and one male, follow her.

The four of them came to party and it is clear from their attire of sequins and glitter, heavy and intricate beading, that no expense was spared to glamour up these four. The male wears a silver sequined blazer which gives him the resemblance of a silver disco ball.

But maybe it's just my jealousy talking, as when I take time to look at them, I appreciate how stunning all four look tonight.

With displeasure, I notice a few male angels watch Lis' swinging hips, while the earlier group of the female modelling crew in floral dresses, scatter out of her way as if she's infectious.

Interesting...

But before I walk toward the audience, which is about to crucify me, Rafe catches my arm and whispers to me: "Do you need her gone?"

He nods his head at Lis' back.

"I don't have the luxury to pick and choose. I need everyone and anyone I can find on my side. I need every able body."

I shake my head in resignation.

"She can stay."

CHAPTER 30

The audience is ready for me.

I scan the wings of the different colours folded behind the backs, the angelic faces of the different races. I'm about to address the exiled United Nations of the celestial world.

There are thirty angels in this room including me, and only two I know are on my side. The remaining twenty seven I need to convince to join me, and even if I manage to pull off that miracle, there's no guarantee it would be enough against Baza and Mik'hael.

"Thank you for being here."

"For the next GA, baby, we have nowhere else to go", one of Sabrael's brothers calls from the back row, his remark is greeted by the thunderous laughter of his brothers.

Ignoring his joke, I answer him: "You do. You can come with me to Uras, all of you."

I scan their faces.

"I'm inviting you. I invite all of you to leave this place and call Uras your home. I'm offering you your way back into Sarukh, as equals."

"What in the name of Hinnom are you talking about?" Another brother calls.

"Mik'hael had exiled you, all of you, for different reasons and sins, some imaginary and some real, and he took your home away from you. He took Heaven from you, the Heaven for which you fought, the Heaven into which some of you were born. He took your home away from you and sent you to this miserable pit to live out eternity, and all because none of you conformed to his vision of "clean" Sarukh, none of you were "comfortable" angels to have around. But I don't care about it. I'd be the last person to hold someone's past against them. I know that no one is perfect and I don't ask you to be."

I scan my gaze over their faces.

"Mik'hael had no right to do it to you, and as a daughter of An, as Uriel: The Harbinger of Chaos, The Keeper of the Gates, The Begetter of Life, The Dam of The Ends", *thank you, Rafe, for reminding me of all her regalia before this performance*, "I want to rectify the wrong and I open the doors of Uras to you all."

As nobody answers my dramatic statement, which I had to rehearse a few times prior, I add: "None of you deserve to be here..."

"Even us?"

Lis' giggles interrupt a fresh wave of my rousing speech, as she sweeps her hand at herself and her companions.

"Um... Yeah. Why you?"

I know a problem is coming my way, I can feel it. I am about to step into it. The cheeky cow is about to drop a steaming pile of shit on my lap.

I look at her face.

Right about now...

"Do you even know, little child, what I'm here for?" she asks with a challenge, narrowing her eyes at me. "Do you know what are *my* sins?"

"No, but I think you are about to tell me", I huff.

"I was accused and found guilty of perverting men. I was one of the first to be cast out by Mik'hael, millennia before the crazy idea of "cleansing" of Sarukh took over his mind. The five of us are the guardian angels of love, in one form or another, and you want us in Uras with you? *Us?* In your precious Uras?"

I sweep my gaze over the gorgeous faces of Lis' companions, pleased to notice that colour touches the cheeks of the two of them at the Lis' disclosures.

Maybe not all of them are into that kinda love...

I dart my gaze to Sam and my gaze crushes at his bent head. He knew it, yet still invited her here. Why? What is he trying to do?

I turn my head and look at Rafe, whose dark face screams clearly at how diabolical this whole idea was.

But I can't turn back, not now. It's a bit too late.

I can't risk losing twenty six strong angels over four, and if Rafe did his job right, the constitution that he had drafted would govern and judge Lis and her behaviours from now on.

It will be out of my hands.

It will be up to her, how she decides to live in Uras.

"The doors of Uras are open to every one of you, and An be my witness, we can use more love in today's Sarukh."

I'm pleased hearing myself.

My voice is decisive and strong. I've manage to turn that curve ball into an asset, and I've begun speaking their lingo: *"An be my witness"*, blah-blah.

But above all, this baring disclosure has suddenly made me feel sorry for Lis. Suddenly I see her through a different prism of a different light and I wonder how much of this "perversion" was of her making, how much of it was her instigation, or maybe she is another victim of male power games, just as I was once.

I look straight at Lis, as I continue: "Everyone has a past and I'm not going to stone you for that. The past is gone and no one, not even An, can change it. But the future is what matters. The future is what we can change. I'm offering you a chance but it's up to you what you'll do with it. I'm inviting you into a new, fresh world, which we're going to build together, a fresh world where no one will be judged on their past but only by their current deeds."

I scan the faces of the angels in front of me, pausing.

"I invite you to join me in Uras. I'm inviting you to come with me. I will give you your home. No!" I cut myself short. "I'm inviting you to make Uras *our* home, a home which will be built on trust and honesty and care for our home and one another. We will be equal there, no one above another. Uras has space for everyone. Uras needs your knowledge."

I look at the group of the angels with Nanael.

"It needs your grace and forgiveness."

I spin my head to the modelling agency in the floral dresses.

"It needs your strength", I say to Sabrael, "and I can swear to An's light, I would never hold your ancestors against you just as I don't ever expect to be reminded of my humanity again."

I stop speaking and the silence hangs in the room.

I want to say something else, to convince them, but Rafe warned me against sounding too desperate. He said if they hear even a single note of desperation, they'll never join me. I guess it's the rules of the animal kingdom they call Heaven.

"Is it something any of you would be interested in?" I ask the silence and the wary faces.

Shit. That's it. I've screwed it. I had one chance and I blew it. What now?

I glance at Rafe. His face is a stoic mask, and by now I know this mask means that I've failed or screwed up. Today, maybe both.

Yofiel stands up.

"I speak for myself and Ophanims. I'll let The Record Keeper speak for himself. I pledge our Qals to Uriel-incarnate, to Rafael the Great Arcanum of Uriel and to Great Uras. We pledge to stand with you. We pledge our undying support to both of you and Uras."

He touches his forehead with four fingers and bows deeply to me, then he turns and does the same to Rafe.

Rafe nods his head in acknowledgement.

The three angels next to Yofiel stand up, then bow to me and then to Rafe.

I reciprocate their bows with one of my own, trying to mirror theirs.

"Thank you, and welcome", I say.

Rafe strolls to Yofiel and clasps him on his arms.

"It's good to have you, brother."

Then Rafe clasps the arms of all three pledged angels, one at a time, hugging them in turn.

The dark-skinned angel, who came with Yofiel and Ophanims stands up.

"The records of Daanom were erased and re-written", he starts. "The accurate records of mine no longer satisfy Great Mik'hael's agenda or reflect the glory of his reign, or the greatness of "The Sarukh cleansing".

There's no longer a place for me in Daanom, and it will never be. Beholden, I would like to accept the offer of Uras' refuge."

The angel bows to me, then to Rafe.

Rafe bows to him and so do I.

I exhale and I feel a blooming smile tug at my lips.

I scan the seated angels, and confronted by the scowls on the brothers' faces, by the fear splashed over the floral modelling crew's elegant faces, by the cautious and calculating glances from Nanael and her crew, my smile weathers and dies.

The five angels probably would be all I win over.

"You have declared yourself against Mik'hael, incarnate. Correct?" Sabrael barks at me from his seat.

"Yes."

"Have you truly killed Mik'hael's assassin?"

"Yes", Sam chimes in. "I saw it with my own eyes."

"Have you truly killed Chamuel?"

"Yes", Rafe answers, before I have chance to open my mouth, "I saw it with my own eyes."

"And you have declared yourself against Baza, yet you have the balls, little incarnate, to be inside the belly of the beast, looking for recruits?" he scoffs, but it isn't a question that requires my answer.

"Aye." He nods his head. "I like that. Very ballsy", he barks and guffaws, and his brothers begin the laugh around him.

"I don't know how capable you are, wee beyelai, but you're spunky, I'll give you that, and most of the battles are won by sheer brassiness."

"You cannot even imagine how ballsy I can be", I huff, giving him a half smile.

He throws his head up and laughs.

"Damiq. We declare ourselves to you, Uriel incarnate, if for nothing else but for a chance to kick Mik'hael's arse. Arllu is incredibly tedious. All that they have here is a handful of decent angels to socialise with, the rest are either scheming sleezeballs or harvesting humans ibnatums. Boring. I think I might die pretty soon of boredom, if I don't have a war."

"Surely, Baza provides you with plenty of wars", I say.

"Nay. All that he fights is humans in Apkallu, but if it's okay with you, I'm not going to call a sheep slaughter a battle worthy of a true warrior."

"Fair enough. Stick with me and you'll have plenty of battles to fight."

Sabrael turns his head and looks at his brothers, and when each gives him a small nod in return, he stands up and announces: "By the will of An, I pledge my Qal and the Qals of Pronoia, Zaazenach, Zabkiel, Tagas, Tartys, Sabaoth, Kafziel, Iaoel to Uriel-incarnate, to Rafael the Great Arcanum of Uriel and to Great Uras. We pledge to stand with you. We pledge our loyalty to you and we pledge to fight with you."

"Thank you", I say when the last words of his oath die.

I touch my fingers to my forehead and bow to him, and then I bow to each of the brothers and every time I do, the brothers stand and give me an answering bow.

I'm elated. As far as I'm concerned, I've scored myself a jackpot of recruits.

Since their military background was revealed to me, I've decided that if I can leave with only one group in tow, it should be this group, a group of the weathered warriors, experienced soldiers, who have a big bone to pick with Mik'hael.

I turn and smile at Sam, then turn and look at Rafe, who sealed in his black mercenaries' gear, looks the part with these fearless warriors.

Suddenly I feel giddy. I feel happy and for the first time in a while, hopeful in fact.

I stamp down my impulse to run up to Sabrael and hug him, so I sober instead, pulling a ruler-worthy broody and slightly sullen expression.

I draw my gaze to the modelling crew.

Under my expectant gaze, the floral girls stare back at me with the fearful eyes of caught rabbits, and the longer I look at their scared faces, the less I want them in my war.

But I'm not going to make it easy for them. I'm not going to set up a precedent. That's the one thing they'd need to find the bravery to do themselves.

They have to tell me "no" themselves. I'm not going to bail them out.

Tired of staring at the floral girls bowed heads, I swing my gaze to Nanael and Co.

Nanael is braver than the floral ones, and she meets my gaze with hers.

"The Puhrumm Ukkin will respectfully decline your offer of sanctuary", she announces as she stands up. "According to our calculations, you're unlikely to withstand the forces of Baza or Mik'hael, let alone the both of them. Your army is disbanded. Your sphere of influence had narrowed to Uras castle, and even this was problematic for you to regain. You are a fresh incarnate, and a *human*, making it unlikely to reinstate the Uriel's dominance or rejuvenate Uriel's powers or control over them under these two conditions.

"As well as this, our calculations have indicated that at the end of this rebellion, everyone associated with the Castle of Uras will be exterminated, with their souls sent to Udhad to be dissolved, therefore we don't want anything to do with this proposition."

She bows to me.

I'm stunned at the beginning of her speech, but the longer she speaks, the angrier I grow.

Using my home grown and freshly learned heavenly profanities, I want to demand to know, as to who the Hell she thinks she is, telling me, just like that, in front of everybody, that according to her *calculations* I'm as well as dead and so is everyone else who pledges to me.

I don't need her logic, her straight talking. This information sharing was done not for my benefit, oh no.

With the rational part of my brain I understand that I need to respect her choice and I do, or I *think* I do, but was it completely necessary? What am I supposed to do with this information? Crawl into a hole and die, just because she said so, because the maths of survival is not in my favour?

I breathe, ignoring Rage, who is crazy dancing in my head to AC/DC.

I breathe out, and by the sheer miracle of self-control, I manage to plaster a calm smile over my face.

"I respect your calculations, Nanael", I say, but I can't keep the frost out of my voice. "And I respect your choice. But before you go, I'd like to point out to you that not everything can be explained, planned or measured. Some things just happen, and some things happen through the sheer determination, bravery and hard work.

"Besides, what about the divine intervention? Aren't you, guys, supposed to be advocates of it? There are plenty of miracles that happen every day. I shouldn't be here. I shouldn't be alive and I shouldn't be Uriel, yet here I am."

She opens her mouth to say something, but I raise my hand silencing her and my large shimmery wings lift me off the ground. The sharp pain burns at the top of the damaged wings but I ignore it.

"I've heard your piece, now it's time for you to hear mine. I fought every single day of my life. All of you can learn a thing or two from humans about their determination. I fought and I survived against odds you've never experienced. I have performed miracles of survival and I'm not going to give up, and most definitely, not because someone has said that I should. I will face my new challenges just as I've faced the challenges before, and I will prevail. You hear me? *Prevail*, as I have done many times before."

I float. My head almost touches the ceiling.

"But before you go, Nanael, I have to warn you, and it's not a threat. It's just a friendly heads-up. When I engage in a war with Baza and it comes to open conflict, I wouldn't be able to protect you or to offer an asylum to you then. Then you will be one of the enemies, and you will be exterminated. Do you understand me?"

I'm using her words against her. If she forewarns the extermination to me and my followers, it's only fitting to offer her the same in return.

"I'll take that chance", she clips.

"Fair enough. Then we have nothing further to discuss."

Sam steps forward.

"Nanael, brothers and sisters. I have to ask you to stay in my quarters until we leave Arllu, which wouldn't be long. I hope, Nanael, you appreciate that we need to take precautions. If you could follow me, I will escort you to my living quarters."

The angels get up and sheepishly scamper towards the door, darting their glances at me, still suspended mid-air, keeping their heads down under the glares from Sabrael and his brothers.

Nanael is the last through the door. Her back is rod straight.

After Nanael's appraisal the atmosphere in the room has turned gloomy.

"I think we're ready to declare ourselves too."

Lis' beautiful melodic voice breaks the silence.

Oh, goody; two for the price of one.

I drop to the floor and close my wings behind me.

"Yes, Lis?"

"By the will of An, I pledge my Qal and the Qals of Theliel, Miniel and Haniel to Uriel-incarnate, to Rafael the Great Arcanum of Uriel and to Great Uras. We pledge to stand with you."

I feel my mouth begin to drop after she has uttered the "I pledge my Qal" words.

I'm not sure if I understood her correctly. I don't understand why she would do it. It's not something I would've expected from her.

I look at the beautiful faces of the angels of love, at Lis', unable to find any sign of "gotcha". I swing my gaze to Rafe, who, after reading the confusion on my face, nods.

"Um..."

I clear my throat.

"Thank you, Lis. Thank you, all of you. I appreciate how daunting it must be, to put your trust in me, especially after everything Nanael had said, and that's why, it is so meaningful to me. Thank you."

I do a set of ceremonious bows to Lis and every angel with her.

CHAPTER 31

By the time Sam came back, the modelling agency had declared themselves too, with the two of them pledging their loyalty to Uras, while the other two shook their heads and fled Sam's opulent room, once Sam came back and escorted them into his private quarters.

With only pledged angels left in the room, I was pleased to tally up my losses only at seven angels. At the beginning of the evening, it would've been the number of angels I thought I would gain.

"Thank you for staying and thank you for your trust. I promise I'll do my best to not fail you."

"As long as you don't chicken out from the battle against Mik'hael, Uriel-incarnate, we're good", one of Sabrael's brothers calls out from the room. "We're here not because we love you, but because we hate him more."

"Fine by me. I don't have a problem with that. I do appreciate your honesty and please don't worry about me chickening out. That fight is not of my making and Mik'hael will be looking for me soon enough, just stick with me."

"Excellent", Sabrael roars, rubbing his hands, and his brothers share excited shoulder punches and some other gestures, although they are new to me, must be an equivalent of "high fives" or maybe something ruder.

"I'll hand the rest of the conversation to Rafe, who'll talk to you about the exit plan."

Rafe steps forward.

"The exodus is planned for five *bêru* from now. You're free to get back to your residences and gather a few essential belongings. But don't over pack. On foot we'll travel to the Gates and from there we'll move to Uras. Please, everyone, be punctual as we need to expedite this promptly, as once Belzeebu will discover one or two absences, the clock will start and we will have a very narrow window of opportunity. Any questions?"

"What about Uras armoury? How stocked are you?" Sabrael booms from his seat.

I want to roll my eyes at his single-minded take on every task, but I manage to hold it back.

"Uras is very well stocked, including Hinnomian weapons, as you've seen."

"I still will bring some of my armoury."

"As you wish", Rafe bows.

Sam walks through the door.

"Is there anything in particular you'd like me to bring?" Lis asks, addressing Sam, smiling seductively at him, and the combination of his shifting gazes, dancing between me and her, and her sparkling eyes on him, suddenly aggravates me.

Not only do I not want to be caught up in any of these innuendo games, but I can't afford alienate her. From now on and forward, she is my ally, irrelevant of my opinion of her. But I don't think I'd be able to handle any territorial games where he is concerned.

I turn away, ignoring the "Flirt Olympics".

"Anyone else? Any questions?" I ask.

The angels shake their heads.

"Excellent", I say. "Then I'll see you soon, at the beginning of your new life. I hope I don't need to remind everyone to be discreet. May An keep you safe and I will see you soon."

The angels get up, and one by one, they leave the room, bowing deep to me and Rafe on their way out and nodding their heads at Sam.

Lis and her mates are the last out of the door, and soon it's just the three of us left in Sam's drawing room.

"Well", I say to fill in the uncomfortable silence. "It actually went much better than I thought."

"What did I tell you, Mermaid? I told you it will be fine and it was. Trust me."

"Thank you."

I turn to the sullen and quiet Rafe.

"Now, we have a fighting chance against Baza and Mik'hael. Thank you for agreeing to accept these angels in Uras. I know how important Uras is to you and I trust you to write a fair constitution, which will serve Uras and its angels' needs. I'll leave it for you to decide."

Rafe jerks his head at me in what I read as agreement.

"Would you mind please to go back to Domiel and Dumah and update them on the progress, check on Jess and prepare them for departure later? I need to make sure that everything's in order."

"I'm sure they have taken a good care of Jess.Any concerns for the departure preparations can be organised by Domiel very fast. I don't see a need to update them."

"Rafe", I say quietly, coming closer to him and taking his hand into mine. "Remember what you promised me?"

Rafe scans my face for a few drawn out seconds, before his gaze jumps to Sam's face then back to mine.

"I will update them in person", he agrees.

"Thank you", I say, but Rafe is already gone and I'm telling it to the closing door.

I turn to Sam.

"Thank you for arranging it, Sam. I know you're risking a lot by doing this."

"You know you don't need to thank me, right?"

He takes a step closer to me, and the scent of him, which I was fighting off all evening, barges into my head, through my blocks and defences, taking over.

"I'd do absolutely anything for you, Mermaid", he whispers. "I hope you know it by now. I hope I've shown you with everything that I've done. I want my actions to speak of my loyalty."

The problem with waiting for an action is, it is like watching a precariously balanced bowl at the edge of a table, waiting, *and not knowing*, if it would fall, shattering into millions of tiny pieces. By then, with that unfortunate outcome, there would be very little that could be done. The bowl would be shattered but so would the trust, the milk would've been spilt and the damage would've been done, and unfortunately for me, in this world the damage could be far more severe than the spilt milk. The damage of misplaced trust would hold grave consequences for many around me, and not just for me, with one of the consequences being death.

"The trust needs to be earned", I mumble.

The things he, and anyone else around him, says have very little to do with how I feel about him. It's as if their warnings and my logic live in a parallel world with my feelings for him. They don't cross, don't impact each other, living side by side, demanding contradictory things from me.

Like a broken record, Rafe regularly repeats that I should be cautious, that Sam is fallen for a reason, but...Hell!

Am I not allowed to be selfish once in a while? Am I not allowed to be a stupid and carefree, and make a mistake, without carrying the world on my shoulders, without worrying about me or someone around me to be killed? Am I not allowed to be a girl, even for a day? Not to be constantly guarded, watchful, suspicious, mature and reasonable, always making the "right decisions"? And if I'm about to die, if these are last few days of my life, of my short and miserable life, can't I have my bit of happiness, a small tiny slither of it? Is it too much to ask?

Am I not allowed to be loved, loved just because, loved because it's me, broken, crazy *me*? Am I not allowed to love too? To throw the caution to the wind and run through a field under a warm summer sun and be happy? Even once in my life?

Was I born only to suffer?

I want to be me. I want to allow myself to be stupid and selfish. I want to enjoy myself and my illogical love.

"There could be another agenda", Rage whispers in my head with a solemn face. *"You're playing in the big league now and, surprising many, you're holding your own. You're still alive, and more so, you're a contender, someone to be reckoned with and someone to watch out for. Baza would've not come at you with his grey soldiers if he wasn't cautious of you, maybe even scared. That move was born out of desperation..."*

I don't see where she's going with it.

"So what?"

My Rage is quiet for a moment, looking at me with her sad eyes. She doesn't rush to say the words, to break my illusions. She doesn't take pleasure in it.

"Sam might be building bridges with a new ruler", she whispers.

I smile.

"Why are you smiling?" Sam asks, coming closer, placing his warm hands on my waist, smiling back, and his glorious dimple comes through.

I can watch him for hours. I can breathe his scent for days.

"Aren't you afraid of me?" I ask.

"Should I be?"

"Don't know." I shrug my shoulders. "Maybe. Some are."

"That's because they don't know you as well as I do", he says, leaning for a kiss.

"Be careful", I say, turning my head away from his kiss, and twisting out of his hold.

I take a small step back.

"Maybe they know me just the right amount."

His hands drop by his sides as he narrows his gaze on me, his smile gone.

I fall silent too, thinking on what Rage had said.

"Do you think I'll win?"

"What? This?"

He nudges his head slightly to the side.

"Yes", I nod. "This, the battle against Baza, then Mik'hael, then anything else that might come my way, the whole lot. Do you think I still will be here a few years from now? Or will I be long dead and forgotten?"

I lift my gaze to his beautiful face. I'm watching it for confirmation of Rage's earlier insinuation, watching for a shifty gaze, maybe a gulp. I want to know what he thinks.

Of course, I'd like to hear a pep talk, from him, from anyone else. It would be so nice to hear that I'm doing the right thing and that I can do it, that my gamble is not that far-fetched and *will* pay off. I want a cheerleader on my side, someone who for once would tell me that I can do it, but, at the same time, I want to hear honesty.

But I have nowhere to get it from. Everyone here lies, and Sam probably would also.

He opens his mouth to answer but I interrupt him.

"Actually, no! Don't answer. Ignore me and my questions. I don't want to know. It's irrelevant what you think, or what anyone thinks of me or my future. Most of you don't even know me, how possibly you can know what I am capable of?"

I look at him and shake my head.

"Forget about it. It's irrelevant. Your words won't change anything, and it's irrelevant what she thinks."

"Who?" he asks, confused, his eyebrows are knitted together.

"No one", I brush it off.

I take a long stride forward, coming close to him, and lifting myself on my toes, I kiss him.

He is taken by surprise by my sudden change of topic, by this unexpected kiss, but he is not motionless for long.

His lips are on mine, soft and tender at first, but as I don't withdraw, holding my ground, they grow demanding and urgent. Living a life of their own, my arms fly up, my hands find his hair, diving into the silky waves of it, and with this touch, his lips intensify their attack, turning merciless and ravaging.

His hands are in my hair. They are stroking my neck. I feel his hands on my waist and at the low of my back. Like the hands of a blind man learning about the subject by touch, his hands are all over me, learning the look and feel of my body.

He tastes of forest and fruits. He smells of rain and storm. He snuck into my head ages ago and I still don't know how to push him from there. The taste and smell of blackberries and pine fight in my head with the scent of the ocean and fruits. My desires and need for freedom fight with the calls of responsibility and cause, my heart and soul fighting my head and logic.

Driven by my emotions, my wings burst open and the nick at the tip of my wing stings, bringing sobering clarity.

I lay my hands on his chest.

His muscles are solid steel under my hands and hot as sand on a beach at midday.

My decision takes the last ounce of my resolve. I ball my hands over his chest and I push him away.

He stumbles away.

His gaze is dazed. His breath is ragged, but so is mine.

He licks his red, swollen lips, and mesmerised, I follow his tongue with my eyes.

"Don't go anywhere. I won't be a second", he says. His voice is rough and low.

But before I can ask him where he's going or answer him, asking where he thinks I'll go, he walks out of the room, leaving me standing in the large opulence of it, breathless, dazed and lost.

CHAPTER 32

"Here's our brave little Mermaid."

I jump up, spinning at the voice. It's not the voice I was expecting.

Although the voice is faintly familiar, I'm still unable to pinpoint the familiarity of it, until I finish the turn and I see *him*.

The breath leaves my lungs in a lost puff.

My head rings and panic squeezes my chest, preventing me from drawing another breath.

The tunnel vision blurs out everything but him, standing by the door in his black leather tunic, the necklace of white human teeth stark against it.

My panic-laden, blurred vision is the reason why I don't see the danger around me, why I miss the attack.

Suddenly, an agonising pain explodes in my right wing, echoing in my head, waking me, and I scream.

With my new and updated survival instinct, fit for this lethal heavenly world, I yank the glowing swords free from my belt, simultaneously spinning towards an assailant.

With a fleeting surprise yet comfort, my brain registers the sight of the Butcher's "little helper". The comfort is because I'm going to kill him.

I cross over my arms, and just as I'm finishing the turn, my arms fly open and wide at the sight of the leather-clad body, as if inviting him into my embrace.

The two deep slashes blossom across his leather tunic and his white chest underneath, and within a second, blood fills the cuts and he cries out a short surprised gasp, before dropping to the ground.

Now I'm awake.

My blood had woken me and his blood energised me.

I spin around, counting five more Butcher's soldiers, scattered around the room like the settees.

They are smaller, projecting less hate and lethality than their fearless leader, but just like him, they are sealed in black, sleeveless, leather butcher tunics, with tightly stocked weapon belts criss-crossing their torsos. All five of them flaunt a pair of grey wings behind their backs, just like their commander.

Fleetingly, at the back of my mind, I wonder why their wings are grey, identical in look and the colour of the Butcher's? Why Baza's soldiers from the clearance had grey wings too? Were these angels bred or changed when they joined his service? Is there a reason for it, a deeper meaning or just a coincidence? Although I have to say, these heavenly worlds don't operate in sloppy realms of coincidence.

My musings are interrupted by the movement of the angels, who slide closer, quiet and agile on their feet.

I spin around. My gaze darts between the six of them: Butcher and his five "helpers".

But Butcher doesn't move.

Patient, he stands by the door, waiting for his minions to do his job, and I wonder if I'm a training tool, seemingly an easy prey to catch that was not taken seriously, as otherwise he wouldn't be away from the action, by the door, cleaning his nails. He would've been in the middle of it.

But lately, I've found a bubbly rush in the freedom of being underestimated.

I've found a heady excitement in it, the excitement of seeing their wide-open surprised eyes the moments before the life leaves their bodies, the excitement of over-powering the enemy that is larger and more experienced than me, the excitement of being the last one standing, as if proving them wrong.

It gave me the edge.

I push at the nearest armchair and it slides away. I nudge at the settee. I pick and throw a gilded chair, for shits and giggles aiming at the one of the minions, and I'm pleased to see him duck when the chair flies above his head and I smile.

Now, I have the space I need.

"Not bad, girl", Butcher calls from by the door.

I don't know what he's talking about. It might be about my killing of his soldier, but maybe my area clearance skills have impressed him, or maybe something else, but I can't afford to stop and chit-chat.

I can't be distracted. I can't afford to pull my gaze away from the tightening ring of his soldiers on me.

"You grew two pairs since the last time I saw you", he says with approval.

Surprised, I glance at him only to see that he is looking at my wings.

Oh...wings...

"Did you honestly think you would get away with coming here?" Butcher calls to me. "With causing trouble, stealing Baza's troops? Baza knows everything that happens in his domain, little human, everything! That's how he stayed in power for all these *GA*."

Butcher maybe feels relaxed and chatty, but I can't afford to stop my spinning. I'm back to my "Ottoman whirling dervishes" dance.

His soldiers are silent and restless. Their advance is ceaseless and unremitting, and before long, with a peripheral vision, I notice one of them on the left, dashes towards me, jumping on the back of the settee I just pushed away.

I turn in time with his landing.

His black axe is raised above his head, and the second his feet touch the floor next to me, the axe screeches through the air, flying towards my head.

I twist at the waist and sideways, away from the axe's wheezing blade, which cuts the air where I stood only a second ago, and when after missing the target, the leather-clad angel rises his axe again, coming closer this time, I drop to my knees and cross my arms over my chest.

For a second I pause, then breathe out, letting my arms spread and my swords glide.

This trick worked once with the lizard. I hope it will work again as it did before.

In a slight downwards trajectory, my glowing swords fly through the air, cutting through the muscle and bone of the angel's legs, and like the lizard before him, he roars.

But his roar does ring in the air for a while before his body crashes to the ground and without looking at him, at his so human face, I reach somewhere to the side of me and sink my sword into flesh.

"That was impressive", Butcher calls to me, and then to his minions: "Hey, useless slugs, watch her and learn, and for Arllu sake, do better."

The remaining four minions take it as an instruction to crank it up a notch, as suddenly all four take to the air, their bodies and grey wings obstruct the light from the chandeliers and the windows.

They are above me like a dome.

Another grey dome above me, again.

I'm noticing the pattern in their fighting strategies and it's good too. It means they work with a handful of "tried and trusted" assault techniques and if I live long enough, I will learn the way they fight, and if I manage to throw something new at them, I might take them by surprise. I might finally get my advantage.

The dome above me is tight. It's restricted by the size of the room and the height of the ceiling.

The angels get in each other's way. The span of their grey wings is wide and there's not enough space, so instead of pouncing on me, they push each other out of the way, squabbling, eager to get to me first and win the approval of their leader.

Using the confusion of their silent bickering, I skid sideways, towards the furniture I just pushed, and once next to it, I slide underneath the golden settee, crawling to the other side of it.

My action has divided the four of them, and while the two drop to the floor and dart after me, the remaining two float in the air like birds of prey, waiting for me to resurface.

But I didn't duck there to hide.

I slide, rising at the other side of the small settee. I turn and with the two easy jumps supported by my half-open wings, I bounce onto the seat, then onto the carved and gilded back of the couch, taking one last jump... upwards.

My wings burst open around me.

I am under a Butcher's soldier. His body floats above me, the side of his laced torso and... his neck.

I don't need to reach high and the slight rise on my wings finishes the job of my arm and my sword.

I'm showered with his red blood and I jump away in time from the crashing body.

Three left and the Butcher.

Rage is excited. She can't believe our luck as she spurs me on.

Do I dare to begin the countdown to the moment when I'll slice the Butcher's neck?

I fly to the farthest side of the room, jamming the both of my right wings on the chandelier, crying at the impact on the already wounded wing, leaving behind a swinging, creaking and chiming crystal.

I grind my teeth at the pain in my wing. I drop my gaze, watching fat drops of blood landing on the furniture and the floor beneath me.

The three "Butcher-in-training" angels fly after me.

Looking at the rapidly growing wall of leather-clad, large male bodies, I begin to wonder if I've made the right call coming this way, when a tentative idea morphs.

The wall...

The idea is crazy and outside of the realm of human thinking or human abilities. It's barely formed, when confronted by the dark gleam of their black weapons, I turn to face the golden wall behind me and I *run up the wall.*

I run up the wall and I run along the ceiling.

The angels are below me now, and I'm above them, upside down, like a fly on the ceiling, while my wings keep me afloat.

The angels' heads are drawn up, looking at me, confusion marries their faces.

Just before I can escape them, one of the angels wakes up to the abnormality of my hair tickling his forehead.

With a phenomenal speed, he reaches to the arsenal at his chest, yanking out a whip, which uncoils to the floor in a black snake. He then raises his arm and sends the whip flying towards me.

But my arms are busy, raised for my assault, and unable to stop the whip.

Following the earlier decided course, my arms descend downwards, aiming at the backs of the angels, leaving me defenceless to the danger of the black whip.

The sword in my left hand sinks into flesh at the same time as the whip cuts through my body and my wings.

Screaming, I crash down and the body of the minion crashes to the floor next to me. My hands open and with a crispy ring of a dropped pin, my sword falls out of my grip, sliding across the polished parquet floor.

I rise up on all fours, try to crawl to the body, reaching for my sword, still jammed into a minion's back, when the vicious hands close over my broken wing and I scream.

The two hands pull at my wings, ripping my wings out of my back, and I feel like a fly, about to lose its wings to a nasty child.

My body is raised off the ground, while my legs are still on the floor, and I push with my arms and my knees, helping my body up, desperate to reduce the cruel pull.

Yanked, I'm up and on my feet.

The two of my wings are held by one minion behind my back, while the other minion stands bravely in front of me, hands on his hips and a pleased, sly smile on his lips.

He leisurely swings his black axe by his hip, while the black whip with its tail painted red is flexed in his other hand.

"As usual, Ariel, the chases you provide are the height of the amusement and excitement", the Butcher's deep voice says from the door.

The parquet squeaks under his heavy steps as he comes closer.

I listen to Butcher but I watch the minion ahead of me. His face is slim and young, although it has small "ratty" features.

"Oh, Arllu!" Butcher exclaims. "What would I give to watch you fight some more, especially against your human adversaries, or ibnatums, or desperate humans", he muses. "Locking you in a cell with them would've provided hours upon hours of entertainment."

The creaking of the parquet grows closer.

"Especially if you fight for survival, or food. And we could've had bets..." he adds, dreamily. "Of course, keeping it strictly as unofficial entertainment."

The parquet squeaks a yard away. My gaze is locked with the minion ahead of me.

"But Baza needs to see you. Probably to torture, following with the public execution, if you ask me."

I can smell Butcher's leather now.

"... A message to Sarukh. He dreamed of it for a while. Finally, he'll bring Uriel, in whatever form it might be, to the end, sticking to Mik'hael at the same time."

Butcher is next to his minion. They're perfect targets: large, close to each other and finally, within my reach.

I breathe out, steadying myself.

My hands dive to my leather corset, finding the handles of the last two knives, and the next second my arms fly out and my knives fly out of them.

I watch one knife sink into the minion's throat and a smile pulls at my lips.

But it doesn't live there long, as a freezing heat spreads in my chest and when I drop my gaze to it, I'm surprised to see blood, spreading over my white tunic.

My confused gaze jumps to Butcher, looking for my knife in his throat.

But Butcher's throat is white and clean, as he stands in front of me. Unharmed, he holds the hilt of a long black sword and it is sunk fully into my body.

BOOKS IN THE "CELESTIAL CREATURES" SERIES:

THE BOOKS ARE AVAILABLE VIA ALL MAJOR PLATFORMS & BEST RETAILERS!

"HEAVENWARD", BOOK 1: https://books2read.com/u/bWzWlx
"HALLOW", BOOK 2: https://books2read.com/u/m2vkw6
"HARBINGER", BOOK 3: https://books2read.com/u/bx8n1l
"HALO", BOOK 4 (AND FINAL): https://books2read.com/u/3nvW56

ACKNOWLEDGEMENTS

All my gratitude goes to my personal cheerleader, my patient and calm husband for tolerating my craziness all these years and for believing in me. For all the encouragement and support you gave me with this book, I will be forever grateful. Love you.

Of course, my deepest gratitude goes to all my readers, to the ones, who supported me and my stories over these years, who believed in Ariel and cheered her on, who spread the word about my crazy imagination.

I write for you. When you read my books, I am truly alive.

ABOUT AUTHOR

Olga Gibbs lives in a leafy-green town, nestled amongst the green fields of West Sussex, England. She lives with her husband, their two daughters and a cat. When not writing books, she is working within adolescent mental health.

Please visit her author website for more information on upcoming books: www.OlgaGibbs.com

www.ingramcontent.com/pod-product-compliance
Lightning Source LLC
Chambersburg PA
CBHW020412180626
46812CB00003B/940